Last Bird Singing

Last Bird Singing

Allan Bush

Seren is the book imprint of
Poetry Wales Press Ltd
57 Nolton Street, Bridgend, Wales CF31 3AE
www.seren-books.com

ISBN 978-1-85411-455-6

A CIP record for this title is available from
the British Library.

Cover picture: John Briggs

The publisher works with the financial assistance of the
Welsh Books Council.

Printed in Plantin by Creative Print and Design, Wales

Bad luck! Bad luck! Now shall we surely suffer encroachment of catastrophe. And there will be no remission, for we have broken faith: this dunce hath slain the singing bird.

Eugene Fish, speaking at a meeting of the Pitch and Toss School on the Old Marl, in late June 1947.

Part One

Chapter One

Christmas is coming. I lie in the dark with my eyes open and stare. It is six am. There is an alarm clock on the window sill; if you press a switch the face lights up. I press the switch and see where the hands are. The line of the plumb bob. Straight up and straight down. It is Saturday and yesterday was the shortest day of the year. The sky I can see through the window flees east. There is cloud with some gaps and odd glimpses of stars. There is pain in my head, a dull pain with no throb.

Seven o'clock finds me sitting with my feet on the floor. My face is in my hands. My eyes are still closed. The room is dark but there are shapes in the dark. Some part of my head is attempting to work out a pattern for the night that is gone. I suck air through my fingers, through the gaps in my teeth. Consumed by a delicate fear and weary to the bone, this is me, a spare bedroom husband in his fiftieth year to heaven. Given a choice, I would not be where I am, but where I would choose to be is open to considerable speculation. My wife Lillian sleeps in her chamber, the room at the front. The cat sleeps in the easy chair. I take my hands from my eyes and look out. Clouds go by, moving fast. Break off and drift before a west wind. The roofs are wet. I dress and go down to make tea. The cat moves and stretches and comes up to look at me. She yawns. Licks at a paw and stares at me, neither love nor forgiveness in her pale green eyes. She yawns again. Then her eyes close.

At eight I leave the house. What little light there is thins dark to blanket grey. The winter mornings come hard now, even Saturdays.

The wind is damp in my face. Lamplight and empty streets. Cars and puddles, the odd leafless tree. Every morning now, it seems, the need to grit the teeth gets stronger. You press on. Turn left at the first corner, left at the next, which brings you to Newport Road. A car goes by, heading east; another heads into town. A bus with faces hung in the windows where hands have cleared the steam from glass. Then quiet. Across the road in a diagonal line to Clifton Street.

The Clifton Café is lit and resplendent in the false dawn. Steam on the windows, a live cell in a dead row. Bernie is there, my old time friend. His eyeglasses catch the light as he turns his head and glitter and flash. J.B. Reilly, a failed and forgotten welterweight with a flat nose and crooked teeth. Long sideburns showing streaks of grey and the other hair combed to hide skin. He shows his teeth to grace a brief smile and nods to the empty chair. He has bagged the table near the window. A damp roll up rests on a box of Swan Vestas. A mug of tea warms his hands. The working bears in their thick check shirts and jeans and muddy boots are deeper into the rest of the cave. They grunt and gesticulate and go hubbadubba and exhale stale beerbreath. Hobbledehoys, Bernie calls them. He hates them. He dresses like them but sees himself as set apart, some refinement, some saving grace. I nod and smile and sit down. Turn to look about the room. Then Monica comes in.

Even my poor worn-out heart attempts to lift itself. Monica Corsi, neé Quinn. She comes in through the strip curtain bearing plates on both arms. Breakfasts to the berserkers. She sees me and smiles.

Tommy, her lips say. Lovely mouth and perfect teeth. She moves through the smoky air like the wind from the sea. My eyes follow her, stay glued to her arse as she leans to place plates for the bears. All eyes follow her and leer. The interior seethes. She straightens, turns, sways and goes out through the curtain again. Strips fly as she passes through, sweep inwards and straighten. Swish!

Getting fat in the arse, Bernie observes. He is fifty four. He gave up all hope nine years ago when his wife died.

A month's wages, I say. It is a game we play. He knows I am in love with the idea of her. A girl like that, I say, that particular girl, if she was to become available and I was gainfully employed...

I suck air urgently and say: I would work a month for nothing to get into her. It means nothing. Talk. Bernie is unimpressed. But when she brings our breakfast I can see how her nipples press out like capbuttons through the shiny black cloth of her flimsy blouse. Slyly glance down to see her high heel shoes and her pearly silver painted toenails where they peep through. Smell her through the baconreek that steams off the plates. Her thigh brushes against my arm. Her hand rests on my shoulder through a pause while the other hand brushes a loose strand of hair. She looks at Bernie. He is shovelling food. She looks at me. Blue eyes. Irish eyes. She smiles.

Okay? she says. Tea after? Her smile deepens and I gulp. What is it? you ask yourself. And what it is, you well know, is the worst kind of craving known to man.

We eat in silence. Everybody in the room eats in silence. The breakfast at the Clifton is the best breakfast in town. People leave and others come in. The hubbadubba rises, falls, pauses and resumes. There is traffic out in the street. The tea urn goes shoosh! Pale light in the sky. Bernie is the first to finish. He wipes at his plate with a piece of bread. Crams it in and pushes the plate away.

Wipes at his lips with the back of his hand. Gazes about him and sucks at his teeth. So, he says, what's new?

I finish chewing and swallow. Let me think, I say.

When I finish eating and lean away there is still a slice of bread on my side plate. He points. You want that? he asks.

I shake my head and he rams it home as if he fears I may reconsider.

The only complaint I got, I say, fucking Wonderloaf. You would expect Italians to know better.

Bernie shakes his head. Swallows hard. She's not a wop, he tells me. That girl is Irish. He purses his lips and nods. Was you drunk last night?

I am drunk every night, I tell him.

Looking about me, I can see it in every face. It is what we share.

Bernie still works. He earns a crust sweeping the yard at the council depot. Makes tea for the management and cleans their cars. Keeps his eyes peeled and listens at doors. He spends most evenings with four cans of Special Brew and a rented video. He talks about the building game during his days of real work and can recite the names of the firms who employed him as if they were the names of famous battles; as if McAlpine was his Stalingrad and George Wimpey might have been El Alamein against the Afrika Korps. He rents two rooms on Sapphire Street and keeps a tabby cat.

He sharpens a matchstick to a point with his redhandled knife. Shielding his mouth, he prods and prises the remnant strands of bacon from his teeth. He folds the blade and puts the knife in his pocket. So, he asks me, how is all going in the happy home?

He picks up the ready-rolled cigarette and strikes the sharpened match for his light. Sucks smoke hard. The Boy still there?

I nod.

It working out?

A shrug, a grudging shrug, is the best I can manage. It is not working out but I am reluctant to admit it.

One evening in the middle of November there was a knock at the front door. When I open the door, roused from the table and still chewing, there he is, my son Elliott, the Boy himself. No suitcase. No hat and no overcoat. No money. The taxidriver wants four pounds. I pay him and we go in without a word. You're a trump, Elliott tells me in the passageway. His mother, hearing her darling's voice, comes rushing out. She falls on his neck. She kisses him hard on the cheek. Holds his face in both hands and her eyes search for signs. She smooths his hair. She steps back and weighs him to the ounce. Her smile flashes through her tears. I look on in silence. This is Lillian, my wife. She was nineteen when he was born. He is twenty four. She studies him under the light. Touches him to make sure he is real. Then the kettle is on, the gas is lit for the pan for eggs, back bacon rashers go under the grill. Soon eggs sputter in the hot fat. The kettle sings. She slices bread. Let me look at you! she says. Let me look at you!

It has been over two years. She wipes away a tear and feasts her eyes. She hands him a clean towel. Wash your hands, she says.

His timing was not good, I explain to Bernie. Christmas is never the best time for us.

Bernie nods. He knows the score. We both smile when Monica brings us our mugs of tea.

It is almost nine and the truck and ladder men are starting to head out. They pause in the door and call back to Monica, joking and flirting. Blow kisses, she blows kisses back. They need money for Christmas. All the civilised world needs money for Christmas. She goes to the door and waves as they get in their vans. Every man in the place would cut off a little finger to fuck her. She *must* know this.

You can't blame her, I suppose, Bernie says. It's her bread and butter.

Monica closes the door and goes back to the kitchen. Her expression is thoughtful, even distracted. She looks perfect to me. Of all the faces I know, hers is the best. If I were still capable of love, it is this woman I would choose to be in love with.

He working? Bernie asks.

He means Elliott. I shake my head.

What did you watch last night? I ask him. His roll up has gone out. He strikes another match. *The Birdman*, he tells me. His eyes light up and he drags hard on the smoke. But I hold up my hand before he can launch himself. Seen it, I tell him. About ten or eleven times.

He sniffs and gives me a sour look and wipes at the window.

We rise from our table just after nine thirty and go to the counter to settle up. The place is quieter now and Monica is upstairs. Phil, the brother-in-law, takes our money. Surly and dull, he rarely speaks. We go outside and stand on the pavement. Breathe morning air. Look one way, turnabout to look the other. Bernie tells me he must visit the sister of his dead wife. He hopes to arrange a place at their table for Christmas Day. He comments on the mildness of the air and heads south towards Constellation Street. It is then, as he walks away, that I notice his boots. And call after him: New boots? He stops dead in his tracks. Turns and comes back. Draws up the right trouser leg to show me the full boot. Halfway up his calf. Not new, he informs me. Refurbished. Almost new, mind. These are the McCoy, genuine German paratrooper boots.

Black leather polished to the gleam of glass. The polishing of boots is one of the major virtues amongst the commonplace tasks that go to make his life. Army training.

How much? I ask him.

Pony, he says. The word slips through his crooked teeth like a lie.

Combat gear is his weakness. In secret dreams he relives the hard and merciless glories of the Russian Front. He believes in his heart the Fuhrer had most things down pat. Yet, in another frame of mind, he will tell you that his mother had been a genuine red who was half Jewish and had visited Moscow in 1934. His father, her second husband, was Irish. Born in Newry. An army man who fought in Burma against the Japanese. Then a labourer in civvy street. Hard drinker. Fornicator. Dead at fifty. My age.

Good leather, he points out. Hardly worn. Keep them for best and they'll last me years.

His voice warms with genuine emotion. The Kraut is his favourite amongst all the nations.

They got leather soles, I point out. That means they must be pretty old. All the new boots got rubber soles.

He looks doubtful. See, he says, they lace up almost to the knee. These boots might have fought at... He racks his brain.

We stare past each other. He allows the trouser leg to fall.

Better get going, he says. Don't want to miss out.

Me too, I tell him. See if the missus is up yet.

Merry Christmas, he says, in case I don't see you.

Same to you, I tell him and stare after him as he goes.

Cross over the road and go into Webber's for a half pound of cooked ham. The shop is full. Faces watch as the three sisters slice at the joints. Narrow their eyes as they read the scales. The fat younger brother works away at a pig's head, his blade, sharpened to a whisker, prising and slitting where cognition once was. Brawn soon. The sisters as skinny as witches. Polonies in redskin coils. Pork pies. Stuffed legs of roast pork. Ham off the bone. Pink meat and white fat. Sausages in shiny skins the colour of hardwall plaster just mixed in the bucket. Piled on white trays in their links to form the shape of a man's brain. We watch and wait. When my turn comes I buy a half pound of shortback bacon to go with the ham. The youngest of the sisters serves me. Nice eyes but a half-hearted mouth, she is the only one still fuckable. She smiles and calls me love as she hands me my change.

Elliott goes past on the other side as I come out of there. He is hurrying, head down, hands thrust into the pockets of his jeans. Skinny and cold-looking in his skimpy leather jacket. I stand still and watch as he goes into the Clifton Café. Curiosity drags me to the window to observe. He stands talking to Monica. There is a tension between them. The mother-in-law, old Mrs Corsi, watches them like a hawk. The diners are watching. It is like a silent film.

Monica's eyes are on his face. Her hands move as if she would strangle him if she had half a chance. Elliott's eyes keep sliding away from her gaze. Then Jimmy, her husband, comes in and they move apart. Elliott sits down at a vacant table. Monica goes out and Jimmy follows her. Mrs Corsi is watching Elliott as she pours his tea. He nods without looking up when she sets it before him. He yawns. Lights a cigarette. His face locks into a mask of boredom. He blows smoke at the ceiling. He looks like he slept the night in a Ford Fiesta. Mrs Corsi is still watching him closely as I turn to go. And I get a glimpse of Monica watching him through the parted strips of the curtain. Her eyes are heavy with the anxiety of love.

Unhappiness settles in my breast like cold tar. Walking Clifton Street, in any direction, is like going to your own funeral. You don't have a wooden cross to carry but what passes for blood in your heart might be damp sawdust. These are poor times; the shops change hands; they go under and empty and change hands again. I retrace my steps to my own front door.

My wife is up and about. She sits in her gown of pale lilac silk and frowns at her hands. She moves her thumbs. Raises her gaze and her eyes stare dully out into the backyard. Not so much as a flicker to recognise my coming in. Then I grunt and she grunts. Once her eyes were lovelier than the most delicious sin, but they are muddy now. A mug of tea steams before her on the patterned oilcloth. Even as I watch, her jaw tightens like a clamp.

Tea fresh? I say.

She moves a single finger to point where the teapot is. You can feel the grinding of her teeth. Back in ancient history when I married her and she was only nineteen she was as vivid as a burning hayrick. Only faint traces of that remain and she is driven to subterfuge. She can still set sail of an evening and pass as a passable fuck, but the saggings are there and the tricks get harder to manage and hold. She has a fellow she sees. She moves in a bubble of glum hysteria. I go to the teapot and pour tea into a cup. Sit to her right so as not to intercept her stare. Silence settles.

Then she suddenly speaks. He didn't come in, she says.

Her voice startles me. I shift in my chair to look at her.

Elliott, she says. His bed is empty. I got up at three. He wasn't there. I couldn't sleep... Worrying my guts out.

I shrug and drink some tea. The tea is stewed.

Why can't he phone? she says. All he got to do is pick up the phone. I got to lie there, can't sleep, thinking all the bad things. The worst things. You were out like a light. Worse than a nightmare. Look at my eyes... all bloodshot and piggy.

She presses her face in my direction and I look.

I had a bad dream, too, she says. He was climbing stairs. Not these stairs. Stairs with no carpet... There was a light coming under a door... I was in a cupboard or wardrobe, or something... I could see him but he couldn't see me. He wasn't wearing a shirt under his coat. His mouth was wide open.

Probably yawning, I say. Probably forgot where he was going and got bored. Probably...

He could be on a slab right now, she says, and I don't think you would give a fuck.

Her eyes close as if she is experiencing sudden and overwhelming pain. She draws a deep breath.

Slab! I say. You mean a slab in the morgue? Whore's bed, more like it. A strong likelihood some flatfoot whore took him home for...

They were after him, she says. Men. Three men. In the dream. He was running up these wooden stairs. It was raining. I remember now, at one point he stops on a landing and there is rain running down the window pane. Men were after him...

She looks at me. I am almost certain he is in trouble, she says.

She sets great store by her dreams. Considers herself some sort of a witch. I say nothing. She reaches into the pocket of her gown and pulls out a packet of Silk Cut.

Look at me, she says. He got me so worried I'm smoking again.

She shakes her head and half smiles. Little bastard, she says. And lights up with her trusty Zippo. This is another thing with her, the ongoing renunciation of the cigarette.

It was sheer murder, she tells people, the first three weeks, but I stuck it out. Hung in there. I had to, she explains, it was ruining my looks.

She means what she says but she smokes on the sly.

Twenty five years ago I was desperately in love with her. I was convinced of her purity, of her rightness for me alone, and vice versa. With this woman alongside me on the buckboard, I told myself, we could have braved the rigours and dangers of a prairie crossing and won through. I was convinced we could have found our place in the sun. The Golden West. Great hopes found their place in my heart of hearts. Once, in the first year of our marriage, I carried a half hundred weight sack of cobble coal from the Daviot Street coalyard to our freezing rooms. Two miles through falling snow. Knelt down to light the fire in the cast iron grate and thanked God for the chance to prove my devotion and love. The world was an imperishable oyster. We spoke to each other of the future, the grand life that lay ahead of us. She was pregnant with the Boy Wonder. What followed on from those times is a long and complicated story.

Our house is poor. I tried to punish her with poverty. Now, when the game is all but over, I hate her like a stepmother. And she hates me for stealing her chance. She is not usually up at this time on a Saturday. She works all week and Friday is her big night. She hates mornings anyway. There is one picture on the wall that is real oilpaint on genuine canvas. It was painted by a man named Stone and we had it framed by another man named Curle. All told it cost £200. In the front room there are a couple of pine shelves that bear the weight of about forty books that range from *The Man in the Iron Mask* to *Moby Dick*; *The Narrative of Arthur Gordon Pym* to the *Sunday School Bible*. There is a television, a radio and a record player. She has a three-sided mirror on her dressing table. I have not set foot in her room for five years. I have the back bedroom. Elliott has the middle bedroom. We provide roof and board for a nervous cat. Once in a long while I might open a book and get through a page or two, but then the words get loose and start to crawl about like wingless flies. I like to think there was a time I could read two hundred pages without even breaking for a piss. Delusions. We have a daughter we have not seen or heard from for over a year. Lillian, my wife, has a fancy man named Bobby Snell. There are lots of things to bear in our minds as the time presses us back. Something went wrong. I tried to fuck her into wifely submission early on and failed. Fell out of favour. Our lives became mysteries to each other. I still see her as she was. She is my eternal source of lust, the way she was at twenty one.

The knock at the door. It is Elliott. He refuses to carry a key. Lillian leaps up and rushes to greet him. She touches him. It was her idea to name him Elliott; she called him after Elliott Ness, that awful actor who played him, the indomitable G-Man, on TV: Robert Stack in *The Untouchables*. I don't think she missed a single episode. I love his hair, she used to say. Such beautiful wavy hair. And his eyes. He looks so sincere.

Elliott, our son, is the beautiful boy. They come in from the passage together. She hangs on his neck. Both smile. She kisses his cheek hard. It makes me uneasy to watch. I stare away and shift my feet like a poor relation. She kisses him again and he wriggles free.

I could eat him, she says. Worrying me sick.

Elliott looks at me. Smiles at me. Points his finger at me.

He saw me, he says. He was watching me.

There is a silence. Lillian looks at me. Icy. Looks at Elliott.

Saw you where?

The Clifton Café.

Lillian turns on me. Why didn't you say you saw him? she demands.

I look away. Say nothing.

You're not a man, she tells me. You just let me sit here and stew... You wouldn't, she says, even make a decent mouse.

Our eyes meet for the first time in days and I wonder if she knows how much I have grown to hate her. If she has any idea of how easily I could kill her; how it would please me no end to attack her flesh with some tool like a mattock or a crowbar; wade into her, bone and flesh, with a well-used garden spade. Draw blood. For years I was scared she might poison my soup.

Her lip trembles. He knew how worried I was, she says.

Sit down, Elliott says. Puts his arm around her. Guides her to her chair. It is worse than being in a bad dream. The sentiment spread like jam on bread.

Just lets me go on, she says. Worrying myself sick.

Bullshit, I say. You are full of shit. The pair of you...

Elliott leans over and takes two cigarettes from her pack.

Lights them both and hands her one. We are a family ruined by bad ideas from rotten films. She smiles up at him and drags deep. Had breakfast yet? she asks him.

He shakes his head.

Put the kettle on, she tells him. I'll finish this and cook you something.

I go out at this point. It is best to leave them to it. Mother and son. Like some nursery story. She will flutter her eyelashes and pout as she warms his plate. As coy as you please. He will wolf away and nod and smile. Smoke her cigarettes and borrow money to keep him going. To leave them is the only way.

It is raining. Not hard rain, but a steady drizzle that the wind picks up and intensifies. The Clifton Hotel is open and I go in. The usual people are there. Tony Jones is there with his tinted glasses and a bow tie on; Paul Driscoll and his brother Jimmy are there; Cliff Warner is trying to ease a way into their company. They turn, nod to me, turn back. Not full yet, the room, but not empty either, only subdued for the moment, a sort of gloom and a calm and the daylight at the windows no more than half-hearted. Mavis the barmaid has already spotted me and drawn my pint.

Tommy, she says, How's things, Tom? You're all wet, she says. I nod and pay her.

Have one yourself, I say. She is a landmark in the place. More than twenty years behind the bar and still not forty. She found her vocation at seventeen. Plain as a pikestaff: popeyes, a pale face and funny hair and a body like a barrel. I take my beer to a corner, as far away from the faces I know as I can get. There are a lot of things on my mind and I need a degree of quiet to think.

There is this friend of mine, Raymond Friend, and he is dying of cancer. This is a kid I have known practically all my life. We grew up together. I called his mother auntie. At one time we might have been closer than brothers. He is dying now. He has cancer and there is not long to go. A lot of people have told me. I bump into the bastards in the street and they tell me about Raymond Friend. How he is close to death. A man named Ware, who knew us both when we were kids, the other day in City Road. Waved his finger in my face and said I should get up there quick. The boy is very rough, he said. He weighed me up and down. And look at you, he said, like the side of a fucking house. A tall skinny man with sharp blue eyes who knew both our fathers. Do your duty, he said.

Raymond Friend. Everybody called him Amigo. Ever since he was a little kid. It must have been some kind of a joke, to do with those Western pictures they had back then with Randolph Scott in them, or Rod Cameron, and a lot of Mexicans and haciendas. Adios Amigo, they used to say. The good gringoes and the bad gringoes and one or two honourable wetbacks to take the bullets and show white teeth with the dying breath. Amigo. I sip at my beer and settle to think.

His old man is dead. Billy Friend. He died just after my mother died. He had played as a pro in the old Southern League. All he knew was football. He knew more about football than anybody I ever knew. He made sure Amigo had a ball before he was out of his pram. Had him kicking a football before he could walk. All he wanted out of life was for his boy to be a footballer. He had this job in the tinworks, sort of odd-job man who ran the tinworks football team. They won the district first division three years in a row. He got this bunch of catchers and fitters and rollermen and one or two misfits from outside the works and made them into the best team around. They had a ground behind the factory yard, on the other side of the river. Amigo and I hardly ever missed a game. We were both mad about football. We lived our lives with a ball in the park. I spent more time in his house than I did in my own. We practised and practised. Billy Friend would watch us. There were other kids, but they just made the numbers up to have a game.

Mrs Lewis, the landlady, comes in and looks around. Avoids my eye. It is she who runs the place. Her husband, the landlord Courtney, will be upstairs in bed. He drinks nothing but white wine with brandy chasers and the mornings are murder for him. She loves him. An indulgent mother could not love him more. She goes out.

Amigo was the apple of his father's eye. There was a daughter, two years younger than Amigo. Father and son could have come out of the same pod with twenty years between them. They both had the same hair. Same eyes. Same narrow view: football to them was like the Blood of the Saviour to monks in the monastery.

People said the old man had been good, but the son was a marvellous player. Even as a child, from the age of about seven, Amigo possessed astonishing physical composure. When he was in a game he had this unassailable equilibrium that kept him safe. It was like he was inside a bubble that stretched the time for him into an endlessly favourable accommodation of his body and his body's purpose with the ball. What was hard for the rest of us was easy for him. He saw very clearly how simple it was. Any fool, anywhere, who has ever kicked a ball more than a dozen times knows how hard it really is, but for Amigo, even at that age, it was like pissing the bed.

But that was long ago. A lot of water has passed since then. I take a sip of my beer. Killing time. A man named Moore comes in. One of the last of the maintenance men hanging on at the steelworks. A man of my generation, who still rides a bike.

Pissing down, he tells me. He points to his parka which is shiny with rain. Takes out a handkerchief and wipes at his face. When Mavis serves him he takes his beer to join the others and I relax. What I am hoping is for Bernie to come in. Sometimes he does. Sometimes not. He is not a drinker in the serious sense and he is mean with money. The price of beer in a bar depresses him. He keeps holding it up to the light to gauge the purity and clarity, then he tastes it like a winetaster and pulls a face. To swallow it costs him pain. But he is lonely like me and sometimes he comes in for the company. To chew the fat. So I keep an eye on the clock and watch the door. By one o'clock I am on my fourth pint and the first of the whisky chasers. One o'clock is the deadline. I go up for another chaser. Mavis looks at the glass.

Beer's a bit flat, I tell her. Or maybe it's me. Needed the livener, you know how it is.

Bernie fails to appear and I am back to Amigo. Things didn't work out. He had not long signed for Swindon Town when he fractured his skull in a car crash. They were coming back from a night game against Luton Town. It was September. He was twenty three at the time and there were some who felt he might be ready to move up a division. The verge of the big time, as they say. I never saw him play in the league, so I couldn't judge, but his old man always maintained that if you were not there by twenty one, you had better forget it.

Then he got married to a girl named Teresa Carey. It was a bad match. She was too lively for him and they never hit it off. I never went to his wedding, and he never came to mine. But I knew her. A lot of men knew her. I bumped into her one night in a place called the Buccaneer Club. She was with Amigo's sister. They were waiting for Amigo to come straight from the game. By eleven o'clock we knew he wouldn't make it. She was getting drunk. His sister was drunk. She was dancing with a man named Bradford. I was drunk. Teresa asked me if I felt like dancing and we danced. Later on we went outside. The place had been a grand house once and there was a terrace with a stone balustrade and steps down to an overgrown lawn. There was a harvest moon. I have no recollection of exchanging a single word with her, but we stood in an alcove for – it must have been – hours, trying to swallow each other whole. My dick then was as hard as it had ever been. My willing compliance is not in question. It was out and in her hand and all set to slide home before the true nature of the moment hit me.

Jesus! I said. I pulled away from her as if she was a snake.

Jesus Christ! I said.

She walked away from me without a word. When she reached the door she turned to look at me – her eyes were like black grapes. Then she went in. Amigo's sister was stood at the bar. Tight lipped.

O yes, was all she said.

The carcrash was the reason Amigo failed to turn up. Another player, John Griffiths, was killed. The driver had both legs amputated. A lot of bad stuff in my life stems from that night. It was almost three am before I got home and Lillian never forgave me. And years later, when Teresa wanted to hurt him bad, she told him I had fucked her. She knew he didn't give a fuck about her, but she was smart enough to realise that the thought of his oldest friend getting into her behind his back would crack him up.

By two o'clock I am starting to slide and half the dead people I have ever known are coming back. I am starting to tell myself how worthless I am. The room is crowded now and the landlady is helping out behind the bar. Courtney, her husband, has come down to oversee. He is in his little corner where the bar runs into the wall, smiling at all. Mine host, in his pinstripe suit, with a glass of white wine to get him into another day. There are even three women wearing paper hats. The daylight at the windows is almost gone. I have switched the chaser from whisky to brandy. This is to commemorate my mother's brother, my Uncle Charles. A drunkard like me. A fool. He had been a prisoner of war with the Germans. I got drunk on brandy at his funeral and the hangover lasted two days.

The memories make me thoughtful. I note the lateness by the light gone from the windows. I finish my pint and stand alongside a man just come in. The rain drips from him. He looks poor.

Raining out? Mavis asks him.

Emptying down, he tells her.

Her expressionless gaze meets mine as she receives his five pound note. Same again, Tommy? she asks me.

While she is on her way to the till I decide to go for a piss. Along the corridor and through a door into a sort of vestibule. Go in through the door and stand at the pissbowl and stare. Piss. When I turn there are two men between me and the door. It occurs to me that they must have been in the cubicle all along and I wonder if they are queers. But as I move to reach the door the man closest to me holds up his hand. He is wearing black leather gloves.

Mr Oliver? he says.

I look past him to weigh up the man at the door. Both men are strangers to me.

Do I know you? I ask.

Best of my knowledge, he says, you owe Mr Twomey the contractor some money. Am I correct?

Who the fuck are you? I demand.

Friends of Mr Twomey, he tells me.

Tell Mr Twomey, I tell him, he'll get his money after Christmas.

Then the other cubicle door opens and Julian Twomey himself steps out. He smiles at me.

Slip your mind, did it? he says. He is an unpleasant bastard and I am starting to feel afraid. The amount owing is in dispute: he says seventy pounds and I think fifty is closer to the mark. His sudden appearance startles me and I can think of nothing to say. A fuck you would be unwise. He holds out his hand.

Seventy quid, he says. Let's have it.

No way, I tell him, am I paying you seventy.

Okay, he says, how much are you willing to pay?

Fifty, I tell him.

Okay, he says, let's have the fifty.

I laugh. Now? I say. It is fucking Christmas. I'm out of work. No chance.

He nods. Small blue eyes and very black curly hair. His lips are clamped tight.

You owed me that money since October, he reminds me.

Listen, I tell him, I'll get it for you.

When?

Next Monday?

No good, he says. How much you got on you?

Bladders, I tell him, and thrust my right hand into my trouser pocket to bring out some change. As I do so the man near me punches me in the stomach. The punch winds me and the change in my hand flies everywhere. The other man grabs me from behind. Together they hold me powerless in front of Twomey. He smiles and reaches into my coat pocket and takes my wallet. He opens it and removes all the money I have in the world: three ten pound notes and a fiver.

This'll do for now, he says. He tosses the empty wallet into the pissbowl. Then he bares his teeth and punches me hard in the face.

His henchmen shove me into a cubicle and they leave. My nose is bleeding and my eyes are blurred with tears. I am not entirely out to the world but neither am I properly in it. I stagger across to the mirror. My face looks like a smashed plum.

There is a long moment. A man named Mason helps me to my feet. He holds my shoulders and peers hard into my face.

Your nose is broke, he tells me. His eyes squint with a sort of concern. It took three of them, he says. He tells me this to make me feel better about it, to console me. Wash your face, he says and leads me to the sink. There is a mirror; blood over the front of my shirt; blood and snot smeared over upper lip and chin. I run the water and wash off the blood. It keeps bleeding.

The faces in the bar stare at me with mild curiosity. Mavis pauses to watch as Mason helps me off the premises. He gives me a light shove to send me out into the rain.

Mind how you go, Tommy, he says. Hard rain that bounces in the street. Almost dark. There is much discouragement in my bones as I walk home. Cold rain on my bald patch.

The house is empty. I take a good look at myself in the bathroom mirror. The face that looks back at me is old and sad. The eyes are full of fear. The face of a man who would put a bullet in his brain if he had the bullet. And could *find* the brain.

A search for booze turns up a bottle with about four tablespoons of British sherry. When I tilt the bottle the sherry shifts about as slow as molasses. When I remove the cork and sniff it smells like ancient jam. A bad moment and I am tempted to hurl the bottle out through the window. It is dark and I am broke and there is nothing for it but to lie down and try to sleep. It will not come. I lie on my back and stare. Weary as fuck, all I can do is listen to the sounds of rain and wait. Shift about in the cradle of discomfort. Sigh and groan and measure the pain in my face. Chew over any amount of ancient bitterness. In the end, after much agitation, a thin slumber settles over me. A sort of fragile veil to cut me off from what ails the stagnant soul.

Chapter Two

A sort of half-hearted dream is set in motion. Not much in the way of action; no excitement or chance of anything good; nobody in the dream seems to be aware of anybody else; just a few faces from other dreams and a faintly familiar landscape, but mainly a dream where the sleeper knows it is a dream early on and recognises the signs of it being low key and waits to wake up. I take my watch from the window sill and switch on the light. Not even midnight. I go for a piss and try again. This time I find something. Sort of crawl into a soft groove and duck down. The next time I wake my eyes snap open as if there is someone in the room. But the room is empty. Go downstairs and see if Elliott is there. Nothing. No wife, no son. Not even a wind under the door. The emptiness is profound. Go back up and leapfrog into the next dark and think about dreams that lead nowhere. Listen to a car going by. The far-off shriek of a woman. The intermittent noises of revellers out in the great night. The same old doldrums. The head perched on the bag of bones like Humpty Dumpty.

It is still the night and there is much to be dealt with. The thoughts are there and it is like moving the load in the hold of a riverbarge in rough water. This thought shifted from here to there, that memory pushed overboard. A particular woman brought out of shadow and re-examined, someone you had known as a girl and maybe one night held her tit at Easter under a cold March moon, how she might have been ten years down the road had you taken advantage of what might have been half a chance. A certain look she gave. Or a smile. On into the dark. Up and down the scale. The maggot that can dream still knows he is a maggot. Think of my mother who is dead. I no longer know where she is, where I might look to find her. When I try to examine her in my mind's eye, it gets hazy. Can't seem to get a good look at her face. Just hear her cough, small cough, a peremptory introductory sound as she approaches, a sort of guarded announcement. And the sound her heels made on a hard floor. In a corridor, say, or a high-ceilinged room.

Then another car goes by in the night. The wind at the window. It is like digging your own grave. My mother. We were such constant companions when I was young. When the world was as new as a morning after overnight snow. We went often to the pictures. We watched all the films and we knew all the names they had given the actors. Then we went home to those rooms and she undressed me for bed. Then we sat at the table and ate buttered bread and took chips from a single threepennorth, a shallow portion. The winter outside and the dark and the wind booming about the roof under which you shelter. The light where you are and the shadows at the edges. The fire out in the grate, but the warm bed waiting when we run out of words.

I cannot see her face. I can smell the vinegar on those chips and still taste the fried potato and hear her voice. Chew again at the bread so thinly buttered and exactly recollect the intimate safety and the happiness. But her beautiful face evades me. You think until the bones in your skull ache.

My wife is not home. I can feel her faraway, a faint signal lost on the airwaves. The cat sleeps on the cushion on the sofa and dreams of grey mice. Twitches and dreams. You can feel yourself sag into the mattress, the elemental bag of shit. You can see where you went wrong: how you did not so much chicken out, but rather turned the blind eye and chickened *in*.

The dull gleam of the damp paving stones out in the backyard at first light. Another false dawn. Snail slime glimmer. Grey broken sky and a wind in the shrubs like a toothless comb. A funny little wind that will often serve to keep off the rain. Listen to the news on the radio. All those words, falling like dandruff. Or dead flies. By the time the next bulletin comes they will have been swept away, so that the great gulp of nothing can go on. The world they try to cram down your throat. We have traffic and drains. Get the shit pumped out to sea and pray.

My nose aches like a bad tooth. The eyesockets are bruised, with blood clotted in the whites. But I am sober for once and reasonably clearheaded and a grim fortitude is upon me. A morning in winter, a Sunday morning to boot, after a sober night, is like washing up on a rocky shore. I eat a round of toast and drink sweet tea. Study the numbers on the clock on the stove. Switch off the offending voice.

The cloud pulls apart to reveal chinks where the sun can leak through. Inside myself, deep down, as they say, I am all hollowed out, worm-eaten from the dull empty days and nights and so little going on. The boredom with myself. How I long to tell somebody about it. The tales of genteel faith and wasted trust. Nobody who will listen anyway and pretty soon you start to dry up like a stream in summer. You ache to proclaim. Long for the power to strike them dumb as jellyfish, for you to climb up into that little pulpit with the spot of God's pure light beaming down where you stand and give it to the bastards *straight*. No butting in. All the doors locked. Here you are, been half a century jammed like shit in a blocked drain – then the release. So many things that come on you late and make it hard and how the good things fade out early and never come back to play again. How the game gets lost. An entire generation who were dragged through the starscope of adolescence and the gaping hole and fed the visions of flesh, Ava, Lana, Rita and Rhonda, as if they were no more than normality, which, in the clamour and scalding gush of the nightly wank, they were. Those images and poses we grappled to hold steady while we worked our meat towards gasp and toothgrind, wince and grimace in the icy dark. How it made us blind and lost us in a maze. How we took the bait and wilted like weeds and fell with the dead seed into the place of rocks. The grinding of souls. Now I have to sit and try to work it out, this thing we lost and where it went to. Skin and time. Find some small thing to set on the scales. It is all interpretation. Jesus, I tell any bastard who will listen, when I was fourteen, I had heroes who lived right here in this town. And reel off the names: Tommy Downey, Mike Hurley, Billy James, and could go on. But no one gives a fuck. They look at you as if you might be crazy. They search in their particular blindness for the nipple or some knob to suck. Sigh and suck and hang on tight.

Meanwhile, the deepness of the empty house. Out in the garden, winter weeds. The moss on the brick. The wet. Within the walls, all the day to day markers of the lost cause. The living proof. The cat, poor, innocent moggie, that has played her part in all the miseries and dull raging and heard all the curses from bitten tongues and caught their bitter songs on the frayings of her nerves. The chairs and the milk jug, the knives and forks in the drawer. The dripping tap. The cupboard that got bare to the last half bag of flour and a jar of currants dried to the point of disintegration and dust. Green mould. The sly goblin in the cold chimney. The curse in the walls. The sky that comes every morning to the window and glares in. The air is cold. Not icy and piercing as needles cold, but dull and bone-ache cold. Dead cold. Damp too.

I leave at two pm and make my way into the town. It's December 23, Queen Street. There is Christmas bustle. The Main Drag. This is it, culmination. Faces and drunken breath. I stare like a clock, hoping to catch a glimpse of a neat arse in a tight pair of pants, or a thigh thrust through a slit skirt. Exciting eyes. Or nice teeth. Not a single thing worth even a half a groan. Mostly that stuff is gone from me now. That cause is long lost. The poor hate Christmas. All that trudging, all that junk. The weather.

The little drunk singer they call Perry who puts down his upturned cloth cap and goes through the entire Como repertoire for hours and hours without taking a piss, closing his eyes and gesturing limply to the air as if his tired little heart was about to break into breadcrumbs any minute, is there. Holding a yellow plastic megaphone to help him out. Boost the weak voice. It is the one about the sweet head and the pillow. These are the messages he sends to the gods of love and misery and loss of the dreams. The voice is pleasant enough in a wavery way, but weak as fuck, even with the loudhailer, and nobody listens. They just go by where he is and stare at his busted shoes and his fat-arse jeans about three sizes too big for the poor little short-arse bastard, with the gut like a bag of shit where the belt should be. And bewigged to boot. This is a genuine star. The wig on his head would grace a ragdoll.

They give him a wide berth, the festive crowds. Skirt about him as if he were a leper. Now and then a child will drop some money in the hat. Small child. Small coin, a fivepence or a ten pence piece. Or copper. Maybe once in a blue moon, a twenty pence. He smiles and nods and works a thank you into the lyrics of the song so it fits the flow. Sings on and on and knows all the words like gospel, rising as sugarsoap bubbles from his mouth to the angels who hide in the clouds, the weak and tireless voice. I gag and throw my last pound coin in the hat. Move on. All I have in the world now is some small change and the carving knife strapped to my left leg like a splint. Nor is there even a morsel in my belly. It seemed inappropriate to eat before going to see a dying man. There was a tin of Alaskan salmon I might have gorged on. Sockeye. Or baked beans. Sardines. But it seemed worthier by far if I could manage the trip on hunger. Nought but a cup of water and the bitter taste of contrition.

My route takes me through the Castle grounds. Go in at the gate opposite the Angel and follow the path that follows the river north.

The river runs south but my path runs north. It is quiet in there and empty. The bare trees and wet grass. Puddles on the path. Some dead clumps of flowers and pampas grass in the old beds. A watery yellow in the sky to the west. No people in this section. The next stage is the nursery wall. Then the rugby pitches. The white posts and the silence of the trampled mud. To the left of the path there is a strip of ragged wood. Sweet chestnut and some evergreen oak. A man with a dog, coming from the riverbank. The dog is black and brown, mixed breed, with retriever prominent. The man wears a Giants baseball hat and hides behind a white beard. He is about my age. We both scowl and move on. How I envy him that dog. He calls the dog to heel. I spit on the path. The sun is dropped behind the trees. A thin pale strip of yellow sky. Certain ideas and memories from childhood come back to plague me. Things to do with a life in the wilderness. A sort of hermit existence as a means to escape, that occupied me a great deal when I was ten. Based mainly on the Errol Flynn version of Sherwood I had seen in the Tivoli. A little pang. Not pain, at least, not exactly pain.

The woods broaden out to enclose the playing fields at the top end. Beyond this is the weir. The sound through the trees is like a seashell up to the ear. You come out of the trees into a thin wash of last light. The water churns at the foot of the sloping stone. There is much that is old and will never change in the dying afternoon. The water amongst the rocks, a white, soiled beard. Three men who lean on the iron rail and stare. One turns to watch my passing. Above the slope of stone the water brims as smooth as glass. I go past the footbridge and enter the corridor of leafless limes. It will be dark long before I get there.

It is Amigo who comes to answer my knock. His chalkwhite face hangs like a paper mask against the dark interior. His hands clutch at the frame of the door. I hear the sharp sound of him catching his breath.

Fuck me, he says.

Ray, I say. We stand there a long moment and simply stare. Then Auntie Ada comes out of the front room and switches on the light in the passage.

Who is it? she says. Comes closer to peer up at me, a short, fat woman I have known all my life. Her face is flushed and her eyes are bright and hard as flints. Breath on her, as they say, like a hot mince pie.

Tommy, she says. Then the sister joins her mother. Leans against the passage wall, sips from her glass and sneers. Look who's here. Makes a noise of deprecation and drinks hard. The wind is cold at the back of my neck.

Come on in, Amigo says.

There is a moment of extreme hesitation, then the crossing over the threshold. The two women melt back into the dark and we watch their going.

Fuck them, he says. Come out the back. He points at the kitchen door. In there, he says. The house is familiar to me. He touches my shoulder. I knew you'd show up, he tells me.

He looks like a bird in a bad winter. Christ, I say. Maybe my mouth falls open. Tears start when I see him clear in the light of the lamp. The dark is at the window. The fire is almost out. He holds out his hand. It is cold and dry as a bird's claw when I shake it. A sigh comes out of him like a muffled sob and I am forced to clench my teeth hard to stop its echo. Tears leak anyway. With my free hand, I reach out and draw him to me in a tentative embrace. He feels like a paper kite, insubstantial enough to float on a summer breeze, light enough to carry on your arm as far as the Toy Bazaar.

Don't cry, he says. For fuck's sake, Tommy, don't start that stuff.

I wipe at the wet cheeks with my knuckles and turn my head away from his steady gaze.

Only the other night, he says, I dreamt of you. You and me were going along together. It was when we were kids.

He sits down in the chair and lets out a gasp as if it is costing him pain. His face is lost in shadow.

Let's get this fucking fire going, I say. And fall on my knees and feel about on the hearth for the poker. There is a faint salmon glow from the grey of the ash in the basket. I thread the poker between the bars and work it to free the powder that clogs the coals. Lean closer and blow softly to work up a revival. There is new coal in an orange plastic sack. Cobbles. I reach in and pull out a couple and place them judiciously. Blow some more. Then find an old *Echo* and hold it over the opening to cause an updraught. It'll come, I promise him. We'll soon get it going.

And in time, a long time, a little flame breaks free. It grows until the newspaper screen takes on a faint glow, strong enough to read the print. Pull the *Echo* away and build cobbles around the flame. Fold the newspaper and put it down. We both watch the flames as they take hold and grow. I draw a deep breath.

I've come up to explain, I tell him. He stares and says nothing. I clear my throat and nod at the fire. It's picking up, I say. The flame now is bright enough to throw my shadow onto the far wall.

I don't give a fuck, he tells me. Don't say a word. What happened, happened.

I didn't fuck her, I say. I don't know what she...

It don't mean a thing to me now, he says.

The fire is taking hold and will not now be defeated. Grab a chair, he says. On your knees like a fucking skivvy there.

It's Christmas, I say, and I didn't bring you a thing. Not even a card.

Fuck all that, he says. What do I want with a card?

We sit there in silence, looking into the fire and momentarily caught up in a solid state of something that had been and been lost and then found again, that might well have come close to the old friendship of our childhood.

Then his eyes soften and he even smiles. Hey, he says, remember Tina Louise?

I nod. Christ, I say, do I!

It was on in the week, he says. One afternoon. Remember her going to the pump in the moonlight?

The images come back. We must have been about sixteen, caught up in the mysteries and dreams of virginal boys. *God's Little Acre.*

Long time ago, I say.

Fuck me, he says, about a million years...

I weighed myself the other day, he tells me. His voice is calm and matter of fact. Just over five stone. Could be an apprentice jockey. There's no chance now, Tom, I'm a fucking goner.

There is nothing I can say. The flames of the fire dance and flicker in the grate. Only dark night at the window.

Then he says: I don't really give a fuck anymore. I did, once, at the start. You want to crawl under the table. Hide under the bed. He looks at me. You got kids, haven't you? I nod. He looks at the fire. Little face almost rosy in the light from the flames. They turn out okay? he asks me.

I shrug. Tina Louise is still on my mind, the white petticoat in the moonlight and the way Aldo Ray tried to grab at her. That vibrant fucking flesh. Tina Louise! I sigh. Imagine getting into that...

I wonder what became of her. I never saw her in another film.

Fuck only knows, he says.

I go to the orange sack and place more coals on the fire.

What happened to your mush? he says. Some cunt put one on you?

I nod. You still drinking? he asks.

Not as much as I was, I tell him.

Is that supposed to be good or bad? he says.

Well, I say, it's not supposed to be good.

I got some whisky, he tells me. Some bright bastard brought me a bottle of whisky. He points to the dresser. Over there, he says. The bottle glints in the firelight.

It's okay, I tell him.

Take the fucking thing with you, he says. I'll drink your health, I tell him. He laughs.

How about you? I say. Could you chance one?

Doctor's orders, he says. Dare not. I'm living on fucking pills. Doctors, he says.

More silence. There is much I would like to say to him. I long for his blessing. To explain and be forgiven whole.

You working? he asks me. I shake my head. Your missus working? I nod.

Good job? he asks.

Not bad, I tell him. We got the boy back with us. Me and him, I say, don't hit it off. Don't often see things eye to eye.

He smiles. Mamma's boy, is he? he says. He points to the bottle of whisky. Help yourself, he says.

I been trying, I explain, to steer clear of the hard stuff. He nods. Then his eyes close. There is a pause, as if he has trapped a new pain and must study its novelty before anything can proceed. His frail body stiffens and the hands clutch at the arms of the chair. I gulp in acute discomfort and get to my feet. He opens his eyes and lets out a long sigh.

Are you tired? I ask.

He nods. Looks into the fire. Fucking *exhausted*, he says. There is a long silence. Then a sudden laugh from the front room.

I'll push off, I tell him. He nods to the scotch on the dresser.

Take it with you, he says. I pick up the bottle and thrust it into the pocket of my coat. Help me up, he says. I'll see you to the door. I offer him my right hand and haul him out of the chair. Light as a sack of feathers. Fingers like twigs. His free hand clutches at my shoulder to gain balance. He breathes hard and we are close enough to kiss. Then we move apart and make our way out of the room. I go before him and open the front door. The night is dark and the night air is cold.

Tommy, he says. We look at each other. The light from the streetlamp catches his eyes in their deep sockets. A faint sob escapes him and I pull him towards me. Stare past him into the dark hole. The sounds of the TV from the front room. Tears flood into my eyes. Teeth clenched, I turn away. Step back. Look after yourself, he says. You too, I tell him. Take another step back.

You and me, he says. Remember? I nod, helpless. We were the best this dump ever saw, he says.

I point at him. You, I say. *You* were. Not me, *you*.

The words fall out of my mouth like stones. I wipe at my eyes, but the tears are still streaming as I walk away.

All the best, Tommy, he calls after me. Merry Christmas. All I can do is hurry on.

It is the only moving thing in the quiet cold stillness of the evening street. A silvery car that comes around the corner and passes through the lamplight where I am waiting in the hope of a bus. It passes by me. Then it stops. It must be thirty yards beyond where I stand. Then the silver car moves slowly backward until it is alongside me. The window comes down and I can see Harry Rivers. He is grinning. He says: How's the boy?

We go into the Pineapple and he insists on buying. The barman is half asleep. There are three men watching some football game with no sound. Two kids in the back room, playing pool. Harry brings the beer to the table. The grin is as I remember it, the old swagger is still there. He sits down and takes a sip from his glass. He points at my face. What happened? he asks.

It is a long story, I tell him. His gaze slips away as soon as our eyes meet. Green eyes like a cat. Beautiful haircut.

You look prosperous, I observe.

He nods, very curt and looks around the room. First time I been in here for a while, he says. Nods. A long time... Must be ten years.

Dicky Wicks' funeral, I remind him.

He nods, puts down his glass, shifts back in his chair. Did someone fill you in?

More or less, I tell him. It was a man I owed money to.

You used to be a hard nut, he says. I stare at him to see if he is serious. Smile. The one thing I *never* was, was hard. Nut, certainly, more often than not. I know what he means though: one night at the old Kennard Rooms, I saved him from a beating. Stepped in when some bastard named Manders was all set to kick his teeth down his throat over some little prickteaser named Penny Gibbs. Harry had fucked her and Manders claimed she was his girl. His words were, I gets as jealous as sin. He cracked Harry once, and Harry lay down. Then he started to put the boot in. Which is where I intervened.

I just been to see Amigo, I tell him.

I been to see the old lady, he says.

How is she? She okay? She must be getting on.

She found religion, he says. Takes a good hard swig at his beer. Then he thinks for a moment. You can watch the struggle going on.

How is he? he asks finally.

Rough, I tell him. He is rough as fuck. Rougher than I thought he'd be. I bet he don't weigh five stone. Looks like he's been stuffed with old paper. Looks terrible.

You working? he asks me.

I shake my head. Not at the moment, I tell him.

You interested in working? He studies me closely. Only, I might have something for you. Be right up your street. You still on the tools?

I afford him a cautious nod and he smiles, a true Harry Rivers smile, the one that got all those girls excited all those years ago; a smile displaying the full glory of his perfect teeth.

Remember, he reminds me, when you were ambitious to be the world's champion bricklayer.

I do remember and the recollection makes me screw up my eyes and almost wince. That was in worthier times, I tell him. A lot of shit flowed over me since then. Rivers of it.

How's the missus? he asks me.

I shrug. Fine, I say. I am pretty sure he will know the score.

How about you, you still in the pub game?

In property, he informs me. The property game. Got five houses packed full of students.

Two pints later and I am explaining to him how it used to feel to go to work with a clear conscience and an open heart. How it felt to burn with ambition at seventeen. How I loved it, the laying of the simple brick. You get the rudiments, I tell him. Anybody can pick up the rudiments in a month or so. Bricks to the line, a monkey can do it. But the finesse is hard to come by. It looks easy. You watch a good bricklayer, I explain, and it looks like pissing the bed.

But it's not. There are the monkeys, a lot of those, but there are only a few magicians. Very few. It takes years. And, don't forget, I was working with the very best. In this dump anyway. It takes years and years. Perfecting. Like a fucking violinist. Gunther Netzer hits a ball fifty yards and it drops on someone's toecap as his foot hits the ground – it looks simple enough, but anybody who ever kicked a ball knows it's not...

The beer on an empty stomach is making me lightheaded. When I was as I was then, young and up and coming, in a sort of primitive wisdom, I fondly imagined that bricklaying might be a way to change the world. That I might graduate and turn into a masterbuilder, become a maestro of better and better walls. Trickier walls, that defied gravity, like Brunelleschi. It is the means to a bad end.

Disappointment is virtually guaranteed.

I smile at him. Mr Rivers, I say. Reach over and finger the cloth of his lapel. Pull the appropriate face to show I am impressed. It is the gesture of a shit-eating lackey.

Look at you, I say. Things got turned around somewhat. Look at me, supposed to be the brains of the attack, a fucking pauper. I should have listened to the old men who tried to wise me up. Frankie Grimshaw and Mike Welsh. This game is no good, they said. Get out, they said, while you still can. I didn't listen. I knew them to be fine fellows, men who could bite the bullet, who did not give a fuck, and so they were... But I believed there was a deeper mystery, some elusive thing. For them, bricklaying was merely the means to lifting the latch. Upwards of a gallon of beer of an evening was all those birds asked of life. Mike worked till he was over seventy. They found him dead in the cement shed. Frankie was a commando in the war, a *real* hard nut, but cancer tracked him down. He died in an attic room in Cross Street. Nobody there to hold his hand and rain coming in through a hole in the roof.

Now, I say, without changing the tone of my voice, I am going to put the bite on you for a small loan that will enable me not only to make it through the night, but even help me survive Christmas and reach into another year... How are you fixed?

Without batting an eyelid, he smiles and pulls out a black calfskin wallet and licks his thumb to facilitate the peeling off of the crisp banknote. Time honoured. Between the leather, as a sandwich with the bread between the meat, there is a thick slice of solid currency. Are those tenners? I ask. He nods. Would ten of those sweethearts be asking too much?

Let's try five, he says. He offers them to me spread like a fan. Here's fifty, he says, tide you over. Come and see me in the New Year about that job. We'll work something out.

I take the money with all the reverence I can muster. Fold the notes and put them safe in my inside pocket. You saved my life, I tell him. I was getting ready to starve. Where was I? Ah yes, the gentle art of the brick in the wall. Once you hit the forty mark, it starts into shallow grave country. The days all get to look like Monday. For me, that is. Some, not many, it don't. Charlie Marley, the old maestro, he saw it as a way of life. Didn't drink and hated his wife, work was the easy part of the day for him. Saved his pennies. Gave his daughter a nice wedding. What a bricklayer! The man was a marvel of accuracy. A fat little bastard, really, and tight as a drum, but put that trowel in his hand and he was like Heifetz. Even my old man gave him best. Harry nods. Takes a sip of beer. Says: marriage don't suit some.

I study his haircut, his fingernails, the silk tie. When we were young men in the hunt for girls, this was the starboy. Blond hair, a Lavernock tan and those teeth, his success rate was higher than anyone I ever knew. All kinds of women, too. He even had a wealthy widow, not *that* old, and smart and knowing, prepared to set him up in a little flat. He would have been about twenty at the time. She took him up to London for a week and rigged him out: a Mrs Gloria Willis. The rest of us, back then, were telling lies about the odd jump. Trying to draw a veil to hide the shame of our prolonged virginity. But this boy was getting into it all over the town. He didn't have any money and he never promised to marry anyone, but they lay down for him like rabbits.

I been admiring your haircut, I tell him, and your manicure. You got that calm look.

He shrugs. Like to look after myself. I got a woman cuts my hair. A girl about twenty five. *See* the arse on her. I got a good dentist; an electric toothbrush. I'm going *bald*, though. He leans forward to show me the top of his head, a tonsured area like a moon through thin cloud. See?

Still got the old choppers, I notice.

He bares the teeth. Not one single filling, he says.

You should be proud, I tell him. I can count my good *whole* teeth on my thumbs.

How's your father? he asks me. I haven't seen him for years.

Still going, I reply.

Is he okay?

Far as I know.

He pulls back the cuff of his sleeve and studies a gold watch as thin as a coin. Crocodile strap. It is on his right wrist, the side William Holden favoured. And I have a sudden and vivid recollection of going with him to see *Love is a Many Splendored Thing* in the old Plaza cinema. William Holden was his idol.

Nice timepiece, I say. What make is it?

Not a Rolex, he says.

Looks plenty expensive, I say.

Where's he living? he asks. He still in the bungalow?

Out in the country, I tell him. Built himself a house in a field.

Never remarried?

I shake my head. How about you? I ask him.

Not fucking likely, he says.

He gets to his feet and goes out through the door at the back of the room. I watch him glance up at the game on TV. The place is crying out for a rock to come sailing through the window, or for one of the kids playing pool to have an epileptic fit. One of the drinkers watching the football stirs himself and goes up to the bar. Then the back door opens and Harry comes back. He walks with the measured tread of the man who is doing okay. He sits down. He looks about him, restless.

How about the women? I ask him. Old age slowing you down?

I keep trying, he says.

I point to his glass and tell him to drink up, but he shakes his head. I got to get going, he says. You want a lift anywhere?

Which way are you going? I ask him.

He shrugs. I could drop you in town, he offers.

He has unbuttoned his jacket and I can see the bulge of his belly. His face has the relaxed jowly look of a run-to-seed Ryan O'Neal and I wonder what he sees when he looks at me. Like Amigo, I have known him practically all my life. My mind goes back to another Christmas, when we were about seventeen, Harry and a kid named Filer and me, just wandering the freezing streets of a Christmas night. Everything dead and locked up. Bored out of our minds. No overcoats on, just gritting our teeth pointlessly, trying to act like tough hombres. Time as slow as a cardboard clock. Filer was the first to crack. Fuck this, he said and went home. Harry and I walked down to the end of West

Road and looked at the canal. There was ice at the edges. We stood there shivering for a long time, neither of us speaking. Then we went to his house.

The fire was burning solidly in the grate. The room was packed with warm air. His father sat on one side of the fire and his mother on the other. Mrs Rivers jumped up when she saw me. She smiled. Harry got his teeth from her. She asked how I was. How my mother was etc. Then she set to slicing meat off their turkey and buttering bread. Can I offer you a sandwich? and all of that. I'd offer you something strong to drink, but you're too young. Will tea do? All the time she is laughing as if she finds herself a scream. His old man just sat there looking into the red coals. My mother had gone to school with his mother. They still called each other by their maiden names. Harry went outside for a piss. His mother came to the scullery door.

Tommy, she said, would you be kind enough to ask Mr Rivers if he would like a cup of tea?

Mr Rivers kept staring into the fire. Without looking at me, he said: Tommy, please tell Mrs Rivers that Mr Rivers would.

I turn back to Mrs Rivers. She is watching me hard.

He said yes, I tell her.

Harry explained to me later that his parents had not spoken to each other for fourteen years, except through an intermediary.

But why? I asked him.

They ran out of words, he said.

Chapter Three

When we come out into the street the air is cold. The dark and the empty lamplight are almost as I remember them from long ago. A vast and sudden lunge towards regret. A car goes by. Then another. We stand there in silence. Then we cross the road and get into his car.

We sit in silence. Harry shifts in his seat. Slides the key in the ignition.

Many moons, I say. The old place don't change much but it feels like being on another planet.

He starts the engine and we move off and I am all of a sudden lifted close to pleasure by the notion of being in this shiny car with an opulent interior. Almost optimism, but that could be the beer. Money in my pocket. The idea of not having to walk. Sniff at the leather.

Nice big car, Harry Boy, I tell him. Nice and comfortable. How many you fucked in here?

Harry laughs and says nothing. This is the kind of car we never even dreamed of when we were young. A car like this, big German car, would have made our lives easy.

It is like a fucking hearse, I tell him. You could lay them out and make yourself the master of their flesh... Fuck them all ways. Up and down and sideways... Move them around like dolls. They would be impressed. I'm impressed. Show them the way the wipers work and everything. Work the windows... Woo the bastards with ease in a car like this one.

He laughs quietly. My words make him happy.

Bit long in the tooth, he says, to be fucking them in the car. Not as agile as I used to be.

You got a girlfriend? I ask him.

Sort of, he says. Sort of on and off. Been going with her for a couple of years now, but I don't want her getting no ideas. Leave gaps, you know, so she knows.

We are passing across the bottom of the park.

I heard you and him fell out, he says. Amigo, I mean.

He turns his head to look at me. Did you make it up?

I stare straight ahead. Trees on both sides of the road. Bridge Road. The spheres of lamplight.

What did you hear? I ask him.

You poked his missus.

He is barely doing twenty miles an hour, the engine soft as a sigh.

The deserted road. I can feel his eyes on me.

Is it true? he asks.

No, I tell him.

We go past the rowing club gates and climb the hill. Stop at the lights. He is watching me like a hawk.

I'm glad, he says. When I first heard it I said: that don't sound like Tommy. No way would that boy be fucking Amigo's wife. You and him was like brothers.

The lights change and we start down the hill. The Black Lion. The Maltsters Arms. A couple of cars.

In my book, he tells me, that's the lowest of the low.

We come to another red light. Harry curses. Two cars cross and head east along Western Avenue. Harry holds up a single finger.

One thing, he says, I never did. *Golden* rule. Never fuck a mate's missus. I fucked quite a few of the wives of strangers, mind, I won't be denying that. A fuck is a fuck and you get it where you can. But I had a code, even a low-life like me: you leave the wives of your mates alone.

Honourable fellow, I say.

I don't know about that, he says, but there were chances.

The lights change and we go on.

Plenty of chances, too, he says. A tone of smugness to go with the virtue. The one I got going now is married. That's why I'm just driving around. She is stuck with her family. This Christmas shit. They got kids coming home and she can't get out of it. He glances at me.

How about your kids?

The boy is home, I tell him.

You don't sound overjoyed, he says.

Thorn in my flesh, I tell him. Lillian loves him. Adores him and gives him money. Cooks him meals he likes. Spoils him. I'm out.

Is he still good looking? he asks. He used to be good looking. Women like him, I tell him. I suppose he is.

He laughs. Must take after his mother, he says,

Very likely, I say. I wouldn't know a lot about that. The whole thing is something I never got my head around. Not properly. Some element in there I could never work out. The superficiality, the high heel stuff, the whore bit, the show, *that* I could get. But the primitive bit, the basics, the cunt and dick and blood part of it, that always eluded me. Red swamp. I think I always respected women too much. Or was afraid of them. I don't particularly like them, but I was always scared of hurting their feelings. Vessels of grief...

Harry laughs at this. Says nothing.

And the way it can chew up the lives of people, I say. That's another mystery to me.

Silence fills up the car like a fog. We go down Penhill.

Next year, he says, I think I will fuck off somewhere where they got sunshine. Florida maybe. Or Southern Spain. Some place where they got nice golfcourses. Christmas got nothing to offer me now.

We turn into Cathedral Road, close to the journey's end. Amigo is still on my mind.

I nearly fucked her, I blurt out. Stare straight ahead. Locked in.

It might be another person speaking.

I must have been less than an inch from her snatch, I tell him. It was in her hand, my dick... Do that leave me innocent?

He says nothing, but I insist: is it only the fuck that determines the guilt?

I'll drop you at the Castle, he says.

We go past Sophia Gardens and over the bridge. Past the Angel Hotel. He pulls into the empty bus lay-by. We sit and stare into the mouth of Queen Street. The Christmas lights going on and off. It starts to rain, a blur of fine drizzle on the windscreen.

He is dying, I tell him. He looks terrible. He is my oldest friend. You were right, we were like brothers... Once. I wanted him to forgive me. Now he'll go to his grave with his curse still on me.

I hear him draw a deep breath and slowly exhale.

I saw her, he says. About a month ago. Terry, his ex. I was going down the hill in Crwys Road and she was coming up. I think she must have spotted me before I spotted her. I am working out what to say to her when she dives into this shop. She didn't want to speak to me, didn't want to explain. She looked rough. There's no words for it. I just kept going. I nearly kept going when I saw you tonight. I still don't know what made me come back.

We are silent again. I don't want it to end. What is it? I ask him. Is it some kind of curse?

I turn and watch him move his upper lip down to cover his lower lip.

He turns to look at me and his face is serious, almost grave.

It is dog, he says quietly. Too much fucking dog. The worst kind of bad luck.

Sackcloth and ashes, I say. Then I open the door and get out. Stoop to look back in. Thanks for the lift, I tell him. I pat my pocket where the money is. And thanks for the bread. I'll get it back to you as soon as I can.

Come and see me about that job, he says. In the New Year. I'm serious, Tommy.

I nod and then shrug. The idea of working for him fails to enthuse me. I watch him glance in the wing mirror. He is trying to look like Steve McQueen. Be careful, Tommy, he says.

It is like a disease and we all have it. There is no known cure. Then the glass slides up to seal the hole and he pulls away.

Adam Street with the lights going out and the east wind coming in. The stagger and stumble jolt through my being like a plague. All the emptiness of the old-time Sunday on the eve of Xmas Eve. I turn my attention to the prison wall. All through my life this has been the most significant architectural feature of a town that was losing. A car goes by; leaves a silence like the hole in a frozen puddle. There is a deeper silence within the walls of The Vulcan.

The jail wall. The sky, with cloud and star. The wind to stir old memories. I cross the road and let my hands touch the stone of the wall. Rough-hewn blocks of Blue Pennant. There is nobody walking. Over and over my thoughts are with my memories of Nat King Cole. The stone under my fingertips is hard, unforgiving, as I try to come to terms.

My house is dark when I reach it; windows like empty mouths. The key in the lock. Enter and pause. Hold my breath. The insistent emptiness of inside the mask. Stillness and cold air. When I switch on the lights nothing stirs. Then the cat comes down the stairs with the slow deliberate tread of Elaine Stewart in that film with Kirk Douglas. The whore in the home of the ham. She (the cat) stares at me hard with bitter and resentful eyes that are the green of the midseason gooseberry outside the black dilation of pupil. Her movements betray sinews stiff with cold and prolonged inactivity. She stops on the bottom tread. Arch of back. Yawn. Then the glare.

There is no sign of my wife. No sign of Elliott. No note.

My stomach, as the old saying has it, thinks my throat is cut, but I cannot bring myself to eat. Not even munch at a cream cracker or chew at a sliver torn from the dry crust in the breadbin. I open the cupboard door and stare in at the labels on the tins. Sauce bottles; sugarbags; mustard jars; salt cellars. This, I tell myself, is not the life. I speak the words aloud: this will not do. The cat is pressed hard against my lower calf. The milk in the bottle on the draining board is clotted. It smells about a week sour. All I can find to feed her is a flat tin of Portugese sardine in sunflower oil. I take down a tin of beans and imagine how they would be, hot on warm buttered toast. But I am unable to muster the resolve necessary to open the tin and spill the beans into a pan. So I stare at the label for a full minute. It feels as if my substance is dissolving into thin air and silence. As if the tin in my hand is the only thing anchoring me to the earth. When I put it down all that I can think of is Nat King Cole.

Then I close my eyes and I can see Christmas when I was sixteen years of age. It snowed that Christmas, a fine powdery snow that lay in the furrows of the field beyond the end of January. The cold wind blew and only the snow that had settled in the pockets and holes and tiny craters and furrows was left when that wind ceased and *that* snow stayed into February. Every night I could see the lines of the furrows in that dark field like a blueprint. It crackled when you trod on it like a crust of salt. No other year was ever like that one in my life: my seventeenth. My first real incoherent drunken episode occurred that Christmas. Unable to stand drunk. This reminds me of Amigo's bottle. I tap my pocket to make sure it is safe. Force my face to smile and take down a nice glass from the dresser. Pour a generous measure. Smell it. Hold it up to the light. The colour of whisky held against the light is a constant comfort. But I feel nothing. I smell it again and sip. Then the stare takes over and I lose where I am. Sip again. This time it colours the interior like thin paint. A varnish over the hole in my head. It tastes of varnish. Or turpentine. Or is it shellac? I put down my glass of whisky and take from the shelf a glass jar of Maxwell House coffee granules. Heft the jar in my right hand, swivel to the left and hurl it with all my might at the point where the cast iron stove pipe dives into the wall. The brown granules broadcast like sorrelseed. Bits of glass. I take my whisky glass and Amigo's bottle with me into the front room.

Stand at the window and stare out. If I am waiting for a message there is nothing there. The street is empty. The sky is black. Draw the curtains.

The arms of the chair I sit in are said to be covered with genuine hide and they are as cold as ice. The idea of putting on an overcoat crosses my mind. Sip whisky. Nothing, it seems, exists that might make any difference. Then I remember Nat King Cole. There is a record somewhere in the house of his greatest hits, but trying to remember where gets to be too much and the notion slips away. Sip at my whisky. The grey cat sits in the dark passage like a thing formed from steam. It feels as if I can hear her heartbeat. My mouth is dry. When I next come to sip I discover the glass is empty. Reach down to grasp at the bottle neck.

Later on, when I bring up my hands to cover my eyes and forehead it feels like a trapped bird is under them. The skull itself seems to be trembling. But I have no sense of personal fear. Under my hand, the mind moves in, then out. A dark seashore. The whisky is a comfort to me but I am not so far gone that I am not aware of its propensity to turn nasty, its ability to overwhelm. I think about the overcoat but find it hard to move. It strikes me that with the overcoat around my shoulders life might be enhanced. The cat shifts her position. Her tail twitches.

I look down and the gooseberry eyes look up. There is no trust in them. Then a great shudder goes through me. I remember how Amigo's mother used to polish his shoes right up till he went into the army. Straighten his tie before he went dancing on a Saturday night. The telephone rings.

For a moment it feels like dreaming. It rings again and the cat jumps. I go out into the passage and pick it up. Hello, I say. My head feels as if it is looping the loop.

It's me, a voice says. My wife.

Where are you? I say.

I've been trying to get you all day. Where were you? Is Elliott there?

What's going on? I ask her.

You sound drunk. Where is Elliott? Let me speak to him.

He's not here, I tell her.

Where is he? she demands. There is music in the background.

Where are you? I ask. Is that music?

It's the radio, she says. I want to speak to Elliott.

A long silence. I can hear her breathing. The music is gone.

What I would like to know is, I tell her, where the fuck are you? What the fuck is going on?

Calm down, she says. I had to get away. Things were getting out of hand. I need time to think.

It's fucking Christmas, I remind her.

Don't swear, she says.

Think about what?

What do you think? I should have thought that was obvious. About where my life is going.

Your life? I say. I can feel myself swaying and I reach out to steady myself against the wall. *Your* fucking life!

Then it starts to clear in my mind. Snell's wife had died at the end of November. Some bug, they said, she had picked up on a Jamaican holiday. Something tropical and mysterious for which they had no name. Now that the coast was clear, they had eloped.

Is he with you? I ask her.

I need time to think, Tommy.

Where are you? Shacked up in some fucking hotel with that dirty bastard? It's okay now, is it? Now his fucking wife is dead?

I stop talking. She says nothing. It feels like looking over the edge of a high cliff. A buzzing starts up in the back of my head and the swaying gets worse.

I don't give a fuck, I tell her. And I am desperately trying to gather more words when I hear the click at the other end. I stare at the door. Stare at the end of the phone from which the words come. Put the phone back in the cradle.

My heart is not broken, I can feel that much, but my entrails are sad. A story that has kept us all going for years, that had all kinds of moments in it, lies and bitter emotions and truths also, is coming to an end. The cat is sitting in the doorway. Her eyes watch me. They blink lazily. Her mouth gapes to accommodate her yawn.

It is too much and it is nothing. A man needs a violent gesture at such times in his life. A tommy gun to hand, or a brace of grenades. He knows (a man of my age does) that nobody gives a fuck. That none of the nonsense we delude ourselves with to get us through the days means a fucking thing in the long run. Then I recall the coffee jar and Nat King Cole and a colossal weariness takes over and I can barely manage to reach down the genuine Crombie overcoat from the coat rack and shrug it on. The grey cloth feels heavy as lead. My eyelids are as heavy as lead. I regain my seat in the hide armchair. There is still whisky left in the bottle but the desire is gone. This, I tell myself, is the stuff that dreams are really made of. No angel for the Christmas tree and no trimmings. Not a scrap of desire for a single thing in the whole wide world.

A knocking at the front door. My eyes open and I can feel straight away how bugged they are. My mouth is dry. My face feels stiff as cardboard. The room is snot-grey, with morning glimmer around the curtain edges. I think it is Elliott. Can see in the mind's eye the snarl on my face as I stagger along the passageway. It is not Elliott. It is this kid I met who sees me as his friend. His father died, an old drinking companion. His mother is some kind of loose piece out of a weird jigsaw. The kid has high hopes for himself. Sees a future where he will write books or make films, and get to fuck a lot of young and impressionable women. There are raindrops on his glasses. Behind the lenses, eyes like an owl. I glance up at the sky and shudder.

What happened to your face? he asks me.

Come in, I say. We go along the passageway. It's a long story, I tell him.

We go through to the kitchen. I point to a chair at the table. Sit down, kid, I tell him. My better half is out of town. Temporarily, so I am led to believe. I drink some water from a cup. Splash water onto my face. Search for a towel. The kid watches me in silence. His eyes are solemn.

You look pale, I tell him. Is that midnight oil? You studying hard?

He shrugs. He is still standing. He is almost three inches taller than I am.

Sit down, kid. I'll put the kettle on.

He is very thin, with bony hands and long fingers. He looks down at me with that quizzical benevolence young men develop when they go to college. They always go away as boys and come back like novice missionaries.

How's life with you? he says. He glances about the place.

Pretty wonderful, I tell him.

I watched *Badlands* last night, he tells me. He wants to describe things for me but I hold up my hand.

Please, I say. My head feels like it is made out of toffee. Brain, that is.

You don't want to hear my troubles, kid, I tell him. You have just seen *Badlands* and you are twenty years old and you want to... There was a time I would have loved to pick over that chicken carcase. It is Christmas Eve, isn't it? Not now, kid. Right now I got to get some breakfast into me. There is a place called the Clifton Café where I go occasionally to eat breakfast. Have you had breakfast?

He nods. I was just passing on my way into town, he says. What's with the overcoat? And the beard? You look like one of those old guys that sleep in shop doorways.

You are very polite, I tell him.

I go to the bathroom and stare at myself. Dismay like a wave of nausea. It starts in the pit of my stomach and rises steadily. I come back, shaking my head. It's hopeless, I say. Smile at him.

I'll put the kettle on. Do you want a cup of tea? Coffee?

He shakes his head. Do you want to come and watch me eat? I say. You can have a round of toast, or something. A milkshake.

Then, when I have eaten and regained some measure of personal integrity I'll tell you all about the first time I saw *On the Waterfront.*

He stares at me as if I am quoting from the good book. In a different life this kid might have become my first disciple. The kettle comes to the boil. Kid, I say, go into the front room and look on the floor by the chair and you should find a bottle and a glass. The glass will be empty (probably) but there should be some liquid, colour of weak tea...

Is it whisky?

Elixir of eternal... Just bring it to me, *s'il vous plait.*

He goes to fetch it. Comes back holding it by the neck between finger and thumb. It is a quarter full. I take it from him and pour a generous measure into a clean glass.

Let me show you something, I say. I put two heaped teaspoons of demerara sugar into the glass and top it up with hot water from the kettle. I sniff at the fragrant steam. Smile at him.

This will restore life to the corpse, I tell him. I drink down a good swallow. Add some whisky. Another swig. Close my eyes and try to hang on to the genuine pleasure.

Is that a hot toddy? he asks me.

I drain the glass and smack my lips. Stare at him as the infusion takes place. That, I tell him, is known as hair of the dog.

We come from sad worlds, I tell the kid.

He makes no reply. We are sitting in the Clifton Café and the breakfast is inside me. Monica is silently enduring her morning with a black eye and many bruises to show for her husband Jimmy's attentions. The kid stares at me, waiting for me to start.

I was about your age, I tell him. It was winter. A Saturday night. I saw it in the Tivoli. Of all the buildings in the whole fucking world there is not one that will afford more pleasure to me than that place did. They sell Mercedes cars from there now. Vehicles for shitheads and pimps, to go with the gold Rolex. But when I was seventeen it was this outpost at the edge of the wide world. Like a trading post on the prairies. By this time I have seen thousands of pictures and not had my first jump. Just a Saturday and I was supposed to meet this girl in there, was supposed to be a cert.

Myrna Baird. She was a sort of pale blonde. Plain featured but nice tits. One of the boys had fucked her. I can see her now. As I came down the aisle she stood up and looked around. She had on a pale blue sweater and the light from the screen fell on her tits. I didn't really fancy her but my continued virginity was starting to bother me. She waves when she sees me. I been keeping you a seat, she says. She looks a bit like Jan Sterling: plain, with a good body. This friend of mine Harry Rivers had set me up. She had her hair cut short like Doris Day. Hard eyes, though. Her father was Scotch, a hard-looking bastard. He reckoned he had played for Third Lanark. I sit down. Cannot think of a single thing to say to her. She is looking up at me with these seen it all eyes. She is eager to be with me. My eyes are on her tits and I am weighing the ordeal of the cinema against the time I can get her in some shop doorway...

At that moment I chance to look up and catch Monica's husband staring at me. I nod and smile. The kid turns around to see who I am looking at. Jimmy beckons to me. I go over to the counter.

Your boy, he says, you seen him today?

No, I tell him. He didn't come home last night.

Was you aware, he says, the little prick was fucking my missus?

I stare at him. Glance at Monica's bruised face.

That's right, he says. Two and fucking two. It was only my mother stopped me from... He starts to wag a finger at me.

I got no quarrel with you, Tom, he tells me, but I get a hold of that kid of yours, I intend to fuck him right up.

I can think of nothing to say to him. He is a belligerent man with a genuine nasty streak.

The best thing he can do, Jimmy says, is fuck off. Out of town. Far away as possible.

I go back to the table. Freddy Clark, a friend of Elliott's, is over in the corner.

Kid, I say, I got a small problem to clear up. I am just going to have a word with that man over there.

Freddy, I say.

He looks up. Tommy. How's it going?

I sit down. Did you know about this business with Elliott and Monica?

He nods. Forks in some bacon and eggs. Chews and looks past me.

Do you know where he is? He didn't come home last night.

He shakes his head, still chewing hard. Then he swallows and lays down his knife and fork.

He been fucking her for a coupla months, he tells me. Jimmy was bound to find out. We all warned him.

He pushes his plate away and stands up.

I got to get going, Tom, he says.

Do you know where he is?

He shakes his head. Honest, he says. I'll see you. Merry Christmas.

Who was that? the kid asks me.

He's a hodcarrier, I tell him.

What's that? the kid asks me.

That's a long story, I tell him.

He's got a hard face, he observes. Worn out with experience.

Well, I say, he is in a hard life.

Hard? How?

The whole business, I tell him. A man who carries bricks up a ladder and earns bladders for it. Lives in rooms with a kid in nappies and a pregnant wife. He is in a tough spot, believe me.

The kid laughs. It irritates me.

What are you laughing at? I say. Fucking college boy, what the fuck do you know? You live to be a fucking thousand, you will never have the faintest inkling what is going on in that man's head when his eyes open in the dark on a Monday morning. The sheer ingenuity and endurance it takes for him to hang onto where he is, which is nowhere... He don't need a torture chamber. He's a bright kid, but he is slack. He is a friend of my son's. He is another bright one. My son, I mean.

Kid, I tell him, I kind of lost the thread of *On the Waterfront*.

He stares at me. His eyes are solemn.

Don't waste your life, kid, I tell him.

It is still raining when we come out into the street. Cold on my bare head and all of a sudden the inside of my skull feels like a barn at midnight in a high wind. Old decrepit slatted doors are swinging and banging. Straw is flying about in the dark. Chickens are squawking with terror. I glance about me; look up at the sky: it feels (my entire being, body and soul) as if the flooded gutters and the dirty brick are starting to get the better of me.

The kid stands beside me. He is waiting for me to do something. Or say something. I look at him and try to speak, but nothing comes readily to mind. He walks with me step for step as far as City Road and we stop at the crossroads. At this point the rain is caught up in the tangle of winds. The traffic grinds on. We press back against the wall of the bank.

Well, he says. He is nonplussed. His big glasses make him look like an owl in a comic book. He hesitates because he is lost. Raindrops on the lenses. Pale blue eyes in pale sockets. A milksop who would be a man of the world. Beautiful silky skin. He takes after his mother and it crosses my mind that she might once upon a time have been a woman of genuine radiance. I nod at the weather and pull a face of final resignation.

You better get going, kid, I tell him. Don't let me detain you from the – Merry Christmas, I tell him. We shake hands and I push him on his way. Stay where I am and watch him dwindle and get wet and find I am once more alone in a town that is running down like an overwound Timex watch. It feels as if I have a private view straight up into the arsehole of futility. A massive frog is sitting on me. I struggle weakly to remember sunlit times, but memories are hard to find. The ugliness, in all the complexity that goes to make a dump like this, closes in.

There are sums trying to work themselves out in my head. Whisky is in them and coins in pockets etc. There is enough for a full bottle. My eyes stare towards the southwest where the lighted windows in the vast grey walls of the office buildings rise like tiers of candles into the dull wet ceiling of the morning sky. The rain falls harder still. The blood inside me goes round and around. Throbs at my temples. Finds a place to pronounce dull pain at the point where the bone at the back of the skull runs into the neck.

All over the town men of my age will be getting into chairs in barbershops. Pausing to stare deep into mirrors before sliding down into the comfort of closed eyes and clean warm bibs and sweetly perfumed oily atmosphere. Settling for the sag and slump of unctuous paunches while the loquacious son of a genuine Athenian with an opinion on everything under the unseen sun will chatter and bellyache and comb and snip away. Men that I know, that I have known since childhood, men that I know to be my natural inferiors in a fairer world. Men who can draw on all the comfort that a Rolex might appear to guarantee. And Christmas with a genuine tree and a bright silver star. Perhaps a Durex and some wishful thoughts. At mooring, an obedient menial providing close attention and the neutral intimacy of the purchased touch.

But I am too listless to hate them much. Men like that deserve the barbers they end up with. Give it up, I tell myself, as if some wandering spirit of vague generosity had gotten into me. Too weary, almost, to give half a mind to the Christmas I am in. Whatever it meant whenever it meant something is long since lost in me. Conviviality, smiles and the warm embrace, all gone. Another year done for is all. Another pisspot filled to the brim. How crimped and shrunk the heart is. Sourness eats into me hard and all trust tends to dissolution. What used to act as counterbalance to the shit has lapsed, and in the places where a so-called good might once have lodged, is only vacancy.

Playing safe, the first thing I do is buy three loaves of white bread. Sliced bread. This is the way you start a curse. My father would not have sliced bread in the house. A man who hated Jews, he would walk miles to buy bread from Moses Zembla's bakery in Eldon Road. He swore that all the bread with names like Meadowblest had secret chemicals to keep the nation on its knees. Then two tins of corned beef and a pound of Canadian Cheddar cheese. A tin of English mustard powder. Two tins of baked beans. All these things as tokens to sustain me while I wander in the rain until the supermarkets will sell me my bottle of Scotch. Queen Street and St Mary Street. Lighted shop windows and the wet pavements. Shoppers and buses. Cold rain falling onto my bald patch. All I am longing for is the time when I am drunk. Maybe even run a hot bath to draw the chill from my bones. Try to find some of the old records and fuck about with the record player until it works again. Sarah Vaughan. Nat King Cole. The ancient sounds to tear at me and open ancient wounds. Gush of blood. Hot tears. The man alone is besieged on all sides. He keeps on squinting to take bearings and pinpoint what he ought to do. I know, when I reach this point, that I am coming to my mother. The voice of Nat King Cole is entirely to do with what my mother was. And where she is, some five miles north by northwest of where I am through pouring rain. A small white marble tablet eighteen inches by eighteen inches with names and dates marks where she lies on a bare hill under squalid grass. It is years since I have been there. Not even a bunch of flowers.

The full weight of morning in winter. Rubbing your nose in it. Close my eyes and think of what I am. Stendhal fell over in the street and died of apoplexy. Keats' lungs, when breath ran out, were like a pair of moth-eaten socks. Clutch at my bottle and think – can it all be wrong when I have you for comfort? The loss is in its proper time. Amigo comes to mind again, then fades. My wife, the same clock but some other morning. My son, vanished like a puff of smoke. All you can do is surrender.

I go home and the solitude burns into me like acid. The bare trees in the road. Sky like soiled bedsheets. In the clear glass bottle the whisky is the colour of weak tea. There is much that bewilders me. Muscles, bones, organs are not easy in my skin. One by one the squeaking mice come creeping in to fill the cavern of my head. The shit stays. I sniff at my stained fingers. It *is* shit. This is the game we are in and we can't get out. We cry out to ourselves: what a fool! What a fool! Women and warmth and their special luxury gone forever: the gravy train. High heels and silk stockings and the gearbox pelt barely a memory. Stuck with the sackcloth. The wet ashes.

The light going down at the window and no song. Only fear. More words of four letters. *fuck; twig; leaf; love; pimp; bell; ball; baby; star.* I sit and drink my whisky down and start to feel sick. This is the time I would press buttons and make cities disappear. *Skin; scum; kith; kind...*

Time it is time. No wife around. The Boy Wonder nowhere.

I begin to build my fire at five o'clock. It is black at the windows by this time and I am charged up with a fierce hilarity. This is an old dream. Take the dining chairs and break them; tear off the horseshoe rail of the back and pull the spokes from the holes in the seat like teeth; then the legs, the footrails. Bare hands is all I need. Snap them like reedstems. A mad fucker with the strength of ten. And the sweat builds beads on my head and I am sucking the whisky straight out of the bottle's neck. And laughing and laughing, the way the wind laughs in a chimney flue. Then I stop and the sound of the laughter goes on in my head, a melodious insistence to it. There is no hesitation. My cause is virtuous. My blood is pumping. I can feel it sing and hum in my heart, inside the bone of my skull. Feel it gather. More and more.

There is an art to building a fire, a rule of procedure that must be obeyed. The place to start is under the stairs. Clear out the junk. Newspaper. Take some pages of the paper and crumple them into balls. Make a heap of these paper balls. Then you make a wigwam structure with the sticks, the kindling, over the pile of the crumpled paper. Then you strike the match and watch the flame leap out of the wood, squirm in the dark air and right itself and burn. You hold the flame where the crumpled paper is. And watch it catch alight; watch it leave the paper for the wood. Take hold. Dry wood with varnish; the flame and the crackle and snap and pop. It is as easy as pissing the bed once it gets going. Just feed it junk. The house is full of junk. High heel shoes and old petticoats and suit coats and brown leather belts from the bottom of the wardrobe and the books on the shelf and the curtains torn down from the front room windows... A box of sweet-smelling candles my wife had bought that had lain in a cupboard for years. Stand back and watch them melt and run. The flames change colour and intensify and leap up to the soffit of the treads and lick like fuck at the wood and the cobwebs. I can smell the perfume released by the wax, attar of roses, perhaps, or Parma violets, or some such shit. I am pretty calm now. Still joyful, but calming down. Serious now.

Nat King Cole is singing. The flames are secure. The wood in the staircase is old; the treads and the risers, the strings and the banisters, handrail and newel post, the trimming joist and the boards that make the landing, all have been hanging on their nails a hundred years since the carpenter drove the last one home. Waiting for me. Yellow pine from Riga. The Baltic in winter. Before the axe, the tree in the forest, the hundred and fifty years it took to grow.

This is Life! I roar. This is fucking History!

Then it starts to die back on me. By this time Nat King Cole is singing *Unforgettable*. Air, I think. A fire must have air. A draught. I charge up the stairs and open the window in the back bedroom. Glance around the room. A lot of lonely nights and a few bad dreams. A bed. A few books. Scraps of paper. Nothing I want. No time for leavetakings or ceremonial routines. Go back down to my fire. Open the back door. Open the front door. The game is dead serious. But I am laughing. It is bubbling out of me. Now the fire really starts to roar. Take up my whisky bottle and drink hard. Head back and three good long swigs. The heat is on my face through the door. Then the paint on the outside of the string starts to blister and bloat and pop. The dry wood crackles. Yellow tongues of flame as agile as eels slip out through the cracks. They are searching for air. Sucking the oxygen out of the dark. They grow big and roar and leap up in the well and the shadows dance. And I dance too. And the air rushes along the passageway. Then the back door slams shut and the air dies down and I have to wedge the door open with a brick.

Now the string on the passage side is alight and I have to edge past and my eyebrows are singed. I reach the front door and stand on the threshold and survey my work. I am still laughing. I had forgotten I was laughing. The air from the night is sucked past me. The staircase climbs high into the well like a burning tree. It is Christmas Eve.

Then the cat leaps suddenly out of the fire and goes past me with a frantic howl. The wet night swallows her. And at last I am all alone. I take the last swallow of whisky and bowl the bottle underarm into the heart of the fire.

There are people gathered in the street. Others come to watch the fun. I go to mingle with them. Walk amongst them. Point to the house with the fireglow framed in the doorway.

This is the fucking game! I tell them. Burn it down! Burn it all down!

The rain starts to fall harder. It will not quench the flames. The flames will search and search and thrive and cannot be stopped. The faces are staring at me. The laughter inside me is stopped now and I can hear myself scream. Flames appear at the front windows. I point and laugh. And dance. Then scream again. Then, again, another scream...

Part Two

Chapter Four

As a man gets older he dreams himself into a second life and takes a position from which he can observe at leisure his flaws and failings and their progression from childhood on, with a dispassionate eye.

He has a second chance to bite the cherry; this is the theory. All journeys home are without mercy. No place can bear the weight you carry home with you. Pearl Street, like an unbuttoned fly. Then the bridge, the fundamental Splott Road Bridge. I get up and walk along the aisle to gain the vestibule. Stare through the window. The backs of Railway Street. The barren fields: plough, sow crumbs and wait for loaves of Wonderloaf. The wet *Echo*. You turnabout – that used to be the York Hotel – and stare along St Mary Street. The buses and the roundabout. The corner of the Royal Hotel. The station, when you disembark, stagnant from disenchantment. The ancient stink. The inevitable, innate provincial second rate. The hills afar, as ever, quite unmoved.

The travellers vanish down the pockets of the stairs. Not one face I know. But the voices are familiar. And the atmosphere, a certain tone of atmosphere, comes back. And the faces: on every face, the leer of the mountebank in the low wage economy. Nothing changed in that respect, only the range of servility is wider spread. Vittori's poem comes to mind.

> ...spittoons that fill
> and overflow and spill
> where pearldivers abound

who plunge and search
the warm grey spit
and nothing ever found
of any worth – just shit.

Every day, you know, will be measured with the same unctuous deliberation, like the coffin of the midget's bride.

When I wake up I am blank. I just lie there. It is May, getting close to the middle of the month, and this is a month I have never had any confidence in. May is a month that can lead any man astray. Time runs out. Each day is a new desert. Each day finds a new hole in my left shoe. Or pebble in my right shoe. And each new day presents the dusty road for me to walk. Day in, day out, the streets in their grimy and provincial familiarity rise up like the demented in their padded cells. I long for the so-called open road and the starry sky and the pale sun at dawn in the silence strewn with the songs of birds. Blackbird and goldfinch and yellowhammer. Robin redbreast. I would gladly trudge my way to the world's end but my knees ache worse than rotten teeth and the corns on my little toes are more tender than ripe boils.

I stay where I am until the need to piss moves me. When I come into the kitchen it is as if the Oracle has managed to elude time. He sits in the same chair. A can of Stella nestles in his right hand exactly as it did last night. His eyes rest on me as I come into the doorframe and a sigh of an immense weariness escapes him. He gestures with the can-holding hand. He has turned into a drunk.

How come, he says, everyone you talk about's a cocksucker?

It is as if the seven hours I have been asleep have kept him spellbound with that question on his lips. I puff my cheeks and shrug. Smile. Bear with me for a moment, Bob, I say, the bladder bout to bust if – and hurry past him out into the backyard where I let it flood out amongst the red roses and the weeds. Coming back into the kitchen, I say: bravado, mainly. It is a word I grew fond of. It seemed to be right for any number of people I was forced to deal with back then. People I was forced to deal with but had no reason to admire. People for whom I felt contempt. That's all it is, a grand word for the expression of contempt.

He grimaces and puts the can down on the table. You called me it, once, he says. I smile. I must have been drunk, I say. I have called most people I know it, one time or another. Sometimes it don't mean fuck all. Just an expression of familiarity.

He shakes his head. I'm not so sure of that, he says. I think you got a downer on the world. You live too much in the past. You want to wise up.

Well, I say, nodding thoughtfully, wisdom is something I always found in fairly short supply.

He nods towards the empty chair. Sit down, he says.

I'll put the kettle on, I say.

He picks up his can and sips. Puts it down again. He is still drunk from the day before. He tries to keep it going for as long as he can. Hates to let it peter out in sleep. The entire trick, he claims, is one of equilibrium. Just little sips, spaced out to keep it on an even keel. Delicate attention to detail.

We used to be good friends, but I fear this friendship is close to ending. I told you, he told me when I turned up at the door, as long as you want it, you got a place to lay your head.

His partner, which is what he calls Martine, stood back in the shadows. I couldn't see her eyes but I could feel the glare.

I don't want to pose no problems, I said. Just a coupla nights... Get myself, you know, sorted out...

She turned away and went into the kitchen. He looked past me. Then he turned to see if she was still there. Pulled a face. Then he said: Aw, come on in. Fuck it. Let's have a drink, I got a stack of cans.

He was disappointed when I told him I was no longer a drinker.

How long will *that shit* last? he said.

It's my only chance, I told him. If I get back on that stuff, it will finish me.

Martine never said a word. Just kept turning up the sound on the TV while me and the Oracle were trying to converse.

It's not the same, he said, when one is sober.

And he was right. This was my third morning. Things in general are not going as smoothly as I had hoped. I had hoped to move on after the first night but I was still hanging around. It is a chemical thing, he says. With me it is a necessity. How else do you fill the time?

I have heard this tale before. There was a time I might have believed it myself: the man powerless before the massive forces of the chemical world. The needs of flesh and mind and imagination; the soul struggling to find a way in the hopeless battle.

Drunkenness, he says, the type I am seeking to embrace, is like a branch of metaphysics. You run on and on like a clock in an empty house... a delicate... a sort of...

He looks at me. I no longer get about the town much, he tells me. I got hardly any interest left for the wide world. Don't need to be out in all that bustle and blare, arguing the toss and fighting people. Just want to stay forever cool. Juggle the magic ball.

Don't we all, I say.

When you go out, from here, I just wonder where you go all day. You just wander round, or what? I fill the kettle at the sink and switch it on.

Are you going to have a cup? I ask him

He shakes his head. Holds up the can. Best to stick with this, he says. He sips at it to confirm his choice.

When the water boils I make tea with a single teabag in the chipped china mug allocated for my use. I move the bag about with a spoon to hasten the release of the teabag's potency.

I was never, he says, a great lover of the cup that cheers. I think it was my old man. His devotion to his cup of tea was downright slavish. Could never even wait for it to cool, but had to be slurping at it.

He sips from the can and holds it at arm's length to study it. Then he sniffs, pulls a face and puts it down.

I get them cut price, he says. This fellow I know goes back and forth to the continent. It is how he lives. People are being forced to take measures of evasion, the taxation in this country is nothing short of punitive.

I sit down and sip quietly at the tea. It is too hot.

I walk, I tell him. My legs just carry me where they will. The edges of town, where the cemeteries are. I am making a walking tour of the cemeteries. Checking all the names on the new gravestones to see if my enemies are lying in them.

Found any? he asks, smiling. But before I can reply I see his gaze shift and I know Martine is standing behind me. As I alter my position to turn, she says: a pity you wasn't looking for a room to sleep in.

I stand up. Her presence confuses me, the palpable hostility. Almost before I know it, I am leaving the house and I have pulled the front door shut. The tea is still on the kitchen table.

And the morning is truly immense. There is a sense of true vastness and newly ordained possibility as I stare up and see the bright blue and the swift white cloud from west to east.

Here I am, I tell myself, with no roof to call my own. Can't even fart in my own darkness. Once, when we were getting towards old, she told me of her fears of death. Lillian. I clammed right up and could not meet her eyes. In the widening margin of our vital years, only fear and vileness. Sorrow still burns me. The times, I used to tell myself, are good for the pimps and the bitches of the pimps. Old songs can still bring back the aches of little memories.

It is almost nine o'clock and there are children passing on their way to school. Workmen are plastering the walls of the big house on the corner of the avenue. I watch as they move about their tasks with the ponderous deliberation of mechanical beings. One, unseen, works away at the front of the house; the steady taptap of lumphammer on cold chisel as he seeks to chip away the old stucco from the stone walls beneath. The work has gone slowly, the Oracle informs me. I watch them, he told me, from the bedroom window. They go about their tasks with a sort of lugubrious dissonance. They are like surly bears in a failing circus.

The labourer who is the ground crew glances up from his mixer as I pass. His eyes are heavy with disdain that has its roots in the certainty of infinite boredom. He has a weatherbeaten face, much wrinkled and showing the signs of wear that solid drinking brings. He is very thin, with long legs and a small body like a jockey. His face is that of a jockey at the end of a long and largely unsuccessful career. The top of his spine curves quite sharply where it passes between his shoulderblades, so that he resembles a question mark as he leans to peer inside the mixer's revolving drum. He is wearing tight blue jeans that are drawn up almost to his chest and held there by a tightly buckled leather belt. His black baseball cap is worn with the peak tilted up, so that the three letters SOX, embroidered in white cotton, are almost obscured. Now and then he taps at the shell of the drum with a brick hammer as he waits for the mixing mortar to achieve consistency. He adopts the attitude of keeper or guardian; the sand is heaped neatly on a spread-out layer of stout blue polythene sheet; alongside the sand, a tidy stack of six polenta yellow cement bags; there is a forty-gallon butt to hold the water. Aware, perhaps, of my attentive gaze, he picks up his shovel from where it leans against the waterbutt, studies it briefly, then, with a soft, loose-armed and languid movement, flings it into the heap of sand. A gesture to mark a stage of some forlorn finality. Then he stares away down the street with eyes that are accustomed to expect the worst and are dully resigned to meet it whether it comes or not.

The plasterer waits up on the scaffold. He stares down into the street with the face of a contented man whose mild curiosity has been stirred. He is waiting without anxiety for the day's first batch of mortar to arrive. He, too, wears a black baseball hat. But the insignia on this hat comprises the letters SA, which is the name of a local beer much favoured by drinkers who seek to maximise the assault on their sobriety. The side of the house, with its skeletal framework of scaffold tubes and boarded walkways, gives the impression of a temporary theatre. The scene reminds me of my father. How he would have weighed things up in a flash. He would have called it a 'hospital job': a place not unlike a sanctuary, outside of time and real life. His face comes before my inner vision. I can see the twist of the mouth; the hard mockery in the eyes that missed nothing; hear the harsh certainty of his pronouncement. In his prime he was as neat and hard as a tight knot in new rope. The same weight to the ounce at forty as he had been at twenty one. A man of colossal dedication where his own ends were concerned. A true man of the single mind. A kind of integrity, perhaps, or maybe something that he saw as honour that only found a dishonourable place to show itself. Men of this kind, the prisoners of the buildings, will always be measured by me according to my father's gauge. He would know them instantly. Passing along the pavement opposite, all it would require would be the most cursory of glances and their essential calibre would be exposed to him. And his opinion would be as if he had spent years in their company. And he was never a man to fight shy of a poor opinion, or give some luckless being the benefit of any doubt. His image comes back to me as he was in his prime; his black hair glistening in summer sunlight like newcut coal; his face dark as any dago. He used to wear bib and brace overalls that faded to the colour of a marl road in dry weather. Eyes like a cat (grey green, flecked with hazel) that flickered with a fierce resentment at the passing of every single minute of the working day.

A shuffling sound behind me causes me to turn and I see the Oracle coming towards me. The fresh air seems to bloat him. He is hurrying as fast as his broken slippers will allow. He has brought his can of Stella.

You didn't drink your tea, he tells me. He pauses to gather his breath, smiles at me through his discomfort.

Try not to be so touchy, he says.

Touchy? I say. What I am doing is reacting to plain hostility. She is like fucking Lady Macbeth.

She's not *really* hostile, he says. Irritable, maybe, now and then.

I hold up my hand to stop the bullshit. Hey, I tell him, let's not kid one another, she hates my fucking guts. She must think I want to break up the happy home.

He shakes his head. She suffers from nerves, he tells me. I want you to understand that I can't take sides against her. She is devoted to me. She believes in me.

Well, I say, you are a lucky man.

He studies the can of Stella and sips at it to distract himself. Turns to stare at the corner house and nods to encompass the activity going on there.

Been watching points? he says. Smiles and shakes his head. Those boys don't intend to kill themselves, do they?

Look, I say, I'll be moving on. This is used up here. I think it's for the best, don't you?

He nods thoughtfully, staring past me. Draws a deep breath.

Well, he says, I won't shake hands with you. People like you and me should never feel the need for shaking hands.

His gaze seems to pass in and out of focus. Then he moves back towards his house as if to create distance. The run up for a thirty yard free kick. He takes a good hearty swig at his can. I can hear the glug glog glug in his throat. Then he staggers slightly and squints up at the sky and seems for a moment to have lost his bearings. Then he puffs his cheeks and blows hard, as I have watched many a cherry-nosed drunk do in other settings. His eyes close, the lids as a sheet thrown over pain. Open and stare.

Life, he says, is never really much cop for the likes of us. Big talkers. Auspicious beginners... We don't really *ever* dig the pace... We watch dildos do well and our hearts contract. Rage makes us swallow our tongues. The best, the likes of you and me, can only hang on... grow quiet and hang on like roosting bats. The worst – Christ only knows... Our eyes meet for the last time. There is nothing I can add to this. Far away, as if in another world, there is the sound of the school bell. Two little girls, followed by their distraught-looking mother, come round the corner and hurry towards the gates of the school. The Oracle goes on: It's no good anymore. I have not written a word in more than a year. Not so much as a sonnet. Do you ever write now?

Shopping lists, I tell him. And the names of streets...

Well, he says wearily, that makes you one of the lucky ones. It just dried up. Like I had the blight on me.

I can see that tears are welling in his eyes. His bloated red face gives him the look of terrible vulnerability that is the chief characteristic of the ripe boil. He jerks his head back towards the house. She still has faith, he says. Still believes, you know, one day... Still prays for the miracle. But I don't. It's too late. I told her as much. Martine, I said, Baby, we missed the boat.

I can only respond with a noise in the throat.

We keep searching for things, he says. Old rags to stuff in the holes to keep the wind out. But it's gone, And we know it. People like us probably knew it before we were born.

So we stand there, the latter day seers whose time has come and gone, in penitent silence. Then the Oracle speaks again: She got problems, he tells me. There is a story and not many people know it all the way through. You don't like her, I know, but there are ins and outs of things...

It's okay, I tell him. One of those things. I shrug, more or less eager to be on my way. He looks down at the ground. Throughout the entire exchange our eyes have not met for longer than the briefest flicker. It is as if absence has made us afraid of the secrets we might reveal to each other.

I can see the mother who just passed us coming back from the school. She is blonde and young and slender, wearing a faded cotton dress. She is hardly beautiful, but yet lovely in that miraculous way that only the mothers of young children who still can find love for their father can be. The sight of her suddenly overwhelms me: the astonishing thrust of her flesh against the cotton of her frock, the fabric thin and washed so often that the colours of the flowers in the pattern are faded almost out to shadow and its woven integrity is all but ready to give up the ghost of its purpose. It might even explode and burst asunder in a blinding shimmer of stunned particles, if I could but induce her to jitterbug for just ten seconds. The Oracle, curious to see what is holding my attention so completely, turns his head. His eyes register indifference as she goes out to the crown of the road to give us a wide berth. She passes behind me and I turn to watch and my heart goes out to her as I see the wonderful concoction of what she is and consider fully the stupendous thing she balances on the tip of her nose without even knowing it is there. All that love and trust she will have to sustain in the face of so many dangers and so many threatening factors. Then she is round the corner and gone.

When I turn back he is staring at the can in his hand. There is about him a particular raptness and I can see him briefly, just a glimpse, as he was when he used to come down to visit us in our first home. So handsome and serious about life and its endless possibility; about so-called good and evil and the one true heart. Just before he went off to the university. That big old house whose windows and doors cried out for paint, whose rooms we could not even manage to furnish with secondhand junk. A time of magic.

It's empty, he says.

I stare at him. We are both lost again, slipping away like spirits of the twilight before the approaching night.

The can, he says. He inverts it to prove his point.

Yes, I tell him. I am attempting to make a reasonable shape of the day ahead.

I better be getting back, he says.

Yes, I say.

There is silence between us. The man with the chisel once again takes up with his taptapping hammer. The ground crew with the hat of the Chicago Whitesox baseball team deems the mix in the drum to be just about right and tilts it down so that the mortar flops into the waiting barrow. We both watch him. He is aware of our attention.

Look, I say, I better get going...

I stare at him but he will not meet my eyes. We stand in the second cycle of estrangement. Then I catch sight of Martine. She has come to the door and she is watching him anxiously. She is like the mother who understands that her little boy must be allowed to play in the street with other boys yet cannot leave his wellbeing entirely to chance; who still longs to be where she can protect him always and keep him with her where she knows he will be safe. She holds a fresh can of Stella in her hand. She knows his needs. She calls out to him.

Bobby, are you alright?

The Whitesox man and the SA man pause in what they are about and turn to watch. She crosses the narrow forecourt and offers up the can for him to see. His weakness is her strength. She is smiling at him with eyes that offer an infinite encouragement. I am invisible to her. I am standing not ten feet from where he stands but I might be made out of steam. She takes the empty can from him and presses the fresh one into his grasp. He stands like a man hypnotised. His free hand moves to rip the tag from the can. He raises it to his lips and tilts back his head. I watch his Adam's apple move under the skin on his throat as the liquid passes into him. He lowers the can and sighs. The relief in the sound is palpable. She takes his hand and starts to lead him like a blind man, like a child who has wandered into the dark wood. He has forgotten me. The Oracle, that was my wife's name for him. He could recite the *Pied Piper of Hamelin* from start to finish at six and a half, now he is happy to forget the entire world at the touch of her hand. As the devoted couple walk together back to the house the men in the baseball hats begin to applaud. There is much mockery in it, but along with the mockery I am able to detect something of the awe and deep resentment of the Pharisee on the entry of Christ into the city. And in this applause I see my own loss, and recognise that before a love like this, of this immensity, the Master himself would be powerless.

Chapter Five

This is my first night ever where nothing intervenes between my skin and starlight. I might be a new bride, might be a genuine virgin bride at the threshold, such is the degree and density of my anxious deliberation of the failing light. After a day of reduction, of ever-narrowing circles, here I am, finally, on the point of the pin.

I am in the Castle Grounds. The sun is setting behind the trees that line the riverbank. I am loitering just inside the treeline.

To the impartial eye my presence would be judged along with the more familiar denizens: the child molesters, the arse bandits, the hand-clasping, bug-eyed dog-knot lovers. All those who crawl like insects about the honeypot of particular miseries and wait for the inevitabilities that appall us all.

At first, it seemed as if the railings and the padlocked gates would keep me safe, but as the light deserts me, so the fears swarm. The weather is not inclement, the air is not unduly cold, but there is acute discomfort. The way, it seems, is narrow and I am afraid. Only time and death. What is left of my life is pressing hard against me with its total unconcern. A sharp stick in the small of the back.

There is a longing for something. Some lost connection. Some seashell I can hold to my ear and dream the tides, the moon's pull and thrusting off. Some talisman.

In the few nights spent beneath the Oracle's roof the maggot was already in me. During those long daytimes I wandered about, trying to find the shit of the life that had brought me to where I was. It was a disappointment to conclude that all that had come to pass in my life had only amounted to me – what was in my skin. That experience had washed over me and left a blank. So I wandered about like a phantom who was trying to rediscover an ancient path from the dream of childhood. But the path was overgrown. It proved to be little more than a way of coming to the true wit's end. All I discovered was the sorrow of rust. That whatever had been behind the mask of memory was gone.

I found that the districts where the adventures of my youth took place were subdued. Numb. I spent two sunny days walking from one road to the next, moving like an intruder, an alien, a spy. It brought pain; passing along the fronts of the bungalows and the paired houses with their tiny front gardens and the rosebushes was worse than the visits to the graveyard. The saplings I half-remembered had grown tall. A faint gasp of breeze ruffled the leaves, stirred the dust, set the flowers nodding in their beds. It had all aged badly, much as I had. They seemed, these houses built by the long-dead hobbledehoys, to be the purest expression of the nation's need for the mortgaged sepulchre as a way of life. I walked past houses that my father had built, that I had worked on: these are the truly murderous moments, when you stand back and gaze upon what your life has gone for. I paused before the pair of houses in the little cul-de-sac with some Welsh name. The landowner had succumbed to the old man's badgering and shut him up with the plot nobody else wanted. Charlie Marley, the old Maestro, had done the brickwork to the front. A deep reddish (the colour of dried blood) brick from some brickworks up near Usk, laid in the white mortar from George Tucker's mill. The Old Man had built the four-flue stack. He always insisted on building the stack. It was like placing the flag on the top of the hill. I had simply been around, doing odd bits of brickwork where it (the roughness of my laborious incompetence) didn't matter much; or assisting the labourer, the great hero of my seventeenth year, Ivor Rees, to get a start; or clearing up the debris of brick fragments and mortar droppings. Lew Francis and Frank Yard built the house next door. V.J. Toomis built the row of houses opposite. He had a brother who acted as a sort of foreman, Kendall Toomis, who played the piano in the singing room of the Hollybush Inn of a Friday evening. A tall man who looked like a stork. Vivian Toomis had married the landowner's daughter. He got first choice of the plots. There had been Jack Lane and Barry Blake and Ginger Bool (bricklayers) and the Porter brothers, who built the houses in the adjacent street. Heol something or other. All those roads that ran away from the Common to the south and west had Welsh names nobody understood. How I had hated them back then. It always struck me that they only started when the town was finished as a port. When I was a child the people in this town hated the real Welsh almost as much as they hated the English. Back then, all the people of this town dreamed about was America. What had once been a sprawling stage in a grand theatre of the dramatic confusion of houses built by valiant and heroic men had dulled to next to nothing. The old Maestro's brickwork no longer stood out. These men had been giants to me. I always believed that more care could not have gone into the Chrysler Building, or the cathedral at Chartres, than went into the houses my old man built. Scale alone had made the difference. And the lousy architect. But you come back years later, take a good look around you – your heart hits rock bottom.

The wandering mind is soon jerked back by a whistle, blown three times. A white van approaches at a crawl from the castle and proceeds north. The place always employed a system of eviction at sunset. I step back behind the trunk of the holm oak as the van goes past. Starkweather Security. Two men in uniform. One drives, the other blows his whistle. The face of the whistler (on my side) is stunned with boredom. These are the men of the hour, visionaries guided by the polestar of the minimum wage. I watch the van until the woods swallow it. The light appears to crumble and drift away on the breeze. The leaves rustle overhead. Turning to face the sunset, I watch the scraps of cloud turn to ash in the afterglow. All is quiet; the hushed roar of the water at the foot of the weir scarcely reaches where I am. The whistle blasts grow ever fainter. The intermittent shush of traffic from North Road could be in another life. The cricket ground is no more than pallid vacancy held in place by a fringe of darkening trees. Soon I will be immersed in night. I try to stiffen the weakness of heart with resignation. Attempt to reason with myself that there are no tigers or poisonous snakes, that it will take only a short journey to be back where there are pavements and lamplight and the proximity of bricks and windows affording glimpses into rooms where the TV is going.

Then I hear sounds behind me. Movement through the undergrowth on the far side of the clearing where the groundsmen dump the trash from their labours. Two men moving through the long grass. I can hear their voices without being able to make out words. Their movements are energetic and without caution. I come to realise that I am trembling, but there seems to be no grounds for real fear. It is not, I try to tell myself, as if I am in the presence of the Viet Cong. They start to collect branches from the piles and prepare to light a fire. The snapping of twigs. Laughter. Then a match is held to a ball of crumpled newspaper and two flushed faces are buoyed on the darkness by the sudden flare of light. The voices grow louder. They give no sign that they know I am there. All the time the dark is thickening like soup. I stand seething in uncertainty like a jugged hare. The flames take hold and settle to a steady flame. The two men pause from their activity and I choose this moment to reveal myself.

I saw your fire, I tell them. Neither speaks. I move closer to the fire so they can see me better. I smile to show them I mean no harm. Their stares betray belligerent suspicion. The older man looks to be about thirty. Two days' growth of stubble beard is trying to catch up with the close-cropped hair on his head. Bright blue eyes that keep glancing at his companion, as if to flash signals. He is well built and his movements are deft, as if he has pitched camp in the woods many times. He is dressed in jeans and black sweater and wears working boots. There is a swagger to him and an aura of hostility, a roustabout from the circus or the travelling fair. The other one looks barely old enough to vote. He is tall, thin, yet not ungainly. His glasses give him a studious look.

Look, I tell them, I have no wish to intrude.

I direct my words to the boy. He stares at me. Tosses the branch in his hand onto the fire. I jerk my thumb behind me.

I been stood over there for over an hour, I tell him. I was trying to work out my next move when you two showed up.

He nods. He could be a girl, with his long fair hair, smooth skin, slender fingers. When I glance at his companion he smiles as if he has read my mind.

We are not a pair of fags, he says. He smiles easily and possesses the voice of one who has grown up amongst educated people. Mr Flavin looks after me, he says.

Flavin says nothing. But he stares at me. Hard.

You hardly look the type, he says.

Type? I say.

To be sleeping rough in the woods.

I consider this and shrug; thinking of the day and the wandering that has brought me where I find myself.

Is there a type? I ask him. I always thought it was...

Flavin interrupts me. Did we get the bacon? he asks. He looks at me.

The boy studies him with disapproving eyes. Shakes his head. Takes a package from his pocket and tosses it to him. Flavin snarls something in my direction.

Don't mind Mr Flavin, the boy tells me. He's had a long day.

Then he offers me his hand. Allows it to lie like a boneless thing in my brief grasp before its casual withdrawal. Julian Rimmer, he says. We nod, watching each other with hooded eyes. He points carelessly. This is Daniel Flavin, he says. Flavin and I exchange the briefest of grimaces.

The boy and I watch as Flavin busies himself. They have a sliced loaf and half a dozen boxed eggs. All the time I have been talking with the boy, Flavin has been feeding twigs to the fire. Now he brings two clear plastic bottles of water and a two pint, red tin kettle from his bag. Next comes a frying pan, which he presses down onto the cone of burning twigs. He wipes his hands on his jeans and starts to lay strips of bacon in the pan. They sizzle and sputter and curl up. Flavin moves them with a stick to keep them from sticking. Then he flips them over. His movements betray impatience. The boy is watching me. When our eyes meet he smiles.

Well, he says, I expect you are wondering how Mr Flavin and I are travelling together. Such an odd coupling...

I shrug.

It's a long story, Rimmer says. He turns to Flavin: Isn't it, Dan? Flavin says nothing. He lifts the pan from the fire to save the bacon from burning and gasps as the handle burns his hand. He puts the pan down fast and starts to curse. Rimmer laughs.

Flavin falls into a fierce sulk. Snarls and stamps about, turning this way and that. Rimmer takes two slices of white bread from the wrapping paper, lays two strips of bacon between them and hands it to me gravely. Flavin mutters. His features contort.

Guests first, Rimmer says. Then, to Flavin: Are you entirely stupid? Use your cap.

I close my eyes and bite into the sandwich; close my eyes as I chew to concentrate fully on the pleasure of soft white steam-baked factory bread and undercooked bacon to an empty stomach. Rimmer and Flavin make more sandwiches and we sit there, chewing in silence and staring into the flames. Rimmer sighs and pats his stomach. Smiles at me. He points to Flavin. Never learns, he says. He leans over and takes Flavin's hand, holds the palm in the firelight to study it better. Skin like leather, he says. You or me, we'd have blisters like a string of pearls.

Flavin darts a glance at me and emits a thick, harsh sound from deep in his throat. He stands up abruptly and I think he is about to kick out at the fire. Or me. Rimmer speaks sharply to him. There is an icy superiority in his voice.

Calm down!

Flavin hangs his head.

Dan!

Flavin turns and looks at him with miserable eyes.

Be nice, Danny... Rimmer gently chides. He starts to sing in a sweet girlish voice the refrain from *Danny Boy*. And Flavin smiles as a child rebuked smiles when coaxed to come back into the fold. Rimmer turns to me and winks. He motions Flavin to resume his seat.

Danny, Danny, Danny Boy... he says, and pats his head.

Mr Flavin is a man you have to handle with kid gloves, he informs me. His truculence is that of the rejected suitor. He feels a fool. Feels life has done the dirty on him. A sentimental sort. Listen...

He loves me, though he loves me like an older brother
But loves me not as he loves my darling mother
Who kicks him out of bed to take another.

And bursts into a peal of laughter.

It's a long story, Rimmer says. Long to long-ish, any way. Goes back to my childhood. The first time I laid eyes on Dan I was barely into puberty. And his features were hidden from me by my mother's bush. What I saw as I came into the room from the dark landing was the soles of his feet. Mother was holding his stiffened member in her right hand. Her eyes were solemn. Then there was the slightest flicker to suggest my sudden appearance had offended her. I was always afraid of that – offending her. I just stood and stared. I thought, from the way she sat, that she was shitting into his mouth. Then I saw this hand reach out and feel about for the light switch on the wall. It was Daniel Flavin's hand. No doubt sensible to my confusion and dismay, he turned off the light.

Rimmer paused and gazed into the flames. Sniffed and stroked his chin. He went on: I had seen my mother naked many times. Men were there on a regular basis. It was a more or less practical arrangement. I believe my father encouraged it. He certainly didn't *dis*courage it. Mr Flavin kept coming back and we became friends. The others, for the most part, I despised. Some of them were my father's friends. I think he always knew... He just found it easier to turn the blind eye. He's an artist. I think he felt it was part of the deal – suffering and all that.

What kind of an artist? I enquire.

The kind that paints pictures. He was a painter.

Was? I ask.

Rimmer nods, but offers no explanation.

Flavin, meanwhile, is busy snapping twigs from branches and building the fire into a blaze, so that the dancing flames throw our shadows far back onto the wall of trees that fringe us about. He is cursing to himself and his manner begins to make me nervous.

Don't mind him, Rimmer says. He has got a bottle of El Scotcho in the bag and he is scared you might want to help him kill it. You are not a drinking man, are you?

Never touch the stuff, I tell him. Sworn off long ago. More than a thousand days. I turn to Flavin. Guzzle away, brother. Guzzle to your heart's content. You got my blessing.

I don't need your blessing, says Flavin. From the smaller rucksack he takes a half bottle of Bell's, wrapped in a blue towel.

Now he'll calm down, Rimmer says. A couple of good swigs at his old medicine and he'll be nice as pie. You, though, you packed it in, you say?

Got no vices, I tell him. Don't drink. Don't smoke. I could be a monk if I could find a suitable cell.

Rimmer nods as if he understands what I am saying fully. But I am curious about his father. Your father, I say, you said *was* an artist – is he dead?

He stares thoughtfully at my forehead. Shakes his head. No, he says.

Stares into the fire. No, he says, he is not dead. He is in an institution. Not that far from here. He survived two attempts on his life – both by him. Sleeping pills... then a shotgun.

Flavin laughs aloud at this. Cunt couldn't even hit himself with a shotgun, he sneers. Lost his nerve.

The boy chuckles. There, he says. The final word from Daniel Flavin.

He pauses. But, whether he lost his nerve or not, he did blow off an ear; blasted the flesh right off the cheekbone. It must have been pretty close. Death, it seems, didn't want him.

Flavin grunts and drinks from the bottle of whisky.

Look at him, the kid says, now he got that bottle to nurse – not a happier chap in all of Christendom.

There is silence. Then Rimmer holds up a single finger; stares at me solemnly. You must not, he says, get the idea that my father is deserving of pity. He is, and always was, an all-round bastard. I think I am his child, but the first one, my brilliant brother, was sired by another man. Yet he (my father) sees himself as an outstanding example of humankind. A great artist. The world, he is convinced, hangs on his every word.

Fathers and sons, I venture, is a funny business.

Rimmer shakes his head. Not really, he says. Are you married?

Used to be, I tell him. I watch Flavin tilt his bottle. His eyes switch to meet mine. I experience a sudden pang of yearning for something. A sip. A deep hole inside me.

Is your wife dead? Rimmer asks.

No, I tell him. She's with another man. It is a long story. Goes back a long way. Before you were even born.

Friend of yours? he asks. This man?

Sort of, I tell him. Was... I *knew* him. It was me who introduced him to her, so I thought.

But that particular subject was not something I wished to pursue.

I have only been back here a week, I tell him. In this town. It's a funny thing. Funny but it don't make you laugh. The faces in the streets are like balloons. All day long I walk around and around, as if I got no bearings. And this is where I grew up. There was a time I knew this town better than the back of my hand.

Flavin laughs, raucous and unpleasant. Full of shit, he says.

Silence.

Hey, Flavin says, I said you was full of shit.

Look, I tell him, I am not going to argue with you.

Rimmer tells him to shut up. Curt and authoritative. Flavin stares sulkily into the fire.

Were you a virgin? When you got married?

Yes. It was a pact we had.

And you believed her?

Yes.

The kid is silent for a moment. Then he smiles. Hear that, Danny Boy? He turns to me. Explains. All this man knows is women like my old lady. Sluts and whores who are the embodiment of vice and depravity. Virginity seems so... He makes a broad gesture.

Things were different then, I tell him. Anyway, it was the lie that did it. I must have loved her a lot, to be that blind.

I start to feel queasy. Talking about it never fails to do that. Flavin swigs from his bottle and holds it against the firelight to see how much is left. Less than half. I watch as he pokes at the fire with a stick. The structure collapses with a puff of feathery ash, one or two sparks fly up.

Who wised you up? Who was the little bird? the kid asks me.

I shrug. What's the difference?

Suddenly Flavin stands up and hurls his stick into the fire.

Love, he snarls at me, what do you know about love? His eyes glare and, fearful of offering even the slightest pretext for a quarrel, I look away. At this point Rimmer gets to his feet and heads into the trees along the river.

Going for a shit, Flavin tells me. He studies the bottle in his hand. His old lady kicked us both out. It was getting too heavy. I was desperate for that woman. He wanted to stick with me. His brother sends him money. He wants to learn about life. The world.

That stuff about his father, I ask him, is it true?

He nods. The suicide stuff is true. He's a weak man. He goes out and sleeps in the shed when she got men there. In a hammock. But I was there the night the gun went off. Shotgun. Blew a hole in the door.

Flavin sits there nursing his bottle and there is no more talk until the kid gets back. He looks from face to face. You two are quiet, he observes.

We were talking about the loss of love, I tell him, and it has made us thoughtful.

The kid points at Flavin. Grins. On about my dear old mother again? I tried to tell him, how much bad news she is. The worst kind of whore you can find. She is also mad. He won't have it. But I've seen her. Grew up with that stuff all my life.

Ever been in love, kid? I ask him.

He turns to me with a cold stare. Love? What is love?

Well, I tell him, it is not something you can easily explain.

The story is telling itself; it is all I have left; whenever I find myself in company, sooner or later my tongue will find its way.

This is only a little story. Everyday stuff. Nothing extraordinary. All about the ship of a marriage getting onto the rocks. About it not being sturdy enough to take the battering of wind and storm. It don't measure high on the scale of real suffering. Nobody got skinned alive, or had his tongue ripped out. But our lives are small and the ways narrow and the ordinary disappointment is all we have to use for tragedy. I say: I wanted to burn them to cinders in their bed. Everything failed. The house burnt down, but without them in it.

The kid stares into the fire. Nods. What puzzles me, he says finally, is all this fuss about her virginity.

She told me she was, I tell him.

The kid says nothing. Flavin says, you musta been a cunt.

I say nothing. He is staring at me. Did you hear what I said? he asks me. I turn to look into his eyes. They are fierce. I look away.

To the kid: It was to do with honour.

Flavin laughs. A sound like a stone rattling down a tin chute.

Fucking full of shit! Flavin says.

How do you mean, honour? the kid asks me.

Honour is truth, I tell him. In a marriage it is.

The kid smiles. Hear that, Dan? he says. We got a chap here who is an idealist. There is mockery in his voice.

Fearing I may have gone too far, I shake my head and smile. Don't think I am looking for pity, I tell him. I was drinking myself under, night after night. Digging myself into a deep hole...

Rimmer looks down at his hands. There is a silence. Then Flavin speaks. Don't look at me like that, he says. He is glowering at me like a theatre dragon. His blue eyes are vivid with trumped-up hate. He lays the whisky bottle down in the grass and gets to his feet.

I wasn't looking at you, I protest.

You were looking right down your nose at me, he insists. Like a fucking swan.

I watch his fists clench and I turn to the kid. But this time he does not intervene. He stares down at the palm of his right hand the way Pontius Pilate must have done.

Flavin says: I could take a cunt like you with one hand tied behind my back.

Then he kicks out at me. His aim had been for the balls, but I manage to deflect the boot with my knee. Hoping to appease him, I roll on the ground as if mortally wounded. The kid bursts into a peal of laughter. I roll up like a hedgehog. Flavin screams: On your feet! On your feet and fight like a man, you old cunt! I'm going to beat you to pulp!

I stay where I am and plead with the kid to keep him off me. But the kid laughs again. Then I feel the boot going into my ribs. There is a muffled sound inside me of bones buckling. A lot of pain. He starts to stamp on the hands that cover the back of the head.

What revives me is the sound of the kid's laughter. It is receding. My head aches and there is a sound like swarming bees in my ears. When I bring my hand to the back of my head the fingers feel something as sticky as jam.

Chapter Six

I eat well, he tells me. Pats his belly. Smiles. Eat sensible these days. None of the shit. Cut all that out. I walk a lot. Walking helps me think things through. Certain problems I got, walking is a great help with finding the appropriate solutions. It also keeps the blubber down. Wearing out shoe leather is something yours truly does a lot of these days. Rubber, to be more accurate – wear out rubber. Bought these Italian walking boots. Vibram soles. Cost me a lot of money, but worth every penny, as far as an even keel and...

He looks past me and seems to lose his way. His eyes are unhappy. They are unwilling to meet my gaze except for now and then a darting glance. He grimaces and blinks.

I put on a lot of weight. An *awful* lot of weight. Ex-athlete, of course, like yourself. The hard muscle turns into fat. You start to sag and bulge. I got to look like a sack of shit. I was eating shit. Boozing like a bastard. Like a *maniac*... Nowadays, I'm eating, you know, sensibly. Cut out the fat. Cut out sugar. Cut down the booze to the one day a week. One *good* day. Real piss-up. Saturdays. I make a solid day of it. Dawn till dusk... or whenever I pass out. The quacks reckon that's the best way – the body got six clear days to...

He makes the gesture of infinite resignation and points to the bandage on my head. Wounded soldier, he says. What happened?

Little accident, I tell him.

Somebody said you were out, he says. Unfortunate business.

I nod and stare past him. My eyes take in the facade of the old Gaiety cinema, the grey sky. We are in City Road.

So, he says, how you doing? Apart from the mishap, that is. You winning?

I shrug. I been better, I tell him.

He nods emphatically. That's the stuff, he says. Don't let the bastards get you down. Emotion almost brings tears to his eyes and, for a moment, I am fearful he may embrace me. I step back instinctively to preclude this. He offers me his hand instead: this is Peter Eames, the Poverty Poet.

> People said I took a nosedive
> When I lost my house, lost
> My car, lost my young wife
> To a man with a big dick
> One day I was sunny side up the next
> Found me flat as a pancake a chick
> Did it she had her own car
> Own umbrella an Italian
> Leather coat cost me the best part
> Of a grand I was prepared
> To marinate the bitch in brandy
> Let her gargle pink champagne
> And spit it in the sink she
> Used my tongue for arsewipe
> Seven hundred days then
> Blew me out the first pimp
> Came along could make her fart
> She broke my heart
> When she walked out and left
> Me wilderness to search
> To find another soul
> Might fit the bill
> I am searching still...

It went on for another three pages. He used to write stuff like that and pin it on the notice board in the Clifton and the Royal Oak. Used to sing sentimental songs and break down in the street. He had sworn to drink himself into an early grave if she didn't come back. He claimed to be getting through a bottle of Jameson's out of the optic and chasing that down with a dozen or more of Urquell Pils.

It's a race, he told people, between me and the bread. Let's hope I get there first.

He wrote a poem about the heart attack he proposed to, how she kept turning him down. He grew a beard and let his hair grow where it would. He stopped wearing a tie.

That heart attack is my true love now, he told the world. My North Star when I'm heading for the Pole.

His wife (he showed me a snapshot) had been at best a so-so small town piece of arse, but he acted as if he had lost Linda Darnell in her prime, and here he was, Big Diamond Jim, cracking up for all to see. He told everyone he met the most intimate details: how he caught her sucking this man (he was a sergeant in the city police) off in the back of his (Eames') Range Rover. How she had sent him pictures of her and the copper performing unnatural acts.

In my *own* bed, he said.

Like what? we asked him.

Sodomy, he said and almost shed a tear, and stuff like that. The stuff she would never do with me.

Let us see the pictures, Eugene Egan said.

I burnt them, Eames said. He held his hands about a foot apart. A dick on him like that, he said.

This homebreaker was a well known local rugby star, a giant of a man with a sour outlook. Sometimes Eames broke down during the telling and had to be helped down from his barstool. Husband and wife had been reconciled for a time, but then the adultery had started up again.

I promised her a swimming pool if she was good, he told us. And we egged him on. Where is she now, Pete? Two rooms. Two poxy rooms in Arabella Street. Her and the kid. I don't even know for sure that kid was mine...

I go swimming, he tells me. It helps me relax. It's good for the heart. I'm becoming more and more willing to be reconciled. Picking up the pieces... One day at a time, like the alkies say.

Squints at me. How about you? he asks. I heard you had your own little tragedy. You and me got a lot in common.

I nod, look away. Same boat, I say.

What do you think you'll do?

No plans in particular, I tell him.

Will you try to win her back?

I stare at him. Look away. I got to find a roof, I tell him. I been out in the open air two whole nights and it don't suit my delicate nature. First things first.

He smiles the smile of the battle hardened veteran, weariness and pain and irony all mixed up in it. This is the man, I recall, who has gazed at a snapshot of the erstwhile Mrs Eames taking another man's dick up her arsehole.

I did a bit of that, he tells me, roughing it. Only I did it in January. Trust me to find the hard way.

Yes, I say. Trust you.

Look, he says, maybe I can help you out. Remember Harry?

Harry who? I ask.

Rivers, he says. He's a property tycoon. Got houses he lets out to all kinds of people. You remember him, good-looking bastard. Used to fuck all the girls down the beach. He needs a man for maintenance. Odd jobs on his properties. He's a good egg. It'd be right up your street. And he'll fix you up with a room.

My lack of eagerness seems to surprise him.

I'll take you there, he says. He lives in Oakfield Street. He got shot of the Dragon Lady. I'll put in a good word for you.

We are standing on the corner of Glenroy Street. He moves away. Come on, he calls back to me, and I follow like a dog. We walk south and then turn into Byron Street and head east. The place is just coming out of its coma. The Poet is telling me about his life. You know how it is, he says, you had a bit of it... He stops. Gazes about him and sorrowfully shakes his head.

What a fucking dump this is, he says. These streets... I could never even begin to tell you how these streets get me down. You never saw my house, did you? A front lawn like fucking Wembley... I thought I had it all... Now I'm just like any other... Sometimes...

He clenches his fists and grits his teeth. He is wrestling with the meaning of life. Fuck it, he says. You don't want to hear my woe.

We walk on. Everybody he ever met has heard his woe. You get the feeling he might have been better suited to a life as Father Eames, the crusading Catholic priest. Someone who had settled for plain masturbation and buggering the odd altar boy when he got the chance. Since I saw him last he has collected one of the worst broken noses I have ever seen. It suggests that it must have been caused by a blow from the heel of an axe swung hard by a seven foot giant. His face was always long but the broken nose has turned it into a concavity like an upright sickle moon.

How did you get the nose? I ask him.

It was him, he says, the copper. He nutted me. I took a poke at him. Big mistake. I mean, what chance would I have against a hardman like him? No fucking chance. It was the second time. After I took her back. Someone tipped me off and I caught them redhanded. That's when I knew. For sure. I swung at him and he caught my fist like it was a tennis ball. He is laughing. I'm gonna show you something, he says. I'm gonna show you what happens to little boys like you when they fuck around with real men. Then he grabs me by the lapels and nuts me. Head of granite. I go out like a light. Blood everywhere. All over my shirt, my suit... She, my missus, never even stopped to make sure I was okay.

He reaches into his inside pocket and brings out a wallet. Takes out a snapshot and hands it to me. That's her, he tells me. I study the picture of a woman in a bikini. She is trying to look like Dorothy Malone. Her photo don't do her justice, he tells me, but you can see how a man would lose his head over a woman like her.

I nod and hand it back. He puts it away again. We walk on.

That's when I knew it was *really* over, he says. The Finish.

But despite the setbacks of his married life and other signs of depreciation there is much disdain in this bastard. We pass a small Chinese takeaway and he points to the litter on the gutter.

Look, he says. You have to wonder at these people. He points out the houses, a lordly gesture to take in the entire neighbourhood. Look at these hovels, he says. Imagine, if you can, working an entire lifetime to end up owning one of these... Fucking dog kennels.

As a younger man he bore a faint resemblance to the English actor Stewart Granger, a sort of lank-haired version with softer eyes. Eyes exactly like a collie bitch. His father was some small time local businessman. They had money. The sister had married some contractor named MacInerney. I must have been about twenty at the time. A gang of us, all drunk and boisterous and ready to die for love. It starts coming back to me.

A woman in a lowcut green dress. About thirty. At this time the contractor had moved out. She had three kids by him and was convinced the day would come when he would come back to her. Amigo, I remember, had a crush on her. He spent the entire night running after, her to no avail.

How is your sister? I ask him.

She's dead, he tells me.

How about the Great MacInerney?

Dead. Went back to Ireland and took his own life. He owed close to half a million. He ruined my sister's life. Broke her heart. The both of us, he goes on, gave up our lives to worthless people.

He gazes up above the rooftops as we turn into Partridge Road. He sighs. His eyes are wistful and a little bleak. He stops and reaches out to detain me. We never know what's around the next corner, do we? It's all a mystery. I mean, there I was on the crest of the wave. Or so I thought... I worshipped that woman. An old saying, but a true one: I thought the sun shone out of her arsehole. I was in with the Uncle, Jimmy, and making money hand over fist. I gave her everything. A woman who came from a family that had nothing.

He falls silent. His eyes look worn out. This thing will not let him alone. The worst part is, he goes on, I took her back. But she didn't come to me. No. I had to go to her. Was forced to beg her. That was how she got me to promise her the swimming pool.

He shakes his head and laughs. The whole thing has become a routine. Gestures, intonations, pauses etc are as smooth-running as an old vaudeville routine. I would have give that woman the fucking earth, he says. He holds out his hands and clenches them until they shudder. The fucking moon, man. You think your life is like a song. All those words that meant fuck all. Then there was the kid. My little Sophie. Now, looking back, I got to harbour doubts, but back then, you know, I worshipped that kid almost as much I worshipped her mother. She is part of it. I get her to come back. I talk her into it. Give her her own car. The swimming pool... All of it...

We are coming to St Anne's church.

It is not even a month and they are at it again. A fucking month. She couldn't keep away from him... Someone tipped me off and I caught them in the Red House. I couldn't forgive her a second time.

We go around the corner in silence and come into Oakfield Street.

When I met her, he says, you wouldn't have thought butter would melt in her mouth. I thought she was as pure as pure – You must know something of what I'm on about. Have an inkling... He tugs at my sleeve, gazes with yearning into my eyes. Inkling? I say. Nod and smile. Indeed I do, I tell him.

He points. Almost there, he tells me. Jesus Christ, Tommy, you will never know how much I hate these poxy streets. This fucking day to day. What I have been reduced to. Just trudging up and down. Trudging forever and nowhere left to go. I'm like the Wandering fucking Jew.... Seen too much. And this fucking town... I am sick to death of this syphilitic fucking town.

The house we are going to is two houses knocked into one. Old house; stone walls, bathstone bays, plinth and stringcourse; just below the cornice, a frieze of red and black and yellow tile breaks up the masonry. Even from a long way off it was easy to see much work would be needed to bring the place up to scratch. The gutters are the original cast iron, ornate ogee, and, where they are not missing, they support enough green grass for a nimble goat to graze for days. Slates are missing in many places from the roof. The visible woodwork, fascia, bargeboard, window frames and doors, has passed into the region of decay where paint can no longer serve.

The Poverty Poet points and laughs. Home sweet home, he says.

Harry Rivers comes to the door. He smiles when he sees me.

Fuck me, Tom, he says. Then he laughs aloud, as if something wonderful is happening. He turns to Eames. Where did you find him? I love this fucking boy... Then to me: Come in, come in...

He puts his arm around my shoulder and we all go into the front room. A huge room with hardly any furniture. There is a plain deal table with a small pile of papers, a red and black plastic chair; there are two other chairs, so-called easy, odd and dishevelled. Harry sits in one easy chair and points for me to take the other. He ignores Eames. Beams at me. This has made my fucking day, he tells me. The only ones of the old crowd I ever see are the ones I don't want to. Jerks his thumb at Eames.

Like this one here, he says. Eames smiles as if it is a joke.

Tommy is looking for a place to stay, Eames says. I told him you were on the lookout for a handyman.

Rivers eyes him with casual distaste. Turns to me. His eyes are silvery; what blue was ever in them has faded out.

Too bad, Tom, he says, you and your missus. He points to my bandage. What happened?

I got mugged, I tell him. Two blind hooligans took me for a man of means... We both laugh. Then Harry turns to Eames. Points to the door. I want to talk to Tommy in private, he tells him. Eames exits.

Fucking creep, Harry says. He smiles. He tell you the story about his missus and the police?

I nod.

Half the fucking force, he says.

He told me you had a room to let, I remind him.

It's not here, he says. I got another house on the Taff Embankment. It's an attic room. Shared kitchen and bathroom. No palace, mind. And a couple in there should be in the zoo.

I nod. It'll do, I say.

How about the work? he asks me. I shrug. I got a stack of work, he goes on. Fucking miles of it. I got half a dozen houses and they are all falling apart. I'll give you thirty a day, in your hand, and the room is rent free.

I smile at him. The idea of money and a roof bowls me over.

You could have got me cheap, I tell him. A bag of salt...

Harry laughs. You look like you been in the wars, he says. I wanta help you out. He gets to his feet. Come on, I'll run you down there and show you the room.

It is when I see his car that it comes back to me that I had always harboured a sneaking contempt for this flash bastard. To this day I don't know what it was, but, where a certain type of woman was concerned, Harry Rivers was irresistible. And he could weigh a woman up at a glance. The car is parked around the corner in Princes Street. A red BMW, brand new.

As we go along Adam Street he points out the jail. They were gonna sell it, he tells me. The fucking jail. As a development site. We sit in silence as far as the Monument. Then he asks when the bandage is coming off. Couple of days, I tell him. I got to go back in a week to get the stitches out. They had to shave my head where the stitches are. I got a bald patch the size of a saucer on the back of my head.

He laughs. You got a fucker the size of a dinner plate on the top.

You're not doing so bad, I tell him, take away the good barber and that careful comb.

He flushes at this. He was always vain. Always made sure he had an even tan down the beach, and I always had the suspicion that the cunt tinted his hair blond. He used to model himself on Tab Hunter and Troy Donohue, or one of those other blond morons who were the pretty boys then. He used to do sit ups and press ups and he once confessed to me that he had wanked three times straight off just to prove to himself he could do it if ever the chance came along. You know, he said, if I ever get hold of some woman wants to go all night...

I don't expect miracles, he is telling me. There's a stack of work. No fear of unemployment for years to come. Just go at it steady: slap a bit of paint on one day, couple a slates on a roof the next... It don't have to be a pukka job. I got this wall over Penarth, he tells me. Start you off...

I always remember, I tell him, you had beautiful teeth. You still got beautiful teeth?

He shows them to me. They look too good to be true. Taps at them with a fingernail. Not a single fucking filling, he boasts. Nods at me meaningfully. And I can still get it up. Can you?

Well, I say, there wasn't much need, the last few years.

Wasn't there any nice young boys in there?

I got bad teeth, I tell him.

You always did, he says.

We drive the rest of the way in silence.

The house is just this side of a mansion for size, but it is very dilapidated, close to dereliction. It used to belong the Turnbull family when the town was starting to grow. As soon as they realised they were going to be hemmed in by the hovels of the stiffs, they moved on. To the front only a narrow strip of dogshit hummocky grass separates it and the west bank of the river. The view now was empty factories on the far side. Rusted tin sheets to creak and groan in the wind, cracked concrete yards to harbour weeds. We go in. The hall has a marble floor, black and white squares laid on the squint. Coloured glass in the landing light and the thin sunlight streaming through. The sunbeams cut the dusty air like searchlights.

Fuck me, Harry, I say, it is like the Halls of Montezuma.

He beams with pleasure. Got it for next to fuck all, he tells me. A chap named Miles had it. He had plans for a hotel but he ran out of money at a bad time. I paid his gambling debts and he signed it over to me. It cost me less than that car...

Then he takes out his wallet. A deliberate gesture. A tan calfskin wallet which he flips open to reveal a wad of notes as thick as a new pack of playing cards. Twenties. He removes five and hands them to me. Keep you going, he says. Then he shouts out: Wilson!

A man appears alongside the stairs and comes towards us. Rivers says: This is my good friend Mr Oliver. I want you to look after him. He got the room at the top. He laughs. Wilson nods and gives me a particularly bleakeyed scrutiny. I'll get the key, he says.

Rivers slaps me on the back. Now you're sucking the right tit, he tells me. Then he is gone.

There is a bed in the room. It maintains a position aloof from the walls. The place stinks of vomit. Traces of piss, too. There is a washed-out stain, where the mattress sags, that resembles the map of Ireland. The walls encapsulate an ancient sickness and I am ill at ease as I gaze about me. Any man in this room would feel the pressure of his isolation and weakness. Would know his luck was out. Would grasp immediately that he was at the dead-end of some line.

There is a skylight in the sloping ceiling. Light falls through it. Against the wall on which this light rediscovers itself stands a large mirror in a rectangular gilt frame. The mirror is tilted to maximise whatever might make a way through the filthy skylight glass. There is a yellow-topped table and a green plastic chair. In the darkest corner, a pale green bucket.

The walls are painted a blue that grew discouraged long ago. The ceiling is the colour of porridge. Here and there meandering lines of raw sienna show where the leaking water has trickled. Wilson watches my face as I look around.

Not exactly the Savoy Hotel, he ventures. His face hangs slack on its bones. There is no smile to go with the words, only sour appraisal and boredom. He shrugs and spreads his hands. It's a room, he says. He lets them fall back. His face moves towards some kind of grimace that will encompass the human condition. Hope the flimp didn't build up your hopes... That mirror, know where that came from?

I turn to stare at the mirror. Move to see myself in it. I turn to look at him and shake my head.

Have a guess, he says.

I am, I tell him, at a loss. We stare at each other for a long pause. Then he scratches at his temple and says: Regal Ballroom. He crosses to stand alongside me and we both look in. Just imagine, he says, all the young cunt musta looked in here. Just like me and you. In the good old days. Then he rolls his eyes and gazes up to heaven. Nudges me to bring to mind some paradise of long ago.

I point to the skylight. Does that open? I ask.

He shakes his head. We got it nailed up. We had an old fucker in here was throwing his shitbags out on the roof.

How about water? I enquire. If, for instance, I should wake and find myself dying of thirst, where might I find the tap?

He points downward and starts for the door. Leave you to it, he says as he goes out.

It is a room that would require at least a bottle and a half of Bell's to numb the senses of a normal man for him to take a chance on sleep. A nervous man would climb out on the slates and take the dive. But I am past caring. The bed is an army cot and I make it up the way the army showed long ago; threadbare blankets, no sheets and a bolster with bright striped ticking to support my head. Sleep buries me. Sleep that leads no place that dreams can ever find a man.

I sleep all the starless afternoon and wake to early summer twilight. My eyes open and stare. It is akin to staring out from a lidless coffin. The stupor of sleep is still strong in me. The blur of light at the dusty skylight. The cracks in the ceiling stand out like riverlines on a map. Somewhere inside me there is dull pain. It seems to be exploring me, searching for the right place to take hold and amplify.

By this time it is dark. I get out of bed and piss in the bucket. The pain under the heart is still there. I stare at the wall and wonder. Then I look into the mirror. The Regal Ballroom was a place I knew. There was a snooker hall on the ground floor and the dancehall on the first. On a Friday and Saturday you could hear the music and the shuffle of feet overhead while you played at the tables. Sometimes the owner would leave his kiosk at the foot of the stairs and you could sneak up two flights to watch. Step out from the narrow well and stare into the cave. I remember watching Jean Harland jitterbugging with a kid named Jack Spargo. She must have been about sixteen at the time. The boy was older. I was twelve. The rest of the dancers stepped back and let them have the floor. The music was from a record player: Tennessee Ernie Ford and Shotgun Boogie. The kid was trying hard to be Steve Cochran. Leather jacket and the haircut. Jean Harland had on a white sweater and a black skirt. Behind my clammy hands I can see her almost as I saw her then and my mouth goes dry. These irrecoverable moments are a great danger to the foolish and unwary. It is things of this vicarious measure that most viciously lacerate the mind, if you give in.

I sit on the side of the bed. Noises reach me from the rooms below. Other lives. Doors bang. A metal pot clatters on a hard floor. Voices are raised, followed by brief laughter and a cistern being flushed. Footsteps along the passage underneath, then descending stairs. The money has given me a small foothold. I take the notes from under the pillow and feel them. Crisp new banknotes with sharp edges. I get up and cross to the door. Feel for the knob. Open the door and listen. It feels funny, like the house where Fagin lived. I touch at my unshaven face and start down the narrow flight. The treads creak and the handrail is unsteady. There is a broken pane in the fanlight of the landing window. Air like grey fur in the well as I descend. A door opens as I cross the second landing and a single eye watches through the crack. The newel at the foot of the flight in the hall is as big as a totem pole. When I finally find my way to the kitchen, Wilson is there with another man.

Just about to have a cuppa, Wilson says. Can I interest you?

I nod, stare about me. Wilson points. This here is Mr Foley. Tenant, like your good self.

While I am thinking about offering my hand, Foley turns his back on me. Wilson looks at me and raises his eyebrows. I better give you a front door key, he says. He takes a key from a nail and hands it to me. This is where we cook. Points to the stove, the kettle. Opens a cupboard to reveal a single saucepan. Or, he says, you can eat out. There is an abundance of cafés and chipshops in the neighbourhood. But, if you are willing to part with a tenner per week, Maestro Folio, our resident chef, will rustle you up the full English of a morning.

Mr Foley turns to look at me.

I'll think about it, I say. I take a cup from a sink full of dirty dishes and wash it vigorously under the running tap. Run water into it and drink. Wash it with care and set it down, inverted, on the draining board. I smile at Wilson.

Could you direct me to the bog? I ask him.

He jerks his head towards a yellow-painted door. Out the backyard, he says. Follow your nose.

Coming out through the front door there is a small stage paved with stone, and from this to the pavement six broad stone steps descend. In another age I could almost see myself as a gentleman; buttoning my tan calfskin gloves and glancing left and right where the lamps light the embankment. I suddenly feel like a cigarette. It must be twenty years since I last drew smoke into my lungs, but at this moment I would give a finger from either hand for a good long drag on a Capstan Full Strength. Then women thoughts. A woman. Flesh off the bone and some hole to nestle in. Slipshod and loose. But my nerves scamper about and I quickly lose heart. All that iniquity and only me. My featureless body in the windless night goes down the steps and saunters left.

I move away from the house and stand on the corner as the dark crawls up through the sewer gratings, falls out of the sky. As the polluted river runs on and on into the polluted Channel. Everywhere, like in the secret world of insects, the deep and hidden filth, the veins full of shit being pumped into water where no fishes swim. Soon the grey turns into bruise blue and the lights make yellow space that hangs in the air like sick balloons sagging with pus. The air is warm and clammy. I try to work out where I am on the map that is beginning in my new abode. All about me is a wilderness that is familiar but lacking any comfort.

This is a town that started to die when the world moved on from coal. It always felt to me like a hand-me-down. They keep trying to revive the corpse and maybe now and then an eyelid will flicker or the lips move to hiss some obscenity, but there are no hardons left: the flesh can only languish and putrefy. My grandparents arrived here when the place was coming to life and by the time they were dead it was all over. All the walls are blank and the words search for new meanings. The pinnacle of local lore was knowing how many fourfaced clocks there were between the river in the west and the railway that swung off the mainline in the south to head north through the Queen Street station at the eastern edge of what was and still is the town proper. That was forty years ago and little has changed except half the clocks are gone. That and the running sores of the suburbs in the dreamless fields.

These streets hold, for me, an element of strangeness. What must a man do who has only himself to consider? How to conduct what is left? A foolish man who has made fundamental errors, how should he proceed?

In the end, all you can do is lay your dull little mixture of apathy and humiliation and set it against the measure of the life and final mutilation of Our Lord. And the Miracles. And the mysterious piercing of the hymen of His earthly mother. Mary and Joseph, when they were trying to make a go of it out on the desert edge. When it was winter and the land was cold and inhospitable and not yet Holy and there were hardly any builders looking for carpenters and Christmas not yet a thing to keep in mind and the nights were long for man and maid. When the fire went out and the cold kept them from sleep, what went on under their blanket? All those highs and lows of saintly life. I am thinking about the time when Jesus was a kid, when they were a family living in a tent or some poxy room, with the tools under the bed and the crib in the corner and Joseph, back then, before they knew they were going into the scriptural Hall of Fame.

Maybe that is why the priest steers clear of the frau. They are only designed to make fools of men. That's how the system works.

He looks up as I walk in the bar, Terry Mack, and his features almost manage a smile. To those who do not know this man it might have looked no more than an adjustment within the permanent grimness, but they would be wrong. This is a man who has been brooding over the prospect of disaster since puberty. The face is, as always, tilted down, so that he looks up from under bushy eyebrows at everyone who is not a dwarf or a child. He is the only man in the world to whom I would entrust any secret worth keeping. He straightens up, takes a glass from the shelf and pulls a pint of beer.

Someone told me you was out, he tells me. I been expecting you.

The room is quiet, two men sitting separately at tables, a third sitting on a stool along the bar with his elbows guarding his glass.

Terry Mack studies me and shakes his head as if his worst fears were confirmed. This is the man who had predicted great things for me. My oldest friend and the truest, his judgement was always distorted by love, so that he missed the flaw. Seeing him again is like finding safe harbour and I want to reach out and touch him.

His hair had been a dulled bay the last time we met and now it is solid grey. His eyes are muddy from strong liquor as a lifetime pursuit. He points to the bandage. What happened? he asks. Someone set about you?

I nod. How many of them? he asks. I hold up a single finger. One too many, I tell him and reach out to take my pint. The beer tastes flat. I take another sip. The first for many a long day, I say. I hold up the glass to the light. It tastes funny, I tell him.

That's a good pint, he assures me. I try another sip and then a gulp. That's better, I say. I suppose I had something more auspicious in mind. I raise my glass to him and smile.

I'd a broke out the champagne if you'd a said, he says. You got money? he asks me. I nod, pat my pocket.

I got a start, I tell him. Remember Harry Rivers? He is a man of property these days. I point up to the top shelf where he keeps his own bottle of Bushmills. Give me a couple of tots out of that bottle there. I want to get drunk, I tell him. I held out all these years, but now I am looking for the works – complete inebriation...

I clench my fist and beat at my chest like Mighty Joe Young. You are looking at a desperate man, I tell him. A man who has seen the folly of his temperance ways and no longer gives a fuck...

He listens to me patiently. All his life, on and off, he has listened to me talking bullshit and never complained. His honest and pugnacious Irish face registers a numbed compassion that I know to be boundless. He alone understands my terror. I pull out the banknotes and wave them under his nose.

Put your money away, he says. He takes down the bottle and pours. And while he is pouring one for himself I catch a glimpse of myself in the mirror: the sight jars me to the bone. We touch glasses and down the whisky at a single gulp.

Like fucking Randolph Scott, I say, rapping the glass down hard. He only pulls a face and swills out his own glass as if he means to give it up forever. He looks at me. I been warned off, he tells me. It is stick to beer, or else...

He sniffs and puts the bottle back on the shelf. But it's not easy.

How's the missus? I ask him. He shrugs.

What's been happening? I ask.

Not much, he says. Amigo died.

I know, I say, you wrote me a letter.

He nods. Of course I did, he says. I get confused. I am just waiting for my wife to die. Or me. I don't care. She is worse than a bad conscience, Tommy. Look at this place, worse than the fucking morgue.

I thought you just wanted the quiet life, I remind him.

Not *this* quiet, he says. I think the brewery is keeping tabs on me. It is only a matter of time. Pubs like these have had their day.

He changes the subject to Harry Rivers. Big-headed cunt, he observes. I never liked him. He stares at me. How is your father? You been out to see him?

I shake my head. No, I say. Never been in the new house.

How about the boy? he asks.

I shake my head and push my whisky glass towards him. Give me another go at the firewater, I say and lay a note on the bar.

I point to the glass. Fill that there crystal glass and have one yourself.

Then I pick up the note and fold it three times and press into his breast pocket. Do not tell me, I say, of his troubles, whatever they might be. I don't want to hear.

He takes out the folded note and places it in my hand.

I thought blood was thicker than water, he says. There is a tone of gentle chiding in his voice.

Since when? I ask.

It's a woman. He used to come in here with her now and then. Norman Appleby's wife.

I shrug and look away. I came in for a quiet drink, I tell him.

He pours whisky into my glass and moves away to serve. More people come in through the Bromsgrove Street door. I sniff the whisky and blink. Three men and a woman with ginger hair. Mr Mack serves them. Then he comes back to me.

Smart woman, he says. Money to smooth her out. Hard case, though, and too old for him. He is a nice-looking kid, your boy.

He takes after his mother, I say.

Appleby is no fool, Mr Mack says.

I thought he was queer, I say.

Mr Mack shrugs. He's a rich man and he's a nasty bastard, he says. He is the sort of person you don't want to upset. He looks at me and I shrug again. He goes away and leaves me to my thoughts.

Chapter Seven

There is a breath of rain in the air, a faint damp breath coming in with the tide. Or is this is poetic fancy, the way jerks like me, men who grew up in the town when the docks still worked, will now and then seek to identify themselves as sons of the salt wind. There was a time when it was no great surprise to come across a man who had been a deckhand on trips to Fremantle, Yokohama, Three Rivers on the St Lawrence, or even some dull old European port like Antwerp, Rotterdam or Ancona.

Now I feel dislodged into a late night melancholy. This is not unusual, but it affords at best only lopsided awareness. I wander past the stunted trees. Paget Street. I stop outside the Albions' Club and stare about me. The pie shop on the other corner. After this comes the thinking about death. You take that and balance against what you got. Try to imagine you got a cut-throat razor in your hand, or a loaded gun. Take the muzzle in the mouth... Just a touch on the hair trigger. *Bammm!* No more Mondays!

It is a temptation. Also something you can always fall back on.

Then I consider the question of work. This is something that I have hated all my adult life, yet it has followed me like a dog. Dull work, the kind that wears you down and they pay you bladders. This is the way the poor connect with the upper world. How they play their part in the grand scheme. The drudge. When there are no wars for them to die in, they drudge instead. Much bitterness accumulates. You have been sidelined while lesser men get to the point where they drive nice motor cars and can afford haircuts from real barbers. You have watched the advancement of pimps and arsehole bandits to honourable estate and it has crushed your spirit. Many lose heart and end up driving bread vans or carrying the hod. Men who know the works of the Masters, from Stendhal to Boccherini, Mantegna to the Book of Job. Edged out and lost, while the streets of the towns choke with the cars of men who know nothing but the colour of money.

Come finally to the riverbank, where the water holds the dull light of the night sky between soot-black banks. A bitter moment. The room awaits my return; implacable as a gintrap, with its iron cot and the bucket to piss in. I close my eyes and listen hard for the music of the stars. Looking up I see a cloud like grey dough. A faint shiver runs through the leaves on the trees along the pavement edge. Faint river sounds. What is to become of me?

It would be nice to lie down in the dogshit grass. Or slip into the river and drift far out to the ocean stream. I feel like the watchman at the beginning of time. Waiting for dawn. Some battle to start. The first step of the enemy to start things off. Sometimes the heart fails. This is not uncommon.

My father would not eat supper because a man who lived to be ninety five told him this was the best way to ensure long life. My father thinks he will live to a hundred. Says life is grand. Watches the pictures of the international disasters on TV and is convinced God is working to preserve him. Prays to the Good Shepherd after seventy odd years of total disbelief. Notes the fatal languor of the starving children in Africa, how the bodies are not comfortable with the weight of the heads. How big the eyes are as they stare at the lens. They are no different from you or me, he will tell you, except for the colour of their skin. Nods like a wise man to emphasise these words. Blesses the dying and gains redemption with a single gesture. Discovers a generosity of spirit in his dotage.

Poor little buggers, he says, they never did no harm to you or me. Then pause to think deeper. A bit of fire, a bite of decent food, a roof over your head... And gaze earnestly into your eyes.

This is a man who saw work as the noblest thing of all.

I remember him and it is like starting a book at the end. A weariness settles over me like a cloak soaked with the sorrow of hindsight. Get a picture of life as a blindman clumping up wooden stairs in his hobnail boots. Dull and commonplace as bricks in a hod. And turn for home. The boarding house, a single window lit, comes into view.

At eight sharp a man knocks at my door. The sound of his steps coming up the last flight has already woken me.

Who is it? I call out.

A pause. Then: It's me. This is Arlington, he says. Factotum for the Rivers operation. He climbs the remaining steps. Knocks gently. Speaks gently through the crack on the hinge side: It's gone eight, mate. Can I come in? Standing out here on this landing is making me giddy.

He tries the door but the chair I have propped under the knob holds firm. I get out of bed and take it away. Put my head around the edge of the door.

Wait downstairs, I say. I haven't had a piss yet.

Be fucked! he says, and barges into my room. A man more or less my age, wearing a wig that makes him a redhead like Rita Hayworth. Long-faced, skull the shape of a sugared almond. The stubble on his chin is white. He puts on his glasses to look at me. Grins abruptly. Lights a Gold Flake and sucks down the first drag. Glances about the room. Let's go! he says. Gives the room a quick scrutiny. Claps his hands. Showtime! he says. Let's go!

Then he takes the chair I am still holding and sits down. Blows the smoke up at the skylight.

You don't want to upset Mr Rivers, he tells me. Shakes his head. Studies at his cigarette. You don't want to incur his wrath, you better be sure to be up in the morning. Lack of punctuality is something Mr Rivers dislikes with his heart and soul.

I pull on my trousers and push feet into boots. When I piss into the bucket he turns his head out of modesty.

You look rough, he tells me as we go out through the front door.

How you feeling?

Rough, I tell him.

Night on the piss?

I nod and he gestures towards a white van. A boy with hair like black velvet and eyes like a cat sits behind the wheel. Arlington pushes me ahead of himself. Sit in the middle, he says, and don't fart.

Where we going? I ask. The van is caught in the flow of traffic heading west.

Penarth, Arlington tells me. We got a big stone wall. We got to knock it down and put it up again.

Harry Rivers is waiting for us. He is sitting in his car. The other two get out of the van, one on either side, and dart through the gateway into the garden. I stumble after them and stand staring towards him in some confusion. He gives me a hard, scant smile as he gets out of his car. He makes it plain that he is holding back, curbing his sharp tongue, making allowances for old times' sake. Permits himself a quick glance at his watch. German car. Swiss watch. These are what the dreams are about. He looks past me. He is dressed as if I have been keeping him from a round of golf with Dean Martin's ghost.

Let me show you the strength of it, he says.

The wall is of grey Penarth stone, with bathstone copings; four foot wide piers at twenty foot centres. The wall is about four foot high and bulging badly from the pressure of the earth behind it. He motions for us to walk south. He lights a slim cigar and sucks at it with hunger. The wall runs for close to a hundred yards. Looking beyond I can see the sea, the colour of new lead under a pale sky.

The garden is huge, he tells me. You got the same length the other side. All the work you want.

This is a man of simple pleasures who has done well. Sees himself as a chap who can still manage a roguish twinkle in his eyes when some lump of underage meat goes by in tight pants, and yet escape the opprobrium that might befall another of his generation (someone like me, for instance), who would simply be a dirty old man. The girls he picked out would go along with his seduction procedure as if he had hypnotised them. He would steal something from their handbag, a comb or a powder compact. Once he stole a lipstick and proceeded to paint his own lips. The girls would try to get the item back. A physical struggle would ensue. This might be a week night, a group of us standing outside the café in Station Road after the Tivoli. It would end up with Harry putting some sort of a wrestling hold on them where a certain pain was involved. Perhaps more discomfort than real pain, but humiliation was in there. It used to embarrass me to watch this corny bastard with his little act, but it worked. His judgement as to which girls would play his game was unerring.

It was as if they had a secret sign language. The rest of us, mostly no-hope virgins, used to hate him for his success. He worked in some dead end factory on some kind of machine but on a Saturday night he could pass for Tab Hunter.

This is the girlfriend's, he tells me. Home for the old folk.

Nods towards the house. Used to belong to a shipowner. He grins. Big money in this game, he tells me.

We reach the corner and stop. The wall turns sharply and runs for a similar distance into a cul-de-sac. He points. Same thing this side, he says. I had a bit of luck, he says. He looks down at his hands. The old lady died and left me the house. It was a turning point. I know you shouldn't call it luck when your mother dies, but it was. She cut my sister out. I coulda sold it and gone on the piss. There was a time I would have. Money for jam, it's always a temptation. There was a time I woulda blown it, but I saw the light. Now I got eleven houses and other stuff going.

He starts to walk back. You got to grab the chance, he tells me. Then he points through a gap in the hedge. Lawn like the Arms Park, he says. Huge development potential. We got to do this job right, Tom. We got to take the old wall down and clean all the shit off. Put in proper foundations. Then it got to go back like it was. Same as the original. He points to the piers. These things in the same place. He looks at me. Okay?

I think I can manage it, I tell him.

Attaboy! he says. Do it in bits, he says. So much at a time. he smiles. I mean, you know what to do...

We walk side by side back to his car. Arlington and the sidekick are there.

Leave you boys to it, Harry says, and drives away.

The three of us stare at the wall. Arlington mutters: no good looking at it. Nobody moves. What about tools? I ask him. He jerks his thumb. In the van, he says. He jerks his chin and the kid brings out an assortment of hammers and chisels; a crowbar; a wheelbarrow with a pumped up wheel; three pairs of brand new working gloves in bright orange.

I stare and begin to lose heart. It is a little after nine am and already the air is warm and moist. I can anticipate the feel of sweat on me like warm grease. The work is waiting. This was shit I had hoped to miss forever.

Soon real sweat gushes from my pores. Soaks my shirt and runs in my eyes. The hammer glances off the chisel head at the third blow and takes a piece of skin the size of a postage stamp off the main forefinger knuckle. There is no blood. A pale stickiness oozes. I drop the chisel. Curse.

That's what the gloves are for. Arlington tells me. He is about to add further comment, but I hold up my hand.

Please, I say. Spare me the wisdom.

He laughs softly and goes back to hammering. The kid keeps going. The wound is oozing white syrup like maple bark. I attempt to slide the flap of skin back into place before easing on the yellow glove.

This is worse than the fucking pyramids, I tell them. There is no response. Only the sounds of steel hammering steel. I draw the deep breath and try to come to terms with the moment I am inescapably caught in. It is not easy to become reconciled again with this awful confrontation. Arlington offers encouragement. It'll get easier once we get the copings off, he says.

Is that a promise? I ask him.

My hands are soft. Time and inactivity have diminished me since the last time a lump hammer was in my hand. After ten minutes my arms feel like rags. The temptation to throw the tools into the bushes is strong. I pause and straighten up. Wipe the sweat from my face.

Hard going? Arlington enquires.

Killing me, I tell him.

He smiles, a sort of icy smile, purses his lips and nods.

Keep going, he says, they got three prizes. The kid stops and studies me. He is not even breaking sweat. Eyes like a cat. He turns back to the wall. Tap-tap. Arlington too. Tap-tap... This stone monstrosity, with its mortarless joints and beerbelly bulge, that had promised to collapse in a heap if the three of us farted in unison, is now solid granite.

Pride, Arlington says. Swallow the pride. Just keep going at it steady.

It is years, I tell him, since I did this kind of shit.

You'll get into it, he says.

I show him the blister in the palm of my right hand.

Well, he says, this is what we got. He jerks his chin to indicate the wall. This is what our man wants done. Just keep going at it nice and steady. It is either this or fuck off home.

When the time comes to stop for a cup of tea, Arlington asks how I feel. Old and weary in a loveless land, I tell him.

For the rest of the morning I creak like new shoeleather and my mind dwells on the building of stone edifices since time began. Roman aqueducts. Egyptian pyramids. The labour of the slave. All that anonymous sweat and unmeasured pain. At half past twelve the kid goes to the shop for food and his daily scratchcard. Arlington lights up a Gold Flake and strolls down to the seaward corner. When the kid comes back he hands me a package: brown bread with tuna and lettuce filling, a smear of mayonnaise. The kitchen of the old folks home provides the tea. It is sweet as honey and this, along with the weariness of bone and sinew, is what brings remembrance of my father and the Maestro. I finish chewing bread and start to doze off. They all come trooping back, the long-lost actors from the time of faith. I see my father again, as he was then, the essential man in his place, like the knot in the new rope for the hanging; the old Maestro, with his tendency to hardpacked stoutness. Thickset, he used to say. With bright eyes of unusual blueness, with long, fleshy lips and black hair with a white parting as straight and precise as a line on a blueprint. He modelled himself on Clark Gable without the moustache. My father said of him: I never came across a finer bricklayer than Charlie – Anywhere...

Yet, for all his skill, he was a man leading a double life. He was a vain, weak man who had married a woman as bad as the news can get. I met her once. She was plain and sour looking. He had a daughter who was the light of his life. At seventeen you are on the lookout for heroes and it was hard to balance this marvel with the trowel with the henpecked ninny he turned into the minute work was done.

But Ivor Rees, the hodcarrier, was heroic in every way. He was a thing of beauty, a miracle of the absolute essential. Dark auburn hair that came out of his head thicker than a beaver pelt. Red skin where the sun reached, face and arms, the rest of him as white as milk. Eyes that were clouded grey mottled with amber and shot with flecks of jade green. A stub of a nose that gave his face a blunted look. Few words escaped him. His motto:

talk is cheap. He weighed about ten stone. About five ten. A natural welter, as he put it. A body as neat as a nail. Astonishing strength. Charlie, who had seen any number of hodcarriers, described him as the little gem. Only, of course, within the frame of eight till five: the world of scaffold planks and the monkey and up and down the ladder as a way of life.

I had been in his room once. Sent to rouse him, clumped up the stairs in my hobnail boots and banged on his door. With his landlady scowling at me from across the landing. He was still drunk when I burst in. Lying on a mattress on the bare boards, a single sheet to cover his nakedness. He sat up and blinked at me. One chair in the room. An upturned applebox held an empty beerbottle and a packet of Woodbines. His clothes lay in a heap in the corner. Bare bones. He got dressed and I rode him into work on the bar of my bike. Once he was there, though, the world fell into place again. The sun was shining on the heap of pink bricks; there was white mortar in the bay and bags of cement in the tin shed. Charlie muttered about *up* in the mornings and showed his false teeth. Ivor lit a cool Woodbine and surveyed the scene. An hour had been lost to the demon drink. He stood there like Caesar, newly come to the edge of Gaul. Then he started and from then on the day went like a sewing machine. It was a game we played. The seasons came and went and we adjusted our sights. Everything fell into place.

But where I find myself now is a long way down a bad road. I come out of the reverie and sigh. Fuck work, I mutter. A different calibre.

What? Arlington says.

Happy days, I tell him. I was dreaming. Fucking miles away...

The heat, he murmurs. I was dozing off myself.

The kid is searching his paper for any scrap he might have missed the first three times. At nineteen years old he finds it hard to come to terms with our age. It comes out that the kitchen had been providing them with a cooked lunch before my arrival and he fears that my joining the company has altered things. He tells me of his fears and stares at me as if he expects me to do the decent thing and shoot myself. I close my eyes and pretend to sleep. Arlington snores softly. The sweat has dried on me. The warmth of a lovely summer's day soaks into my bones. We are sitting on a ten foot plank supported by three piles of three bricks. Our backs are against the stone wall of the old coach house. We sit down in shade where the cool air is almost liquid while the rest of the garden is stunned with heat. No breeze. The apple trees within the rectangle of the low box hedge might be made of stone. The espaliered pear trees hard against the rear wall take the full brunt of the sun and sag on their staples like the dying Christ. My eyelids flicker. Open to allow light in like grit under a door. Heaviness drags them down again. I think about prising them open but the effort is lost in the swoop of the sweet restoration of dark dozing. There is even a vague promise of the picking up where some dream left off, but the entire scene is scattered by the rearrival of Mr Rivers in his shiny motor car.

He sounds the horn thrice and Arlington and the kid jump up like yanked mannikins. They start back to work as if it were fornicating. They apply themselves with the unblinking concentration of true converts. Dogs to the master's whistle. My movements are slower. Mr Rivers is looking across me, avoiding my eyes. He is smiling, but the smile is not amiable. The suggestion is that I have behaved badly, almost to the point where it has dishonoured our ancient friendship.

Then he changes and becomes a hard nut to crack. He comes closer; the glance at the gold watch. What else is a gold watch for? They are not good enough to time the Olympics. They are for bossmen to show which way is up. The steel and gold strap on the tanned wrist.

Fuck me, Tommy, he says. Sighs and shakes his head. He has changed his clothes of the morning for an outfit even more suited for a life in California. His hair is freshly cut; a pale pinkish periphery like a nimbus at the nape of his neck and where the hairline curves up behind his ears. And the ears like jug handles. A casual wellbeing sits upon him. We are almost the same age, but he looks more than ten years the younger. It is as if he has managed to switch horses in some miraculous way.

Look, he says, I'm not out to play the cunt. I'm not coming here to catch you out *dead* on half past. He points to the watch. It's almost fucking two o'clock...

The other two are going like the clappers. The fullest of swings. It is like a scene from a bad English film where frenzied activity is called for. Two men who have discovered a revivalist aggression towards the wall's destruction. Their hammers ring out in the languid heat. Stiffness at the knees makes my standing up a slow business. I turn to face my employer. Wince. He stands in the sunlight. Puts on dark glasses. My feelings tend toward mortification. Shame, and a dull, grating anger. Like having to chew a wineglass. Given a gun at this moment, I would have shot him between the eyes and then put the muzzle in my mouth. I clear my throat and say nothing. Wince again. We are like statues. The pause is brief. Then I lower my gaze and go back to the wall. Take up my tools and start again.

And such is the intensity of my concentration on the block of worthless grey stone that it might have shamed Michelangelo.

Mr Rivers turns away and heads towards the house. Half way along the garden path he half turns his head and calls back with the last word. Just play the fucking white man, Tommy. That's all I ask. He has crossed the small courtyard and is skirting the flowerbeds on his way to the rear porch. My chisel point seeks out the pale blue-grey mortar of the bedjoint; blue lias lime and crushed ashes mixed with water in a mill more than a century ago, it runs out like fine powder for timing eggs.

You're learning, Arlington tells me. You bit your tongue.

It wasn't easy, I tell him.

Yes it was, he assures me. It's fuck all. All we got to offer is our labour. He is not a bad bastard, as bastards go. Look upon it as a way of life when times are bad.

Are they going to get better? I ask.

We have to pretend, he says.

Like Nat King Cole?

Now you're sucking the right tit, he tells me. Just take the money.

Once again I turn to the grey wall. Hammer to chisel. The mortar runs out as a fine lilac dust.

Part Three

Chapter Eight

Elliot P. Oliver, *alias* Polly

Don't worry, she told me once, with you I would live in a shack in a shanty town and survive on a handful of bitter rice.

But later that afternoon I'd be polishing the car, or maybe I'd be down in the cellar Appleby had specially built under the house, and I'd see all the bottles. The wines and the different whiskies and stuff, all the shit she would never have with me in that shack. Doubts would loom. I could never see her making do with ladders in her stockings and scruffy old shoes on; or wearing knickers that were not Italian silk. Also, I tell myself, Appleby's no fool.

I am in love. The woman I love is Sandra Appleby. Sandra Appleby is the wife of Norman Appleby, who has been paying my wages for almost two years. Mrs Appleby was unhappy and this made me happy and we are meant to be running away to find a new life that is nothing but day after day of quality time.

This is not a game. This is definitely not a game. The difficulty, you might say, is Mr Appleby and who he is and what it means to get on the wrong side of who he is: a man who occupies a position of some importance in the workings of the town.

Mr Appleby stutters when he speaks, so he doesn't speak much, but were he a speaking man, he might say: This is a little runt I have took in and sheltered and fed and let him drive my cars on his nights off... and this is how this runt pays me back.

Then he will be lost for words. But he will point and make eye gestures and may even mutter or grunt to indicate displeasure.

Mr A is a big man like a bear, with hair of strawberry blond and freckles on the backs of his hands. He moves like a bear, slow and very fastidious, taking his time and choosing the way he will go with great care through the days of his life. He lends money to people and rents out rooms and organises people to organise the distribution of many things the man in the street don't find on a supermarket shelf. He lives in a house like a castle and his wife, the former Miss Cold Knap, Sandra Saunders, is there to look nice on his arm when he goes out on the town.

When he signed me up it seemed too good to be true. His wife had looked me over and sent out signals about all kinds of marvels and amazements when we got to the Red Swamp.

You will be a lackey, she told me. Don't let it bug you. *Be* a lackey. He is paying you to say yes and do the odd jobs. Drive his nice new car and take him places. He goes away a lot and we'll be left alone. Don't worry, I'll show you the ropes.

This was the miracle of the man who was offering me a weekly wage to get into his wife. He looked like Dan Dailey, the old tapdancer, and I wondered if he might be queer. But she said he was just weird. He had never fucked her. She swore on her mother's life he has not so much as touched her tit in amorous contact. A kiss, she said, at the wedding and that was it. But I don't see him fucking men. Just weird.

She is not there. We have arranged to meet in the Virgin record store in the Capitol Centre. The sort of place where you can walk in through one door and out the other side without breaking stride. The sort of place where kids hang around all day and every day. The first time, I am early, sort of hoping she might be there but not hoping too hard. Enter from the arcade and exit onto Churchill Way. Walk over and sit down on the edge of the bandstand. From there I can keep an eye on the *Western Mail* clock on its iron pole in Queen Street. Wait five minutes and go back in. Still no Sandra. A degree of uneasiness sets in. She was nearly always early. She loved going to the dirty little flats I borrowed for the afternoon or evening. Or the hotel rooms we sometimes rented in another town.

It makes me feel clean, she told me, fucking in a dump like this. There was dust like grey fur on the sill, and a plumber had left his toolbag in the wardrobe.

Like we were meeting on our first date, she said. That's how I see it in my mind's eye. I like to be a little bit early and a little bit anxious. As if I'm not sure you'll turn up.

Music is playing. Kids wandering about; stopping and staring at the stuff on display. It is Smokey Robinson. My mother used to have the record. I come out for a second time and look up at the sky away to the south. Out over the Channel the big white clouds are as unmoving as a chalk cliff. The sky overhead is pale and it is warm for early summer. I wait and wait. More time goes by. Very slow and irksome like it is dripping out of a busted pipe. I am in love. I am lost and adrift in a sea of love. I am this man who drives a car and cleans a car and fucks a woman who is the wife of the man who owns the car. By now I know with certainty that she is not coming. But the inability to give up on the forlorn hope makes me hang on. You consider your investment and you can't give up. You are on the hook.

Time is going on. Late afternoon. The weather is nice. Pretty soon it will be the hour when the clerks and the counterjumpers are locking up shops and preparing to wend their ways homeward. I study the faces as they pass me by. Many faces. The flocks of the unremarkable. Or is it shoals? Herring. They drift east. The sickness of the longing is like indigestion.

Then I spot a man I know: Robert Berry. He is a wild and unruly young man who works at odd things for Appleby. His more or less constant companion is a man named Tony G Harris, alias the Pieman. This is a twenty-two-stone mass of meanness and spite and not all of it blubber, who is the muscle end of the Appleby Enterprise. My eyes search for him. A picture is taking shape. Fear makes my mouth dry. Then I spot him. Face like white dough and eyes the colour of barley sugar. He is looking right at me. He grins. This is a man who would chop off your feet and force you to climb a ladder to cheer himself up. Then chop off both your hands and tell you to try again to see if it could still be done. Then cut your throat because he was getting bored.

Then I spot her. She is coming out of the arcade. She calls out to me. Her face is bruised. Polly, she says. He *knows*...

Her eyes are full of despair and her voice is thick with sorrow. Then she sees the Pieman and she points.

Run, Polly! Run! They are gonna kill you!

Without a second thought, I dive into the Park Lane Bar,

cross the floor, vault the counter and go straight through the passage that leads to the main hotel on the other side. The foyer; late afternoon sun flooding in through the fanlight and onto the leaves of the rubber plants. The leaves rustle as I rush by them. I even manage to knock over an old lady as I barge through the doors into Park Place. Mike Stevens' taxi is at the head of the queue. I went to school with his son Carl. Fuck me, Polly! he says. What's the rush?

Mikey, I say, get me out of here!

Chris Poyner is my oldest friend. The one I always turn to in time of trouble. I jump out of the taxi at the Halfway Hotel and cut through the network of streets to his lodgings in Severn Grove. He is not pleased to see me. His eyes are dimmed, the aftermath of strong drink at lunchtime, and when he speaks the sound comes out from deep down. The words struggle, as though crawling through spit.

Fuck you! he says. He sees me as a fairweather friend. Thick-lipped and bleary, he turns his back on me and goes into the depths. I follow him along the passage to the room at the back of the house. There is a girl sitting on the table. She looks about seventeen, but worn. Plain as a pikestaff, with bitten down nails, bad complexion. She nurses a can of Stella and stares at me.

Chris scowls at me. Then he jerks his thumb for the girl to get down. She complies and takes a glug from her can. Her eyes move from my face to his.

You'da knocked five minutes earlier, he says, you coulda saved me the trouble.

The girl glugs some more and lowers her gaze. Chris prods her and tells her to get dressed and beat it. She seems briefly confused, then she starts to search for the articles of clothing strewn about.

She can't find her left shoe and he begins to shout at her. This brings tears and I intervene and assist her in the search. Find the shoe and help her to button the blouse.

Try some old world charm now and then, I tell him. It works wonders.

I touch her tit inadvertently and she gazes at me like a grateful bitch. She reaches to cover my hand.

Give her one, if you want to, he says. I'm going for a shave.

I look at the girl. Smile at her. Sympathy, the odd kind word, is all she needs. I escort her to the front door. Back in the room, I reproach him for his boorishness.

You're a fucking prick, I tell him. A girl like that is so miserable, so down in the fucking dumps, you could get her to come with a nice smile.

Fuck 'em, he says. Fuck 'em all.

Then he stares at me and asks what I want. I explain the situation to him and ask if he will put me up.

How long? he asks me.

Couple of days, I tell him. I'll have to work out a plan of escape... Week at the most...

He picks up the can of Stella the girl had put down and shakes it. It is empty. He crushes it in one hand and hurls it into the corner. Belches and frowns. Stares about him as if seeking hidden enemies. He has a massive head with ginger hair cut short so that it stands up like a hard bristle broom. Pale pink complexion and dark eyes. This is our first meeting in months. Without looking at me, he says: You only ever see some people when they want something. Put the bite on you for some favour...

I have been remiss, I say to him. I been tied up all winter.

He says nothing. Studies his hands. I let him sweat. He would cut off a finger before he'd offend me.

We met for two pints in the Clifton on Christmas Eve. The Sandra thing was just beginning to blossom and I was on the crest of the wave. He was going to watch over cement bags and bricks and drainpipes down at the Session's Building Supplies on Schooner Way. While he was making the rounds of the perimeter fence, with a bit of luck I'd be eyeballing hair on the mound of her cunt. Genuine blonde. My stars, back then, were big and bright and I was deep in the heart of a kind of Texas. Chris told me about his workplace, how much he hated it. How lousy his life was.

It's like a fucking stalag down there, he said, but it beats that room. He had this Tesco bag with his sandwiches and his flask of coffee, and alongside it a bag from Asda that he picked up and held open for my inspection. He took out a peaked cap; shiny black peak and the rest dark chocolate brown; just above the peak there was a gauntleted fist clutching two bolts of forked lightning

embroidered in canary yellow. Over this insignia, the words:
Starkweather Security. Two eighty five an hour, he told me, and
sixteen hour shifts. He had volunteered for the Christmas shift.

See, Poll, he explained, it don't make no difference to me. I
don't give a fuck where I am. At least they pay me for working.
Sitting on my arse and picking up the phone is all it is...

He had never married. There was a child, a little girl he
seldom saw. Others in the class had done better. Even a fucking
hodcarrier, he used to say, is one step up the ladder over me.

Back in the room, I say to him: You still the Kommandant?

He nods. Does not look at me. Still sulking.

Who was she? That girl? I ask him.

He shrugs. What do you care who she is? he says. You don't
give a fuck. I got to work, how else can I live. He nods to the pile
of crumpled cans in the corner. I need a lot of them things, he
says. Then he gives me a quick glance and grins.

I hear you been fucking the boss' wife, he says.

I think that's why I'm here, I tell him.

Nobody's blind forever, he says.

No, I agree. Can I stay here? I ask him.

He nods. I'm on permanent nights, he says. The sofa's the
bed. It's yours till eight am.

He studies his watch as if he expects it to speak to him.

I am on in a couple of hours, he says. Then he goes across to
the fridge and brings out two cans of Stella. He hands one to me.

You're lucky, he tells me, usually it's that cheapo supermarket
shit. I'm seven till eight now. They cut the hours to thirteen.

Unlucky for some, I say.

He shrugs. I wish it was longer. I'd work the full fucking
twenty four if they'd let me. Long hours don't bother me.

You still with the Starkweather outfit? I ask him.

For life, he says. They got me for life.

He looks at me, sips at his Stella. How did all this come
about? he asks me. Is it serious?

I consider for a moment. I fear it is serious, I tell him. We were
thinking of running off together, but something must have
happened.

What will you do?

I don't know, I tell him. I'm nuts about her, otherwise I could just fuck off to London. I'll have to try to get in touch with her.

We sit there in silence, just the occasional glug at a can while he mulls this over. Then he stands up, tilts back his head to empty his can. Straightens up, studies the can and then throws it into the corner. Well, he says, it's your funeral. Women were always your downfall.

Then he goes over to the wardrobe and opens the door. Stares in. Drags out the uniform.

Every day, he says, the same bad dream. On parade. One day (I got this dream) it'll be this huge redhead will step out and grab me and suck me right in like a fucking boa-constrictor.

When he takes off his jeans his huge dick flops out through the fly of his old-fashioned underpants. The uniform is ill-fitting, tight on the body and short in the sleeves. There is a cheval mirror against the wall, a cracked looking glass in a tilted frame. He studies himself in it.

Fucking look at me, he says, his face a mask of self loathing.

He stands there in the gloom of an all-embracing self disgust, staring at himself.

I look like a bag of shit with a belt in the middle, he says.

I cannot disagree. He sighs, sullen and brutish and lost, as if he never knows when he will be coming back; as if, when he leaves this time, it may well be forever. Then something stirs in his brain. You can watch it happening, like a change in the weather.

I meant to tell you, he says, I bumped into your old man. About a week ago. He goes in the Bird in Hand. Terry Mack got it now.

I find this news slightly disconcerting and can think of nothing to say.

You don't look overjoyed, he says.

I look at him. He has known me and my family for most of my life.

No, I tell him, I am not overjoyed.

Explanations concerning the nature of affairs peculiar to my family are not necessary. But he is also curious about Appleby, so I tell him what I know.

Jesus Christ, he says, it looks like you may have a few problems. There is a long pause. Well, he says, with a last look around, time to get going. He looks at me. You okay for bread?

I nod and he leaves.

Chapter Nine

My old man is looking straight at me as I come into the bar of the Bird in Hand through the open door. He is wearing blue jeans and a white shirt with black band on his left arm.

Well well, he says, the young Master Oliver. He empties his glass and hands it to me. I get the beer and sit down.

What's with the black armband? I ask.

Funeral, he says. He sips the head off his beer. Old Charlie. Kaput. The old Maestro... I must have told you about him. He falls into a reverie. Great man, he says. Him and your grandfather were the best in the town. The best team. The happiest days of my life, he says, back then when I was a young boy trying to learn how to lay the brick. He looks at me. Now he is dead, he says. Old Charlie, a real fucking star... Put that trowel in his hand and he was just like another Paganini...

Work, he says, back then I was in *love* with it. It is something even a worn-out old fool like me never forgets. Like your first love. Happy days when the world was almost new.

He wipes at his left eye and looks down at his hands. Alcohol was always his main problem. That and sentimentality. I sit there and wonder how I ever imagined he might be able to help me. His face is starting to bloat and he has grown a gut that shoves out just below his chest then sags like a sack of corn to the point where his belt is drawn through the brass buckle just above his dick. Wearing jeans don't help; blue jeans are the worst thing out for a man with a beerbelly.

It is not a beerbelly... not *exactly*, he once told my mother. It's more of a paunch. A paunch is something a lot of ex-athletes get.

Once you stop playing, see, all the stomach muscles relax.

Relax! she said. *Muscles!* You are sagging like a sack of shit. And don't give me that *ex-athlete!* When were you ever an athlete? *Paunch* be fucked! Stop drinking beer, you fat sod! Get off your arse once in a while!

He was never what might be called a happy man, but now his face looks angry from the effort of living. Bitterness in his eyes; and his mouth possessed by an almost convulsive twitch.

But all I can think of is Sandra: the way *her* arse is in a pair of jeans. The way her waist grows out of a pair of jeans. Like a white lily. Her grey eyes. The way her mouth is when she eats...

So, he says, how are things? You working?

Was working, I tell him.

Norman Appleby, wasn't it?

Yes, I tell him.

He shakes his head and closes his eyes as if there is much pain at the thought of it. Jesus Christ, Elliott! A pimp like that! What were you doing? Washing his car?

I washed his car now and then.

And fucked his wife?

That too.

You may have problems, he says. He is just like his old man, dull but cunning. You don't want to think you can fool him just because you read a book.

I don't think I can fool him, I tell him.

What did you think, then?

I don't know.

You got money?

I got money. Some. Enough for now.

Then what's the problem? Just disappear.

Where to? I ask him.

Anywhere where he can't find you... Just get on a train.

He looks at me with undisguised contempt. Women! he says. Don't you know? Hasn't life taught you anything? Do you think you can fuck a woman – *any* woman – and just walk away? Fuck me, Elliott! The complications your mother and I managed to make out of that proposition must have taught you something.

It is not that simple, I start to explain. I cannot bring myself to say I am in love with her. I just can't say the word.

He laughs. What? Are you heartsick for her? In love with the wife of another man? Some piece of arse that was doing it with the hired hand? Jesus fucking Christ, Elliot!

There is nothing to say. He gets up and goes out for a piss. I turn away and look through the window at the evening sky. The sounds of the bar; a place that is drowning in its own wet boredom. Like a barrel of bad beer, forty thousand nights of guzzling have dragged the place down to the bottom of the well. The window I look through faces northwest, so that I get a glimpse of the sky above the sunset. The glow is still there. Roof line and chimneys darken against it. Small flecks of cloud, high up, still holding sunlight on their bellies. A quiet takes over the street outside the door.

When he comes back he brings two whiskies. Bushmills, he says, compliments of Mr Mack. We drink them down.

Let me tell you something, he says. Let me tell you what living through the last thirty years has taught me. Every day I get up and look back. What do I see? *Look at me!* he snarls. I look at him.

I didn't even have a suit for the funeral, he says. Every morning I look under the bed. There is nothing there, not even a chamberpot. Then I go outside and stand on the corner and wait for a van. Do you want to end up like that? I can barely climb out of bed. People looking at you, standing on the corner of a morning, with your little pack of sandwiches and dusty old boots and anxious eyes, do you fucking want that? Look at me... what I am now. What am I? Even *I* don't know what I am. Do you think I was always like this?

He leans back in his chair and groans. Jesus, he sighs. You are looking at a man who has seen pimps get the better of him time and time again. And watched moronic scoundrels rising to the so-called top in droves... In *fucking droves*. He drinks some beer and glares.

Poor as piss, he says. This, he says, and holds up the glass of beer, played its part. Shakes his head. The fundamental defect.

He drinks some beer and wipes at his mouth with the back of his hand. Don't laugh! he says, then he mimics the action of a man pointing a pistol at his own head, the thumb cocked: Remember that?

It was his Polish joke. It concerns a man who suspects his wife is fucking around and comes home in the early afternoon and catches her in bed with his best friend. He bursts through the door with a gun in his hand. I knew it! he says. He shoots the man immediately. Then the wife starts to laugh at him. Hard hysterical laughter. The husband grins at her. (Raises the gun to his right temple.)

Okay, he says, you can laugh now. He grits his teeth. But you won't be laughing soon. He cocks the hammer. Because you're *Next!*

It was a joke he used to tell us on the nights my mother went out. It was like a game. The clock would be ticking. She'd be done up like a sore thumb. The air would be tight, like we were all suffocating. He would be just like a bear in a cage. As soon as that clock hit half past seven she'd be gone. She'd kiss me and my sister goodbye and she'd be out of that door in a flash. You could smell her perfume. Her lips all soft and puffed up like silk pillows.

Then he would turn to us. The Mask. She thinks I'm dopey, he'd say. She thinks I don't know what's going on.

He'd be whispering. He was afraid of her. Scared she might be listening at the door. Then he would wink at us and smile. Tap at his temple. Don't worry, he'd say, *I know*... The same performance, every Friday night. It went on for years.

Still, he goes on, we mustn't complain. As far as my present life goes, it might even be said that I am at last achieving a certain eminence: I am living in a fucking attic! Ha Ha Ha! Room at the top. My employer owns the roof over my head. Owns the bed I sleep on. Real company man, these days...

He avoids my eyes. The ghastly grin. He goes on. The roof leaks. It is an ancient roof. For more than a century it has borne the brunt of wind and rain. And I get it first. God's chosen. It comes in, the rain, at some unknown point, some cracked or missing slate, a loose flashing, or some errant ridgetile, the joint loosened after years of baking summers and frosty winter nights, the differing co-efficients of linear expansion between the red Bridgwater clay of the tile bonnet and the hard grey Aberthaw cement and Channel sand that went into the mortar mix it was bedded in. Finally achieving the fracture they have been mutually striving for since their rude joining together when the world was young.

He almost beams at me and gulps some more beer. He is beginning to sail now with the wind from the beer driving him on.

Old houses, he says. Houses that got a tablet built in where it says 1904. Or 1896. You are wandering along a street in the twilight, and you pause to wonder about all the shit those rooms inside the walls have seen. Old walls... Food for thought, wouldn't you say? The bricklayers who built them have been dead for fifty years. What miseries, I often wonder, did they nurse in their hearts? He smiles at me. Old houses, he says. They ought to be compelled to blow them all to smithereens. Suffice it to say, my boy, he says, this room I am in, it leaks like fuck. Rain enters and runs down the hip like a skier on a snowy slope. Drips through a crack and I collect each drop in a pickle jar. When there is a west wind and the rain is heavy, it is one drop every twelve seconds. On the nose. A fucking metronome!

He grins at me. His little speech has cheered him up no end.

My round? he says. I hand him my glass and he goes to the bar.

The Bird in Hand is very much like the Royal Oak. A long room designed for working men to line up at the bar and guzzle beer. On the lines of a cattle stall, with the counter as the trough. There is a door at either end. A hatch in the dividing wall and mirrors behind the bottles on the shelves behind the bar. Something about the place reminds me of the night I first set eyes on Sandra.

The party came into the bar around nine o'clock. Six of them. Obvious slummers. We had a lot of slummers in that place. The landlady, Iris, was a minor celebrity; her father had been a star rugby player and she had known a genuine featherweight champion of the world. There was a gym where a couple of fighters trained at the back and the signed photographs of many great champions on the walls. She knew Appleby, who was the only one sober. He laid five twenties on the bar. We'll drink that up, he said. Have one yourself, my dear. Have drop of brandy. He wagged a finger. And the staff, he said. A face like a Hereford bull.

The place was heaving, a Saturday in March after a big rugby match. I served them. Sandra was wearing a black leather jacket. On her it didn't look corny. I like your jacket, I told her. You got anything on under there? The leather was so soft and paperthin her nipples showed through. She looked at me. She was drunk but her eyes were beautiful. Grey eyes. Blonde hair cut short. Lovely mouth.

You're very pretty, she said. Deadpan. She tugged at Appleby's sleeve. Look how pretty this one is, she said. They all turned to stare at me. I'd like to take him home with us, she said.

My father comes back with the beer. I can feel in my bones, he is going to ask about my mother, and he does. Do you ever see your mother? he says. His face looks like he is flinching from a blow.

Now and then, I tell him. Not often.

He looks down at his hands. Says nothing. He turns them palm up, his grimy hands, as if he might discover some message in the lines.

Did you go to the wedding?

Yes.

And your sister?

No.

What was it like?

It was grim.

She's your mother, he says. He looks at me. What's to be said, he says. Nobody's perfect.

He looks around the bar. They had this secret, he says. When they were setting out a house. Your grandfather, the Maestro... He holds up three fingers. Like Steve McQueen. Three numbers, he says. An empty field; a couple of wooden pegs to show the building line. Magic numbers. They were like fucking witch doctors. They had water levels and sprung steel tapes. Accuracy had to be absolute – the cardinal rule. Lines strung from point to point as tight as bowstrings... He stares away, dismembered and lost in reverie.

It was what set them apart... from the rest – the aborigines...

I hold up my hand. This is a story I have heard many times and I am not in the mood to hear it again.

I know this one, I say. This is the one about Pythagoras and three four five to square the crooked world. The square on the hypotenuse and blah blah blah.

The old man looks at me from under his brows. Bloodshot eyes and a lot of anger. Have I told you this before? he asks me.

It is not exactly a secret, I say.

He smiles. He says: You don't have the slightest idea of what I am talking about, do you? I am talking about nineteen fucking fifty four. No one had ever heard of Elvis then. No James Dean. What we had was fucking Dicky Valentine. Primitive fucking times, my bright-eyed boy. His fists are clenched. He would love to sock me right on the jaw. Those two, he says, what those two men could do with lines and tapes and wooden pegs was as mysterious as the moonshot to the rest of them. All those other bastards, when it came for them to set out a house, used some wooden square some halfcut woodbutcher had made from four by one... they had linen tapes all ragged and stretched and half the markings worn away. They didn't care. Did not give a fuck. If they got it in the right field they thought it was a minor miracle... But with the Maestro and your grandfather, accuracy was a religion. The one and only dead true square and the perfectly perpendicular were what they earnestly endeavoured after every working day of their crummy lives. They were the last of the righteous, lost amidst the savage heathen...

He drinks down half of his beer in two swallows. Why did you come here? he asks me. What is the real problem? His eyes are cold.

I tried to run off with his wife, I tell him. He knows and he is out to get me. Or his musclemen are.

He closes his eyes like man with a bad headache.

You are just like your mother, he tells me. He opens his eyes. Looks at me, then looks beyond. I am sick of it, he says. He stands up and empties his glass. Puts down the glass on the table. The froth slides down the sides. I've had enough, he says. I am going to get myself some chips, he says. He cannot bring himself to look at me. I have had a long day, he says, and I am fucking starving. I have been around this sort of shit all my life and I am tired of it.

Then he crosses to the door. Turns and gives me a last look. He looks old and weary, ready to give up.

You can paddle your own fucking canoe, he says. Then he is gone.

As I come out of the door he is disappearing around the corner into Paget Street. Sandra is still on my mind. I had wanted to talk about her. Say her name a few times so he could know she exists. I stop and reach out to touch the wall. The bricks are smooth and cool. It is as if I can taste her. I try to concentrate on her, revive our miraculous thing. And I almost moan aloud at the idea of losing this woman, this amazing contraption of flesh and depravity whose cunt I believe to be capable of making pearls. It is love. I am *hooked* on love.

Trees and lamplight. The Albions' Club on the corner. The church. The street is quiet in the way streets are quiet when the dark is still new and there is a moon. There is only one customer in the fish shop when I look in. A stranger who is not my father. He turns to look at me.

The intervention of houses hides the moon, but I know it is there. I am almost happy to be alone. Almost lost. A part of the night. I wander my way to the river bank and stop to stare. The bridges. The edges of dark things against the soft blur of the city lights. Make my way to the Penarth Road bridge and lean against the stone parapet. Deep thinker in his immemorial pose. A moon, a man against a parapet, a river flowing under him as black as crude. To the south all is hazy and softly grey around the couple of tall smokestacks and the factory roofs; the distant headland beyond the bay.

You keep looking for signs. The next step and other mysteries. Is that moon a full moon? What is this thing called love? I think of my mother and father and their plights. The one washed up, the other trying to hang on in a second marriage with her old fancy man, Bobby Snell. The memory of their wedding cannot come to mind without a shudder. Time to move on, I tell myself. Cut your losses and move on. Take out my dick and piss between the stone balusters, the stream of piss a filament in the moonlight as it falls. Traffic at my back, a car or two. Just drunk enough to conjure with the night's soft roar. The moon's soft dazzle in the vault of endless space. There is a sort of ache in the deep emptiness of my heart for some lost thing. I think of Appleby's wife the night we stood in the orchard amongst the leafless apple trees and kissed, her face when we drew apart in the light of a feeble January moon. I recall the way her back curves and grows like a lily from the cheeks of her arse. The backbone's smooth ripple beneath my fingertips. The wonders of her being alive. Close my eyes and recapture the miracle of burial dark when she sits on my face.

Go past the southern fringe of what is the town. The brewery. Bute Terrace. All is quiet. St Mary Street is in a kind of midweek stupor. All I can think of is what might have been. Of the times of being in a room with her there and the enormous possibilities of the unbridled lusts. On equal terms. The tip of the tongue and the salt taste of limpet in the shell. Sea-salt succulence and my cup runneth over and over. Even the idea of being no more than a dick is okay. I would settle for a week. A day, even an hour... Locked up tight in some room in some dilapidated hotel in a meaningless town. A box of pills to keep it up and a bottle of Wild Turkey for the proper effect. the light of day coming in through dirty windows of a hotel that overlooks railway lines.

Can this be what true love is? Is this what locked my folks in the clamps of their miseries for all those years? What happens when the well dries up? I look up at the sky. Some stars, some cloud. A big moon. Love, I whisper, it is like nothing else. You can dress it up and you can sell it. But you can't weigh it, or put it in a bottle and take it with a spoon. And it is hardly ever sweet.

I turn right into Bute Street and then left and go under the railway bridge, then right into Collingdon Road. Then head for the compound where Chris keeps his watch. Keep in the shadows and breathe the night air. Enter a call box and try to phone her. The phone rings and rings. I can feel the dead space where the sound is.

It goes on and on and nobody picks it up. I write her name in the dirt on the glass. Count three more rings. Give up. Come out by the potato warehouse wall. Shadow and light. The factories stretch away like a filmset, as far as the eye can see.

Chris is not pleased when I rattle the compound gates and call his name. I am almost sober by this time, but he is drunk. He cannot let me inside, he tells me, because of the complicated rigmarole of switches and alarms and automatic locks. There are connections to the police station. His face is held in the arc light and his eyes are peevish in the yellow mask. The idea of lying between sheets where he has lain seems less and less like something a sane man might choose to do. Then the beeper goes on his mobile phone. I can read in his eyes how he hates me being there to watch him jump. He turns away from me to answer. I hear him grunt. Midnight and the hourly check. He reports: Nothing to report. The compound lights flash on the peak of his cap as he turns. The belt cuts into his gut. By now I can smell the beer on his breath. He clips the phone back on his belt and scowls at me.

I went to see the old man, I tell him.

He okay? he asks. Nice to be out, is it? How did he find the life behind bars?

He didn't say.

Probably no worse than this place, he says.

We stare past each other. That was the hourly call, he tells me. They call up to keep you on your toes. He shakes his head and spits onto the concrete. I am losing sight of who I am, he says. It's pathetic. I got to get out of it, Poll.

I stay silent.

It is getting cold, he says. I can't be standing here all night.

The night is warm. What do you do between the calls? I ask him.

Wank, he says. Wank and wank. I got a stack of dirty books. That's how I make sure I can sleep when I get home. It's a great life.

Again the silence falls between us. I'll leave you to it, I tell him and walk away.

I come to the place where Collingdon Road runs into Tyndall Street. The whores are gone from under the bridge. I pause to consider what to do next.

Sandra is a tough baby. Very realistic about the nature of life.

Don't go building your hopes up, she told me once. Day at a time.

This was after I told her that I loved her. We were in a flat that a man named Maurice Swann had let me use. Early one evening in August, with the room ablaze with the last glow of the setting sun. The words just came out of my mouth. She went stiff on me and pushed me away. Then she got out of the bed, got dressed and left without another word.

The next day she said: Ellie, you are very sweet and I like you a lot, but you are not the first and you won't be the last... We can't afford to be getting too emotional. Okay?

The city is dead now. It is the middle of the week and times are bad. Outside of the gambling dens, I am not sure that this place ever had a section of the night where an organised way of life went on; where things changed character and became distinctly nocturnal. Places where those who had been nothing but shadows in the light of day turned into beautiful moths, or wise old owls, or even vampires, after two am. There was a dump where people like Chris could go, some place they called the Cabman's Club, where you could drink and drink and they would provide as long as you had money to lay on the bar. He had told me about it. He went there on his night off. Sat there and kept drinking until he melted into his own stupor.

Under the Bute Street Bridge and come to Mill Lane. Empty and still and silent as the grave. There is a sense of suspension, like the wind trapped in a corpse. Not a breath of wind, though. But the fear is building up inside me. Waiting is mainly what always fixes people like me. Those, that is, who tend towards cowardice. Away from where the pain is. The fingertip held in the candle flame was never a game for the likes of me. It was a great time when I was roaring and contorting and coming in the pink pussy, but where am I now? What comes next to fill up the hole? And where are the gravediggers?

Walk on up the dead furrow of St Mary Street. High Street. The flags on the castle battlements hang limp on their poles. A few milky clouds to comfort the cold and faraway stars. A sound in the night air like a seashell held to your ear when you close your eyes. I consider the option of catching a train to another town. Of starting another life anew in some dump where nobody knows me. Think of the station in the early hours and get bad vibes. All those lit up platforms and shadows and corridors. Dereliction and emptiness.

Then I think of my grandfather who is older than the hills and lives all alone in a house in the wilds. Nine or ten miles out of town along narrow and winding country roads. My father reckons the old man is going nuts, but he will also admit that filial devotion with him was never strong. Of the entire bunch of us, he used to say, the only one worth a light was my mother. Me, he used to say, you already know, and as for those other two, the wide berth is what I would recommend, and the wider, the better.

George Borrow once walked from Norwich to London in twenty seven hours, subsisting, so he claimed, on an apple, a smoked herring and a pint of milk. I try to picture the journey to my grandfather's in my mind. We used to go out there every Saturday in happier times. The summer night I am in is vast and I feel very small and almost lost. But it is dry and the air is warm and I persuade myself I can always sleep in a hedge if need be.

I turn and head west. There is, it seems, a constant comfort in this direction. The moon is low in the southwest when I cross the Canton Bridge. I stop and lean on the rail. Then I hear soft footsteps coming from my left. A short and thickset man is approaching. Dark clothes with white trainers. At his heel, one yard to his rear, a black dog. He stops. The dog stops. We face each other. He wears a black woollen hat with the badge of the LA Raiders. By the light of the lamp I note his freckles and very pale eyes. He smiles at me. He looks harmless.

Admiring the view? he says.

Contemplating the moon, I tell him.

He nods and clears his throat. Nice moon, he says. Going my way?

He nods west. He carries a pack on his back. The dog yawns.

Where you headed? I enquire.

Just out of here, he says. Just anywhere west of here. I been here a week and it is time to move on. I come to the conclusion this is a gringe town. All the natives got hostile eyes. You're not a native, are you? I'm not looking to offend. You don't sound like a native...

I suppose I am, I tell him, but not so you'd notice.

He grins and we start very gently into the journey. He tells me that he has been begging his way around the nation. Sort of an exercise, he explains. I been keeping notes. I might write a book about it. Call it *Seeing the World with a Begging Bowl*.

What's it like? I ask him.

Not bad, he says. It varies quite a bit. You are not going to starve. But there is something about that fucking eight hour day I cannot take.

Where you from? I ask him. He walks very steady, with an absolute economy of movement. Small paces and no swing to the arms. The dog falls into step like a shadow. Down the slope from the bridge and past the City Temple. We pause at the crossroads. I repeat the question.

He shrugs. What does it matter?

Just curious, I tell him. You must have been born somewhere.

Believe it or not, he says, I was born right here. He smiles at me. Bad teeth.

You and me could be blood brothers, he says.

I doubt it, I tell him. Is your family still here?

Shakes his head. Four winds, he says. Scattered all over. I don't know if I ever saw my father, and the last time I met mother I was six years old.

I nod down at the dog. What's his name? I ask.

It's a her, he says.

Her name, then? This is an awkward little bastard.

He shrugs and pats the dog's head. She is not really mine, he says. She just sort of fastened onto me when I was in Newport. Looked at me with those big bitch eyes and begged me to get her out of there.

Wise dog, I say.

It is a bit of company, he tells me. A dog is company when you are on the road. And people will often feed a dog when they won't feed you, you ever notice that?

We both study the dog. She's got a bit of retriever in her somewhere, I venture. I lean over and fondle the dog's ears. The soft dark female eyes look up at me. Intense yearning and absolute docility. A long and miserable history as man's best friend.

I had a dog when I was a kid, I tell him. She was a bitch, too. Sally, a great dog. She had eyes just like your dog's eyes.

We cross the road and go on. Past the old St David's Hospital.

The kid points at the stone facade. That is where I first saw the light, he says.

Before it was a hospital, I tell him, it was a workhouse.

A taxi goes by at cruising speed. A clock chimes somewhere faraway.

One o'clock, I tell him. Must be the City Hall.

We have come to the point where Wellington Street veers half left. Neville Street to the left of us. I think this is where we part company, I tell him. I live not far from here. Then: Do you always travel at night?

Mostly at night, he says. You do better mileage in the dark.

Then I ask him his name, which seems to disconcert him.

Why? he asks. His eyes are suspicious for the first time.

Curiosity, I tell him. So I can remember you in my prayers.

His mouth clamps shut and he shakes his head. Backs away from me, shakes his head again. I don't think you're my type, he says.

He walks away along Wellington Street. By this time I am beginning to feel weary. I stare after him. The last of the true pioneers. Keeping forever one jump ahead of the posse. Then I start to walk along Cowbridge Road. Shops and restaurants and all the dead interiors. My skull feels as if it might be filling up with smoke. My mouth is dry. I would, I tell myself, give my right arm for a berth in any steerage section of any boat going anywhere on earth. Even a wooden rail on a slave ship. Shackles and chains. Trudge on and try to build up a measure of fortitude. Think of Mr Appleby. Then Mrs Appleby. Then the minions of Mr Appleby and Mr Appleby's wrath. Grit my teeth and pray that the coming dawn will shit me out intact.

Then I stop dead in my tracks, turn and look down and see the black bitch looking up at me.

Fuck me! is all I can say. The dog pants. Pauses. Pants some more. I rush back to the corner, but by now the kid is out of sight.

Jesus! I say. The dog looks the other way. I start to walk. The dog follows. I stop and she stops. Start again. Fuck it! I mutter. Come on, then! I tell her. In a way, a strange way, I am grateful for the company.

I have not seen my grandfather for a long time. Many years. He is a shrewd old man who moved out to build a house in a field when his wife died. I have no memory of my grandmother. It is a rough old field, as I recall it, grass and bracken and brambles with a strip of wood and a stream. A pond in the middle of a clump of trees. Some oak trees. It lies some six miles from the edge of the town. A long and wearisome way to walk along country roads in the dead of night. To fly would be marvellous. I think of Sandra. Think of my father and what he might say if he knew where I was heading. My legs are getting tired and there are times it seems that it might be better if I simply ran and butted my head time and time again into some sturdy tree trunk. But from the dog, not one whimper of complaint.

The dark loses form and turns ash grey as we are on the last lap.

A car passes as we draw alongside the small footbridge over the river. It slows down as if the driver wants to get a good look at me. Some farmer, perhaps, or a rustic reveller on his way home. But when I turn and jerk my thumb, the car speeds away. Birds are starting to sound. There are still a couple of miles to go. The dog is steady as a rock, but I am just about all in. Ready to turn into the next field and sprawl in the dewsoaked grass.

When we get to the house the sky is pale and there is a kind of hush and solemnity to the morning air. I climb over the wooden gate and make my way up the overgrown gravel drive. Weeds grow as high as my knees on either side of the deep ruts where the car tyres went. The blackcurrant and gooseberry bushes at the edges are choked with honeysuckle and bindweed. Nettles almost as tall as I am crowd around the brick shed he always called the barn. The white-painted door hangs on one hinge. His pale blue car is almost lost in the long grass. A Ford. A dark blue glazed tarpaulin is draped over the bonnet, held down by bricks. There is mist at the edges of the field.

I go along the narrow concrete path that leads to the kitchen at the back of the house. Look in through the window. My grandfather is seated at the table in the kitchen. No light. He is staring down at his hands like cardplayer. For a moment I think he may be asleep, but his head jerks around to look when I tap at the windowpane. The old withered mask. As much as a week's growth of white stubble where the bottom of his face is collapsed about the toothless mouth. The eyes stare hard. Glare with instinctive rage, then alter to allow a faint smile of recognition. He stands up and beckons to me. Crosses the room to the door. He moves very slow, like a man walking barefoot on broken glass. I hear a key turn in the lock; two bolts slide out of keeps. The door opens a couple of inches and he unhooks a chain to let me in.

Good God! he says. It's the last of the Olivers! His teeth are in by this time. Sorry about the delay, he says. He points at the bolts and the chain. I got it like Fort Knox here, he says. We shake hands. Come in, he says. Come on in, I'll put the kettle on.

Then he spots the dog. Points. Whose mongrel?

Mine, I tell him. She adopted me.

He frowns and sniffs and turns away. Give it some water, he says. He hands me a red plastic bowl. I half fill the bowl at the tap and set it down in the porch. The dog drinks as if we had just crossed a desert.

I'll put the kettle on, he says again.
I take a cup from the drainer and drink two cups of water.
You walk? he asks. All the way?
I nod.
You must be tired.
Pretty tired, I say. Then I sit in the chair by the unlit stove and fall fast asleep.

Chapter Ten

The rest of the day goes by like a dream. We sit there and talk and drink tea and soon it is evening and we are sitting by the stove, with the chopped wood blazing and the flames licking out through the open stove door. The last light of the sun is dying beyond the edge of the trees. My grandfather is telling me tales of his days as a cabin boy: a place called Santos, in Brazil; Goa and Bombay; Buenos Aires and the queer priest in the Seamen's Mission. It was just about better than fuck all, he says. Back here, we had nothing. Running errands. Day after day. You scampered about. We used to be a maritime nation. He tells me about huge bunches of pink bananas for so many reis.

About a tanner, he says. He holds his hand to show how high. A parrot in a cage made out of bamboo, that died when the air got colder north of the line.

Then he stops talking and we watch the wood burn. The walls suck in the dark. The last light at the window makes pale lines along the edges of things. Gramps is dozing. Eyes closed like a cat. His hands are loosely clasped, big hands with thick fingers, veins like cords.

The wood in the stove crackles and spits out a spark. His eyes open again. We got loads of food here, he says. He might be reminding himself. We won't starve, he says. Got binoculars, he says. Got a shotgun. Got a bottle of cherry brandy... He leans over to take a log from the brick hearth and toss it into the stove.

In the morning, he says, you can give me a hand. There's a couple of little jobs. Nothing urgent, he says. I got money out here. Got a safe in the floor. Do you need any money? He looks at me. The room is almost dark by this time. You in trouble? he asks me. Only you got a look about you... Like a man who might be on the run.

Little bit of trouble, I tell him. Things sort of got on top of me. By this time the cigarette has burned down to the tip. I flick it into the flames. A fresh start, I say, is what I need. But there is no rush. Nobody knows where I am. No one would think of looking out here. He nods and stares into the fire. Dozes off again. The dog lies asleep on the straw mat on the floor.

But the next day it rains. And the day after that. Time drags. Lucky we dried out that mattress when we did, he says.

We stand side by side, looking out into the field.

Get a lot of rain out here, he tells me. West wind blows straight in from the sea. We get it first.

We have just finished a breakfast of baked beans on toast. He tells me again that we won't starve. He is proud of his tins of food. Enough to feed a small army, he says. The dog has made herself at home. I'll get some dogfood, I tell him, when I go down for fags.

There is a sell-it-all store in the village that doubles as a post office. Get dog biscuits, he says. Good for her teeth. We'll have to give her a name. How about Bess? We could go in the barn and saw up some logs when you come back, he says. I got a radio here somewhere, if you fancy some music. Now that I am with him, company, as he calls it, he shaves every morning. A fine-featured man, with a curved, fine-bridged aristocratic nose, like a Spanish grandee. His hair is still dark, only thinly streaked with grey.

Was my father any good as a bricklayer? I ask him. I watch his face: the pursing of the lips, the narrowing eyes. He takes his time. I've seen worse, he says.

He lends me an old mac and I walk the mile or so to the village store. The dog stays by the stove. The rain is easing off by this time and birds are starting to sing. The odd car passes me on the road. I buy some chocolate biscuits to go with the sliced loaf and the cigarettes. A box of matches, as an afterthought. The village is quiet; all the peons are long gone and moved to the town and the men and women who replaced them are at places of work.

In the afternoon the sun comes out and we rig up an arrangement of ladders to get onto the flat roof over the rear dormer window. He has got a big tin of some bitumastic paint that I haul up with a rope and slap on where the joints in the felt are. Good thing to get it watertight before the winter, he says. He is happy now. Things are getting done and the labour is cheap.

We open more tins for the evening meal. Tuna chunks and chips. I forgot to get milk, so we have to drink the tea black. He moans about this. I like a drop of milk in my tea, he says. Is that too much to ask? For a moment I think he is joking, but he is not. Is it? he persists.

Is it what?

Too much to fucking ask?

The old buzzard is deadly serious. My father always maintained he, my grandfather, was going nuts.

I'll get some tomorrow, I promise.

Tomorrow, tomorrow... *Always* fucking tomorrow...

Then he gets up and goes over to the back door and throws the hot milkless tea out into the weeds. Fuck it! he says. I'll drink water instead... He sits down again and begins to rock. His lips move. He refuses to look at me. The dog watches him warily.

The next morning he discovers this old Mario Lanza record and spends the rest of the day searching for a plug for the radiogram. He goes through sideboard drawers and old biscuit tins and cardboard boxes dragged out from under beds. Tips out the junk of years and sifts through it. I try to find something to read, but the only books he owns are a Gideon bible and Adam Bede. I go outside and look at the sky instead. Rainclouds. Think of Sandra. I know I won't last long where I am. The peculiar quiet in the middle of the night makes me nervous. Only the dog is not unhappy. She has followed me outside. She looks up at me and when I look at her she wags her tail. She licks the slaver from her lower jaw with a salmon pink tongue. Her eyes seem to have joy in them. She, at least, has found a home.

All night long we got Mario Lanza. He sits and shades his eyes and won't even look at me.

Wet days, he says. I hate the wet days. Tomorrow we got work to do. He looks at me as if he would search my very soul. Okay?

Okay, I tell him.

The old bastard got me working like a dog. Got me up the ladder. Scraping the loose paint from the wood. Bargeboard, he says. That there is the soffit... Fascia... The different names.

Get off the loose stuff. Then sandpaper... Make a block. Wrap the sandpaper around... Like *this, for fuck's sake*... Elbow grease, he tells me. Press hard. Harder... That's it. *That's* the hammer... Keep going. The idea is to keep going.

He has a barn full of pots of paint he has had stored up for years. Paintbrushes in all sizes in packs. Brand new, he says. We got it all. Don't worry. I'll hold the ladder. I won't let you fall. This is your introduction, I can see, to the working day, he says. It was a great invention. I can see you never got previously acquainted... This cracks him up. Keep going, he urges me. The idea is to keep going. Let your mind go free...

So there I am, rubbing with the sandpaper to wear down ancient paint.

We *should* burn it off, he muses. I could find my blowlamp... It's in the barn... Get it back to the wood and start again... That's the *proper* job.

The old man is coming back to life. His head is filling up with ideas of things to do. The old master builder again. He rubs his hands. He got me like a prisoner. Cheap labour for life. *Slave* labour. Me, with my soft shoulder hard against *his* rusty wheel.

And when we stop we got the stories. The history of the Olivers. How his father was a bastard. A real bastard. Unscrupulous. A drunkard and a fornicator. Violent too. But brilliant. A brilliant man. Then the mother, his poor old mother. How she suffered.

Then my grandmother. His dead wife.

You were hardly born, he says, and she was gone. It almost finished me, he tells me. The old songs, he tells me. They are the worst part, playing the old songs...

He looks at me. Moist eyes. He drinks a mouthful of tea and looks away. Life, he says and looks at me hard. Life got body blows you don't expect. He shakes his head. He is searching the nooks and crannies. It teaches you hard lessons, he says. And there is nowhere for you to hide.

After the wisdom it is back to the grind. I am the grinder while he watches and points.

Then there is the evening, out on the terrace with the sun going down behind the trees. The long grass in the field bothers him.

Should get it cut, he says. June hay is the best. A pretty penny. How peaceful it is as he dozes. The peace of the tomb. Then he comes back and there is more history. This bastard, that one. The struggle of the last good man. How hard it is to keep honest in a world filled with rogues. How this, how that...

Sometimes we have a small tot of his special scotch. He hides it, he says, to avoid temptation. A tiny tot in a small glass. Gold-rimmed. Special glasses, he says. Auspicious occasions. Cheers, he says. We touch glasses. Down the hatch! he mutters, but he only sips at it. Barely wets his lips. Sniffs at the whisky and smiles. This is the fucking life, my boy, he says. A wee dram. Puts his nose to the glass and sniffs hard. Sighs. Good for the heart, he tells me. Good for what ails you. Out here, an evening like this, you wouldn't want to call King George your uncle.

We are living on his tinned food. I get a loaf of bread from the village shop when I go down for cigarettes. Hundreds of tins: beans; tuna; salmon; tomato soup. Use them up, he says. Hunger, he assures me, is the best sauce. This and other pearls: hard work never killed anyone, or Rome wasn't built in a day...

He is getting back, he says, to being alive again. A man *needs* work, he says. It is like a proclamation. His eyes are shining. A deep emotion stirs in his heart. He is already working out the way tomorrow ought to go.

Then it is time for bed. The dog is snoring under the table. Gramps makes sure there is water in her bowl. Then he locks and bolts the door. Keep out the nightbirds, he says. He sleeps down stairs and I sleep up. Good night, my boy, he says. Pleasant dreams!

I sit in the quiet room. Outside is the night air. Then I go to the window and look out over the dark field. There is a half moon. The last ebbs of light are in the sky above the trees at the edge.

I say her name softly. SANDRA. Whisper it to myself as slow as I can. S-A-N-D-R-A. Thread each single letter onto the string of my longing. Desire, what is it? Like holding your breath and no ending.

There is an ache in me as hard as pebble. Then I go back to the bed and whisper again and again the name of my love.

All alone in the silence. The deep dark with its silence, that holds each small sound, each creak of the house, each small animal cry, owl wingbeats, the whirring of moths, like jewels in a velvet case.

Will I dream of her? I wonder. Will what she is or was for me ever show up in my dreams? Even to show her face? And will she sing me a lullaby? Listen hard to work out the silence. The needles in haystacks. All hell, as they say, with its monsters is waiting out there.

The next day this man with a red face came with a machine and drove in and went round and round in the field and cut down all the tall grass. He nodded to me and wiped his face with a red handkerchief and went on his way. Jack Butler, Gramp informs me. A good old stick.

And for two hot days the cut grass lay in the field and dried and turned pale. The sun shone down and the dews at night and the grass was like silver. In the light of the moon it was almost white. Or pale grey. Soft feathers of the palest grey.

Then another man, a younger man with a paler face, a fine big lump of a chap, as Gramp said, came. This was the son of the first man. He came with another machine that gathered up the hay and bundled it and bound it with orange cord and shit it out as blocks.

It is like a miracle, Gramp says. The wonders of machinery! One man doing the work of ten.

He is beside himself with a savage joy. He is making plans for the cultivation of the field. Ploughing it up and living off the land. Crops of potatoes, cabbages, swedes and turnips. He is working out yields at so much a pound.

But this is the easy bit. The next bit, the hard bit, where no machine plays a part, is where I come in. Now it is my turn to assist the strapping young farmer to load the blocks of hay onto the flatbed trailer. They are heavy. The cord cuts into my hands and I struggle. The young farmer lifts them with one hand. Swings them up as if they were no more than pillows. He says very little. Just smiles at my efforts. We load the trailer and then stack the hay to make a rick next to the barn. I am worn out at the end of it and my arms feel like rags. The dry seed of the hay sticks to my sweaty skin. My hands are blistered. My muscles are quivering. I gaze away at the distant hills and dream of a cool bar room in the evening and a glass of ice cold beer. I itch like a madman. It makes you want to be forever idle. A life of indolence as a guaranteed way of passing the time.

When it is over, when all the blocks of hay are gathered and stacked and covered with a big green tarpaulin, the young farmer and I sit down and Gramp brings out a tray of tea. Nice cups with spoons in the saucers and a jug for the milk and the sugar in a silver bowl. A plate with six chocolate biscuits as a treat.

Which one are you? Gramp enquires.

Samuel, the young farmer says.

You are all like peas in a pod, Gramp says.

The young man crams a chocolate biscuit into his mouth and takes a swallow of tea and stands up. Puts down his cup and stretches.

On with the motley, he says. No rest for the wicked.

Gramp shakes his hand and walks with him to the tractor. Watches him drive to the gate and disappear. Gramp turns to me and smiles. Points to the hay and rubs his hands.

A perfect day for it, he says. June hay. It went just like a dream.

It is Friday. My aching muscles are still quivering. My heart longs for a night on the town. Gramp comes back. He smiles at me.

A perfect day, he says.

I think I will slip into town tonight, I tell him. Treat myself to a few beers.

He nods. Good idea, he says. I may have a couple of tots myself.

There is a bus at 5.35pm. How will you get back? he asks. There is no bus till the morning.

I'll walk, I tell him.

Then I shine my shoes and take a cold bath and shave four days growth of stubble from my face. Gramp lends me a clean shirt and gives me a twenty pound note.

Have a little drink on your old Grampa, he says. He beams at me. His eyes glow with a benign goodwill. He points to the hay stack.

All gathered in, he says. A perfect day...

We stand and gaze out over the field. It looks softened up and exposed, just like a shorn lamb.

I jump off the bus at the bottom of Cathedral Road and go to call at Chris' door. I do not expect him to be there. I knock but there is no answer. Then I call in at the Conway and drink a pint of lager. The sun streams into the room through the open fanlight. There are people outside on the picnic tables. You would think that all was well with the world. I smoke two cigarettes and move on. The next place is the Romilly. Another pint and another two cigarettes. This is the life, I try to tell myself. Propping up some bar as a perfect stranger amongst strangers.

Sandra is on my mind. I can feel the need in me for this woman like a pebble in my shoe. I tell myself that the world is full of women. That many of these women might make themselves available to me with hardly any real effort at persuasion. I try to list a few of them. It is useless. I am stuck on her and I can't get off. I think of her face. You could never say that she had a kind heart. Or a charitable soul. Yet there is nothing in the world I can imagine that might be worse than losing her for good. I am not talking of crucifixion, or being skinned alive, or burnt at the stake. I sip my beer. Suck down tobacco smoke. I don't know what I am talking about. Some shit I may have gleaned from old films about loves, or songs I may have heard during vulnerable moments. It is as if there were some hole somewhere inside me and some vital thing is leaking away. It is impossible for me to think of life without her as anything but worthless.

So I move on and make my way slowly into town. The evening is warm and there is an air of comfort as you pass the open doors of the pubs on the way. Eager weekenders line up at the bars. Money in their pockets and all set to guzzle. A sort of surrender.

There are certain days that have a character which sets them apart. When I had finished washing the hayseeds off my skin and shaved and put on the clean shirt and was sitting down to eat the corned beef sandwiches my grandfather had cut for me, with the hard work in the past and the night stretching ahead of me like a clear road as straight as an arrow, there had been a surge of elation, as if anything might be possible. But now, as I crossed the Canton bridge and looked down at the river, it was evening and there had been, it seemed to me, a perceptible change. The language of evening differs from that of the day. The town is spread out before me like a corpse on a table. I can feel how alone I am and how open to all kinds of dubious magnanimity and specific woe.

I go into the bar of the Royal Hotel and there is a woman.

Hello, stranger, she says.

Do I know you?

Polly, she says. She knows my name. I stare at her. Her face is a mystery to me. She is not bad looking, a bit skinny and almost as tall as I am and though something about her that makes me think she may not be my type, not *exactly*, I am slightly drunk by this time and later on there will be a big moon in the sky.

You look lost, she says. Were you looking for someone?

You, I tell her.

I'm always easy to find, she says. She smiles, a quavery little smile. Then she lowers her eyes. Very demure. Nice eyes. Sort of gentle eyes. She looks up from under her lashes to steal a quick glance. I don't know her from Adam. Or is it Eve? She smiles again. She keeps her mouth shut when she smiles.

I know your face, I tell her.

You ought to, she says.

I do, But I'm bad with names. The names confuse me.

You can call me Diana, she says.

Where do I know you from?

Think back.

Was it a long time ago?

Long enough.

Are you on your own, Diana?

Not anymore, she says.

I look at her hard and she smiles the way people smile when they are teasing a kid. Her face remains a mystery to me.

Let's get drunk, she says. I'm in the mood. Are you?

Why not?

She touches my hand. No rings on her fingers.

You and me, she says.

Think we could go places?

Anywhere, she says.

Your place? You got a place?

Everyone's got a place.

Where?

Not far.

I stare at her. There is something about her.

What is in it for me? I ask her.

The sky is the limit, she says.

Limit of what?

How high is the moon?

She is watching me over the rim of her glass. Lovely eyes. Eyes that remind me of my mother's eyes. The room is packed with bodies. A warm Friday night after a hot day. The drink is getting to me and I can feel something drawing me in. She leans over and takes my hand. It has been a while, I tell her. This, I hold up the glass, is going straight to my head.

Don't worry, she says, I'll look after you.

Do you want to go? I ask her.

Go where?

You got a room with a bed in it?

It's still early, she says.

So we go to the Angel. Different faces in another room. A deep line of bodies crowding along the bar. She sticks to her vodka and I change over to scotch. I am light headed by now and beginning to brim and flow over with the froth of gaiety. Or is it hilarity?

I touch her arm. I am trying to build up a claim on her, to prepare the way for the intimacy that is to come. She leans over and puts her cool hand on my hot cheek. Draws me toward her and we kiss. Light as a feather.

Let's get a taxi, she says. You wait outside while I powder my nose.

So I stand there in Westgate Street and look up at the stars.

Then a car pulls up. A man who gets out and comes up to me as if he is about to ask directions. Excuse me, he says.

I look at him. He is a stranger.

Get in the car, he says.

What? I say.

Then the driver gets out and comes around the front of the car and stands beside me. Together they take me to the car. The first man opens the rear door and they shove me inside. Harris is there. The Pieman is waiting to embrace me and say hello.

Chapter Eleven

And this place. This car park. This place out of all my nightmares.

This arrangement of drabness about and within the concept of the concrete shoebox. This whited sepulchre. This falsehood. This...

This is the place where my mother died. Where she was brought to out of her own home in a stinking ambulance at the behest of some medical man with bad breath who never deserved the title doctor and put in some bed in some stinking ward at the mercy of strangers dressed as doctors and nurses who did not give a fuck and left her to die that very day. While we, the rest of her family, out of ignorance or sheer indifference or inertia, were busy getting on with their daily business of our worthless lives. So that all that had ever pained her or entranced her or moved her heart in the years since she was hauled into the light was allowed to dribble back into the dark like a lost howl in the bitter and absurd loneliness of her end without as much as a hand to clutch at or a parting glance to carry with her when that shutter came down at the final breath.

All the shoes she had worn out or the cold beds and the icy greys of winter mornings she had endured; all the years spent in the company of those who were not worthy of her time; all the meditation upon pain and its ever expanding emptiness; all the futility of the days of dreaming: all given up at the last gasp to the blank walls from the cold white sheets of a ten a penny hospital iron cot. Her dead pulse taken by some pallid bitch of a strung-out nurse and duly noted down so that the next step of the process might begin. If I ever possessed the brains to make a cataclysmic bomb, then this place, this ramificated structure that I will never cease to hate with all my heart while I am yet able to draw air as breath, is where I would plant it and delight to set it off.

You store a thing. A love? A loss? A burning hate? You hide it away. Or avert your gaze. Cowardice. You endure more than half a lifetime out of the fear of what they have convinced you should be things to fear. And grief confused you, when it might have made you strong. As if the tears alone had sufficient power to obscure the thing. But there is nothing that can heal the wound. The only thing that ever meant a fuck is gone and you are left. It is winter. Not a leaf on any tree and melting snow; a taste at the root of your tongue that is worse than shit. You can only go on burrowing into the cold slime of what lies up ahead. You stare up at the empty sky. No terms of endearment. Only the rest of your miserable and worthless life is left for you to gnaw away at the very roots of loss...

And I come up here again. Make a sudden re-appearance out of some nondescript Sunday afternoon. And run into the wall of all my fears. Try to tell myself that all I want from life is the peace and quiet a nobody should have as a minimum entitlement. The very idea that lives like mine might be more than soiled underwear and holes in shoes and stumbling home and up those stairs blind drunk to throw my carcase on that stinking bed and pray that death will come and show some mercy... cut me short before the morning comes to deal me back into the game. Ties of blood and time. The word son. This is the oldest game in the fucking book.

...walls and shadows and creaks on the treads of long forgotten stairs...

You stare and stare but it goes far beyond your power. Love? Loss? A hate that burns? Grief. The wound still bleeds. You turn away and shake your head and wipe at a tear. There is nothing. These are not, after all, the momentous times. There is no war. It is all commonplace. The world, when you look around, is mean as catshit and commonplace as fuck. But it will not heal.

Then I spot her, my ex-wife. She climbs out of a red car. Blood red. She is wearing dark glasses. Snell gets out of the other side of the car. He is wearing dark glasses. A blue blazer. A new haircut. They look tanned and comfortable. My emotions flounder momentarily and then a degree of detachment sets in and it occurs to me that somewhere there is a point of honour to be sought and found. A sort of justifiable rage to be adopted as a shield or a badge. Perhaps even acted upon. Some artifice.

I watch them start away from the car. She looks easy with the way things are for her. Snell has changed his hairstyle and put on about twenty pounds. I watch her. He does not interest me. Her arse in the white skirt. I can still smell her, the faint underlying scent of lilac has not entirely faded in the absent years. Can still smell the shame of the evenings she went out to meet this man. From under my roof. And came back. She always came back. Ghosts play tricks with me as I turn away.

A man named Hurfoot tells me how it came about. Hurfoot is an ex-boxer with a shaved head and a tremble in both hands. His skin is drawn over his skull and face like a paper mask. His nose makes barely an indent on his line of profile. His eyes shift constantly but rarely blink. He says: Well, Tommy, from what I hear the kid was putting a tail on it: his missus – Appleby's. He is a nice-looking boy. A nice boy. I love that kid. She's a lot younger than him – Appleby. From what I hear, Appleby, he don't touch women. So it is understandable, you know, him (your boy) fucking her. I seen her. In the Oak now and then. Smart. Hard-looking, but smart. You would get that straight away. Not the likes of you and me, but, you know, some good-looking kid. Like your boy. They used to do a fair bit of slumming. Appleby is supposed to be a dope, but he is also quite cunning. Like his old man. Jacko. Remember him? Anyway, he found out. It was his right-hand man. This Tony Harris. Big fat cunt. He been with Appleby for years. Used to drive him about before your boy come on the scene. Probably no love lost. Probably hated it when your boy took over as the chauffeur. A lot of them think Appleby's a fruit. This Harris does debt-collecting. Puts the arm on them for Mr A. By all accounts he was out to finish him (your boy) when this old woman poked him in the eye with her umbrella. Old woman walking her dog. Lucky for him it was raining. Your boy, I mean.

Hurfoot draws in a deep breath and lights a cigarette.

Trying to give these fucking things up, he says. Coffin nails. This Harris gets in The Locomotive most Saturday nights. You can't mistake him. Small eyes. Rat's eyes. Sits there like Old King Cole. Drinks about thirty pints at a sitting. Sticks to Strongbow. Real glutton. He must weigh twenty five stone if he weighs an ounce. Drinks every pint like he was dying of thirst. He is going with a skinny piece named Josie Welsh. She is a lost cause.

Sucks his dick in the bar? I ask.

Hurfoot shakes his head. He drives a car. Big car. They go in his car. He parks around the corner in Nora Street. I am in there about nine that night, so I miss it. But I hear about it about an hour later in the New Dock. He is a fellow you don't want to be fooling with, Tommy. Everybody gives him a wide berth. Except her, this Josie Welsh.

How old is he? I ask.

Not all that old. Under thirty. About twenty eight, I would estimate, at a guess. Got very small hands. And feet like a ballet dancer. But strong. I'm telling you, Tom, this cunt is strong as a fucking ox. If you got plans to, you know, retaliate or anything, take a lump hammer or a fucking pick axe and attack the cunt when he's full of beer. By surprise. How is he, the boy?

Not good, I tell him. He is in a bad way. They broke his jaw. All wired up. Got a fractured skull. Hairline fracture. Broke his cheekbone in two places. Broke three fingers. Broke his leg...

Nice-looking boy, Hurfoot observes. He shakes his head. Those type of women are always bad news.

I say nothing. We are standing at the bar in the New Dock. I signal to Donna the barmaid to replenish Hurfoot's drink.

Have one yourself, sweetheart, I tell her. Lay a ten-pound note on the counter.

Try a Bushmills with your Guinness, I tell Hurfoot. It works wonders.

I notice the long-lost signs once more and try to find fresh hope in the ordinary life. Try to get fit. Cut out Sunday to Wednesday in the Bird in Hand. Tell Mr Mack I am going into training. Mr Mack listens and nods. A life in the licensed trade has made him privy to many such declarations of serious intent. The shedding of the old skin. The new day that is forever getting set to dawn. Nods and smiles his not unkindly smile.

Training for what? he asks me. Try to smarten yourself up a

bit, get yourself a girlfriend. A blowthrough, that's what you need. Even some piece like my old tart. It clears the blood.

Are you pimping for your missus?

She's free, he says. Take her with my blessing. But you know what I mean, something to take the edge off.

Think I should get myself a girl and settle down?

Mr Mack shakes his head. Just a jump, he said. It don't matter who. You could even pay for it.

Fuck that! I declare valiantly.

Better men than you, Mr Mack says.

Men a million times better than me, I tell him. I know all about that shit, but I couldn't bring myself... Out of shame. Do you think I never thought of it? I thought of it plenty of times. Nights I was stuck in that room... Nights I would have cut a finger off my right hand to get into some woman's flesh. The walls closing in and nowhere to go. Your bones ache like a rotten tooth. Your head itches. It is worse than the worst sort of hunger, but I can't do it. Those women frighten me. I have been down to Tyndall Street. Got up close enough to look into their eyes. Too much life and death for me. They don't need me and my pain.

Who gives a fuck what they need? Mr Mack says. That's what you pay them money for...

We stand in silence. Mr Mack stares at the froth clinging to the inside of his glass.

I don't miss my wife, I tell him. Lots of ways I am better off without her. For years she was like a vampire. But when I saw her with him. Up at the hospital. I wanted to cut his heart out.

Understand what I am saying, I don't want *her*. Not for all the tea in China. I have been a fool. I look at where I am and it is all like a mystery to me. I keep thinking I would like to be in some foreign country, Bulgaria or Indo-China, and just live the life of simple obscurity. Wait to die. Wait quietly. Don't give a fuck for no fucker and no fucker give a fuck for me.

Who do you give a fuck for? Mr Mack asks me.

No cunt, I tell him.

And who gives a fuck for you?

Now? I ask. Or ever?

Mr Mack stares at me solemnly and shrugs.

You're getting old and bitter, he says.

I shrug and look around the bar.

A jump, Mr Mack says, is what you need. That'll cure you.

I never found it to be that simple, I say. There is some sort of a code I can't read. It's not easy. Not for me.

What makes you special? Mr Mack asks me.

Nothing, I tell him. It is the ordinary that fucks things up. The ordinary is what makes things hard. Women, all of my life, have been, you know, hard work. Women as the other half, I mean. You think it will just be fucking and they'll cook for you.

Then I cover my face with my hands to show him the conversation is over. When I lower them I catch a glimpse of my self in the mirror behind the bar: eye-sockets like empty oyster-shells.

The old tenderness born of infinity, I whisper. Some kindly soul to stroke my bald head when I come is what I need. Fry onions to make gravy for me on dark winter nights. Or a bacon sandwich once in a while. Put the kettle on for tea...

The voice is mine, a voice grown hoarse with a lost emotion.

You are my friend, Terry, I tell him. Got to mend my ways. Lay off the beer. See if that works. See if there's anything left.

Just get hold of a woman, Mr Mack advises me. It don't have to be anything special. Just so long as she got that gash north of her arsehole.

Go to the place of work. Patch a ceiling. Build a partition wall of brick and mortar. What is this shit? The early summer comes in and leaves like a hogtied bride. You walk out about the town of an evening. The setting sun. The long shadows. You stand and stare at the new season cunt in those summer frocks and white high heel shoes. No stockings on and gold earrings. It ties you up in knots. Sniff at the air and prowl about on the edges and try to avoid the licking of lips. A dirty old monkey out on the ledge. Staring. Eyes like pissholes. You know you will never make the scene of skins that touch again. Is there any other miracle that even gets close to the miracle of the skin? I doubt it. All of you is in there. All those functioning parts, the bits that we spend our lifetimes fucking up. Lungs and kidneys and liver. All it can hope for now is the sag and the wrinkle. Flake and fall. And fail.

You get up in the morning and pinch yourself. Stare at the skylight. You can hardly believe it is another day. It is a mystery where the fortitude comes from. You have seen through all the hocus pocus yet you still go on. The old heart leaps not even once in a blue moon. You try to recall the old hunger dreams for Ava Gardner, say, or you went along the street at night, trying to sing a song like Nat King Cole. Back in the first world. Before you came to realise how vast all this shit really is.

There are days you wake up and the room is grey like a November fog. It is just you and the dust and the silence. It baffles you. There is no way you can discern the means for things to proceed. The next move daunts you. Then time moves on. There is the ride in the van. The company of virtual enemies. Those pair of pricks... You may groan and curse but nothing can alter. Or the employer, Mr Rivers, with his new haircut and the weekly manicure. The air is loaded with the corruption of irony. You – you go on. You go out the door.

I point at a bottle of orange pop. Give me one of those, I tell him. Lots of ice. Think I'll go on the wagon.

Carry the glass and the bottle to a vacant table. Sit down and stare. Sip soda pop and gaze about the room. Begin to hum a tune, very softly, almost under my breath. *Paper Moon*. It is a song I have always loved. Try hard, but I can't remember the words.

The next morning I get out of bed as the dawn is coming up. The grey before sunrise. Sit on the side of the bed and try to meditate. The morning after a sober night. A brief shudder, very intense.

I stand up and stretch both arms above my head. Strain upwards. Grit my teeth. Then jack-knife down to touch my toes. I barely make it. A lot of the gut has been sweated off with work and warm weather but I am stiff as a board. Next, I move my arms in a sort of backward rotation. Then my head. The way boxers do when they come into the ring. Then I lie on my back on the bare floorboards and try sit-ups. Gasp from the effort and fail. Fall back and stare at the skylight. See how the sky pales beyond the layer of dirty glass. Motes dance. Then try another way, with my feet hooked under the rail at the foot of the bed, something (an anchor of kinds) to pull against. This proves easier. I clasp hands at the back of the head and try again. Keep going until I notch up ten. And end up out of breath, with a semi-stiff hard-on. This is a miracle. I touch it to make sure. Jesus, I gasp aloud. Sit up and look at it till it dies. It is Wednesday. Here I am, the lone avenger, in singlet and underpants. I shadow box for about ten seconds. Jabs and uppercuts and hooks from right and left hand: a painless parody. There was a time I knew all the names by heart, the hungry fighter stuff. Then I lose my balance and fall back onto the mattress. Then I go over to the mirror to see myself in as I go through the snarls and killer stare routine. Close my eyes and try to concentrate my attention on a tiny core of calm purpose I was sure was there somewhere. There is a faint pounding inside my skull. Open my eyes. Reach over to fetch the socks out of my shoes where they were stuffed. Pull them on and fall into a reverie. The mind wanders like a butterfly. The working day is still a long way off, but there is no escape. Get dressed and go over to look up through the skylight at a blue sky. Not much wind. Fill the kettle and set it on the gas ring to boil. Make a pot of tea and then half fill the kettle for shaving water. Find a blade that is almost new. Lather the stubble and drag the razor over chin and cheek and upper lip. Feel for smoothness with fingertips and make sure to keep the eyes away from the face in the broken looking glass.

I found out where Reilly was living: a flat over a failing hardware shop in Stockland Street. 35 A. I go to knock on his door one Thursday evening. The last week of July. Grey and humid. He is a long time coming. I wait and then knock again. There are sounds on the stairs; the door opens a crack. An eye glitters in the slit.

It's me: Tommy, I tell him.

The door opens wider. Fuck me! Reilly says. He stares hard at me.

How d'you find me? he says.

Judicious enquiry, I tell him. I got lonely. Missed your wisdom.

Come in, Reilly says. I'll make some tea.

I brought this, I tell him, and open my jacket to reveal a bottle of Jameson's whiskey.

Bernie nods approvingly and licks his lips. We go upstairs. The living room is plainly furnished, uncluttered by ornament and clean. The TV is going with the sound turned down. Reilly switches it off. He points to the Windsor chair. Sit down, he says.

What happened to the other place? I ask him.

He sold up.

This place okay? It looks okay.

Not bad, but the shop's going bust. The landlady's black as coal. I been trying to fuck her for two years. West Indian woman.

Any luck?

Reilly shakes his head. She just laughs, he tells me. She thinks I'm a scream. She's a widow too.

I put the bottle on the gateleg table and sit down.

Never mind the widderwoman shit, I tell him, get two clean glasses. Let us give this fucking bottle a caning. I look at him. You got two clean glasses, haven't you?

Just about , Reilly says. He goes out to find them.

I break the seal on the bottle and pour. Reilly holds his glass to the light. Smiles. I sniff at my own glass before holding it up to touch his. Cheers, I say. Reilly mumbles something and both of us drink it down at one go.

You still sweeping up at the depot? I ask.

Different depot, he says. Same outfit. Same shit. How about you?

Same old shit, I tell him. I'm working for this fellow I have known practically all my life. It's got advantages and disadvantages. Fellow named Rivers. He is not a builder. Property man. We go around patching up his houses. There's this piece he's fucking, owns a nursing home in Penarth, we work there as well. I got a room in one of his houses. On the Embankment. Got a river view if the room had a window. All it got is a skylight. It is not killing work... You know, he's not the type to be on your back all the time... It is just that I find it demeaning to be working for this... I can't think of the right word.

Reilly sips his whiskey and puts the glass down. Looks at me. I love Irish whiskey, he says. I like Scotch, but Irish is better.

Remember my boy? I say. Some cunt nearly killed him the other night. He's in a coma.

He sips some more whiskey. I love this fucking stuff, he says. Got to keep off it, though, because you can get to love it too much. And then it don't love you.

I went up to see him Sunday afternoon, I tell him. In the Heath. He is just lying there with tubes coming out of him.

Plugged into machines. They smashed his face in. Broke his leg. Smashed his hand with a brick. Apparently, he was fucking this man's wife.

Who? Reilly asks.

It don't matter who. But the man who did this was working for the man whose wife my boy was fucking.

He shrugs. That's tough, he says.

We sit in silence.

I saw my missus up there, I tell him after a while. At the hospital. She didn't see me. Mrs Snell now. Mister Snell was there, too. They were holding hands, which is very funny. It don't make me laugh, but it *is* funny. Very. His wife fucking died. He was fucking her for years, my missus. A pimp and a whore. Still got a dream and still hanging on. They got a shiny new fucking Honda. Red, can you fucking believe it?

Reilly moves his glass in a circular motion over the oilcloth that covers the table. First clockwise, then anti-clockwise.

I am bitter, I tell him, staring at my glass, bitter as fuck. But bitterness, as any fool knows, gets you nowhere.

He drinks some whiskey and goes through the motions of a mirthless grin. He nods to show he is listening.

I spotted them as I was coming away. I went down the stairs to miss them. I didn't have the nerve to confront them. I sat down in the foyer and watched them coming out. She is still fuckable. I still felt something. He's getting fat. You know, butterball, like a layer of lard all over. His eyes got that sunbed glare. I could have reached out and touched them.

I pour more whiskey into my glass. Offer the bottle to Reilly. He waves it away.

I am going to kill this man who smashed up my boy, I tell him. I try to speak quietly, in a matter of fact voice. I look at him and smile. How else can I justify my continued existence? I ask.

Reilly puts his glass on the floor and starts to roll a cigarette.

His name is Harris, I go on. Tony G Harris. Ever hear of him? He shakes his head. How? he says.

I don't know yet, I say. Stab him... Axe... Catch him unawares. I am telling you this while I'm still sober. I know you can keep your trap shut.

Reilly lights the cigarette with his lighter. Blows smoke up at the ceiling. I drink more whiskey and gesture vaguely towards the grey evening light at the window.

We go on with these stupid lives that are all fucked up and quietly chaotic, I say, and we never think it will happen to us. Anything bad, that is. We just go on. Don't make a sound.

Then I stand up and cross to where he sits. Place both hands on his shoulders. You can be my witness, I tell him. Then I cross to the window and look out into the street.

I am going to kill this fat bastard just to prove that life is not as easy as he thought it was, I say. I keep my back to Reilly while I speak. They were holding hands, I tell him. Walking across the carpark. I watched them and started to realise all the different ways to tell a lie. How it mutilates us... It is everywhere... It buries us alive.

A cat comes into the room from the scullery. A tabby cat with traces of ginger and eyes the green of unripe gooseberries. The cat stares at me. Yawns. Stretches her back into a concave arc; yawns again and then walks with measured tread to where Reilly is sat. She stares at him for a moment and then leaps lightly onto his lap. Reilly smiles and strokes her head, very gently with his old gnarled hands, with their crooked fingers and broken nails.

She loves me, he says. I feed her out of a tin and she is faithful to me. You should get a cat. Everybody should.

He drinks some whiskey. His eyes beam.

I turn away from the window. He is smoothing his cat. He is content. I'm going, I tell him. I drink off my whiskey. Put the glass down on the table. He looks up at me and we study each other. Then his eyes go to the bottle.

It's yours, I tell him. Don't get up, I tell him. I'll let myself out.

The peculiar darkness of the summer, with its luxury of leaves, its breathless sunsets and deepening mysteries amongst the shadows in the dusk of the days. There are parked cars in the treelined streets and parked cars in the streets where the poor struggle to meet all kinds of payments. All those separate souls and their stories. Knockers to doors, buttons to ring bells. Nights with moons to spread phantom light.

Then the mornings, with the girlish sun shining down on the summer dresses and this year's crop. We gape out from the interior of the white van.

In the evening of that day I am stood in the bus shelter on the ramp up at the hospital. From this place you can easily watch the carpark. I get there at half past six and she arrives about quarter past seven. This was not the red Honda. This time the car is blue. The sun had gone behind the shoebox. I take a deep breath of the evening air when I see her. Watch the legs swing out, the hands move to smooth the white skirt straight. See how she turns to look about her, how her body straightens and adjusts itself. Snell is not with her. She wears dark glasses, which suggests that she had come from the east and driven towards the setting sun. I had searched the phonebook and found the Snells to be unlisted. I watch her stride towards the hospital. She passes under the awning of the basement carpark and the dark swallows her in. Another deep breath. I stand there and gaze about me. The institutionalised artificiality. The structured falsehood. The movement of the people, coming and going, the whole thing like a bad opera without sound. And I am this fool of a man, no longer young, setting himself to watch a woman who has cut him off. My life was emptied of God or gods. Without any emotional attachment. Deep, dreamless sleep was all I craved. The days and nights got racked up like an endless billiards game. But the score stayed the same. Stuck on the zero.

I turn to watch the single decker number eight bus come up the ramp from the terminus on the other side. The driver looks at me but I wave him on and resume the evening watch; note the pace of the people coming and going; try to imagine how it must feel to be trapped into the unnatural life of the medical world, a kind of prison with pain and fear and bad food; the embrace of unified indifference. All those poor suckers, men and women, old and young, who were trying to be brave, who would give anything to be normal again. To be walking along a street, or looking into a shop window at the steam irons and the toasters, or riding a bicycle or farting after a heavy meal. No longer searching for significance or longing for importance, just the chance to go back and be healthy and ordinary: the sick, when they are *truly* sick, would give up the world to go back and just be *well*. All they want is to be found and brought back into the fold from the wilderness. These hospitals are the new deserts for the worn-out world.

I walk up the approach to the entrance and go in through the revolving door. The foyer is crowded, the sick mingling with the well. Like a railway station. I make a path through the crowd and take the lift to the seventh floor. This landing is on the eastern side of the building. Weak light and shadow. Grey floors and oatmeal walls. The variations on the shoebox; a smothering, foggy quiet along the corridors. A nurse comes into view. She passes me on the landing and disappears around the corner. Then the doors of the lift facing me open and two people come out. One of them is Snell. He stares at me, tight-lipped and uneasy. I stare at him. This is the bad dream we both dreaded. Then Snell makes an attempt at a smile. Takes a small step, as if he means to shake hands. Then he changes his mind. Stops dead. He brings both hands up to his throat and straightens the knot of his tie. The third man, who had paused to find his bearings, moves away.

I smile. As glassy and false as I can make it.

Snell says: How's things, Tommy?

I am overwhelmed. I shake my head, as if amazed.

How's things? he asks me, I say. How's fucking things! I suck in a deep breath of stagnant air.

Mr Snell! I say. I try my best to grin; show him my bad teeth.

Where's Mrs Snell, Mr Snell? The new Mrs Snell, how is she? The second Mrs Snell, is she feeling well?

Snell makes a movement with his hands, hardly more than a twitch at the wrists; a small appeal for the seeking of reasonable consideration and understanding, of not expecting miracles from flesh and blood etc. A gesture of appeasement.

I ought to beat you up, I tell him quietly, but I won't. Or I could stand here and call you all kinds of a pimp, but what would that do?

I turn and point along the corridor. I am going in there now, to see my boy, and I don't want you in there with me. Understand?

Snell stares at me. Lil's in there, he says. I only come here to be with her. You don't know how upset she...

You stay here, I insist. You wait here. I don't want you there when I am there. *Get* me?

Snell scowls at me. His hairline moves like John Wayne's and he breathes hard through his nose. Don't push it, Tommy, he says. I don't want to fall out with you. She is my wife now. I got a right.

I glance about me, to make sure we are alone. Then take three short steps and punch this man hard in the middle of the face. Blood comes pouring out of both nostrils. I whoop and leap in to punch again. Snell tries to duck under the second blow, so that my fist glances the top of his skull and dislodges a hairpiece.

A wig! I scream. Like finding gold. A fucking wig!

I try to grab at the wig to tear it completely off. His mouth is drawn open to gasp breath and saliva runs down his chin. I get both arms around Snell's head and try to force him down to the floor. I want to get him down so that I can kick him hard in the face. Know exactly, despite my great anger, how I want the kick to be: the sharp end of the sole beneath the toecap, directed at the teeth. Then into his balls. A sound like a muted siren is coming out of me. My rage swells and I can feel the rediscovery of strength I no longer knew was there. That makes me feel better than anything I have known for years. The sight of his blood makes me feel as if my whole being is singing.

Then the song ceases abruptly when I feel a sharp pain to the cheek just under my left eye. Lillian. My ex-wife had come out of the ward and raced along the corridor to attack me with her nailfile. The hatred I behold in her eyes amazes me. She stabs at me again and the point of the blade gets me on the chin. I slacken my grip on Snell's head, ball my right hand into a fist and swing at her backhanded. The blow knocks her sideways. We stand staring, both gasping for breath. Her eyes are dull with a steadfast hatred. I raise my hand to the wounded cheek, study the blood on my fingertips. Snell tries to resettle his wig. Our bloods drip onto the floor. Lillian goes to stand by her new husband. She brings out a paper tissue and wipes at the blood on his upper lip. I point at them and laugh until I am almost convulsed. Then the lift doors open and out step two men from Starkweather Security. Lillian points at me.

That man there, she says, attacked me and my husband for no reason at all.

Chapter Twelve

Polly

The dull day stacks up like blocks. Can this blood that is in me
be blood that is mine? And is it mine forever? Is it still what I am?
Or am I who I was? And the breath, is it my breath when the
lungs have finished with what air I suck from the room?

Mother of God! keeps running through my mind. Names
crop up that I am hard-pressed to paste meanings to. Or faces.
Swirl in and out of me. Any sort of precision that may have once
been mine eludes me. Edges of things curl and blur. Am I still in
the skin? What there is in my skin, does it all correspond to what
used to be me? No answers, easy or otherwise, come to my aid.
My eyes are tired and my head feels like dough.

I stare at the window; the light fades in, then out. Like a tidal
movement, more or less to the heartbeat. Some sort of shutter.
A degree of sensitivity dips me in a candyfloss. Shrouds me in
cloud. I lose touch.

But I am able to recall the thermometer they shoved up my arse.

Mostly I only stare. Light passes through the intervention of air.
There are groans that I can hear but not feel. My groin is sensitive
to the sounds of feet in the corridor. The different shoes. Shuffles
and clatter and clop and clip. The trolley and its squeal and the
black girl and her trudge behind it. The ruts forming in the floors.
It is all time and windows. I can smell the nurses. Hear the tick of
their watches, detect the rustle of their so-called souls. Smell their
stale secrets and separate them from the face powder. I can even
hear the wingbeats of a passing fly through windowglass. All this
must be part of some compensation.

My mother comes every evening. Sits in the chair and gazes at me. Those eyes. The first to see me in this world.

You feeling any better? she asks.

I nod. I am bandaged like a sore thumb. Her hair is freshly dyed to the colour of limed oak. Streaks of grain. Coffin wood. Powder smooths out the cracks in her face. Sticks to the paste she plasters on. She tries to smile, but happiness will not come to her aid. Any animation makes her face look lumpy. Her eyes are no longer lovely.

Then Snell comes in. The old crooner, with his silver curls and pearly smile, comes briefly hither to my bedside to deliver fresh evidence of his standing as a solid type. That old time smile of his and that pigskin tan and those neat little false teeth that line up when the lips part. Peppermint breath, and, just under it, the four measures of White Horse from the golfclub lunch. Great care goes into every move he makes. All things in life, he feels, call for a degree of strategy.

How goes it, Champ? he says. Touches my hand before I can withdraw it. The wise old smile. He wants to reassure the whole world that he only means well. His entry to my room gives a perspective to my altered circumstance. Part of the frame starts to define itself. Just when I had almost managed to recede to some point where I could observe the action from some middle ground, Snell brings me back into my part in the picture.

The first time I laid eyes on him he was stood in our dining room with his back to me. My mother was supine on the dining table. She saw me in the doorway and shielded her eyes as if a strong light troubled them. Mr Snell did not turn his head, but he stopped his movements. I was seven years old and not without a basic awareness. I turned and made my way back along the passageway to the front door. Stood on tiptoes and pressed the button that rang the bell. My mother had given me my own key. The door was still open. After a while my mother came along the passage. Mr Snell was gone when we reached the dining room. She buttered some bread and put the kettle on for tea. I explained to her that I had left the school yard during playtime on an impulse. She nodded without comment. When we had eaten the bread and butter she took me back to the school.

Mr Snell was a man who drove about the town in a bronze

coloured Jaguar in those days. He sold cars for a living and sang with the band at the Ballroom on the Pier three nights a week. My mother said he sang like Eddy Fisher some nights, other times it was somebody else. He sang *Blue Moon* at their wedding and as he sang his small blue grey pebble eyes were searching everywhere to find my mother's, that they might fuse into some new abstraction on the worn-out theme. But she was drunk from too much champagne. Her hiccups alternated with hysterical laughter. A man named Archie Light played the piano that went with it.

In the room where I am lying in bed their eyes make coded messages and they yawn behind their hands.

He wore a pale salmon pink shirt and a silver tie at the wedding. My mother went for ivory silk and a scarf of lilac gauze. The reception in a small castle had a glass of pink champagne for each guest. Mother and Snell danced the last waltz on the hardwood floor. Cheek to cheek and clinging. Eyes closed. Maybe he was singing to her. The wedding guests who looked on were like the sincere manifestation of some lingering disease.

They glance at their watches. The eyes meet. Get to their feet.

See you around, Champ, says Snell. Mother grips my hand and looks sad, mumbles her words. Then they leave me to myself.

A new nurse. Faintly far eastern. Imported. Probably Filipino. Arse as neat as a thimble and wrapped tight as a Cuban cigar. With her licorice eyes avoiding mine, she moves swiftly about the bed. Crowblack hair. I would gladly render up half my personal fortune if she would agree to finger my balls. But she stays wordless. She does what they pay her to do and leaves.

The pain stays more or less constant. The doctors come in from time to time. In the night there are all sorts of cries to decipher. And the variation of the light at the window brings certain dramatic nuances to bear. You get to hate all the things that surround you in an even-handed way. You dream of remote log cabins and snow and endless winter where the air is made of bandages and lint.

Old Chris is my only ray of hope. He comes in the mornings, fresh from the nightshift at the compound. He alone shares my sense of disaster. He drags with him that mantle of the quietly tragic. His general stupefaction is like a halo. His belly bulges and his shoes don't shine. All he lives for is booze. Our

friendship, he tells me, is the only thing that keeps him human.
It is a sort of love.

I am gonna get that bastard, he promises me. He means the
Pieman.

Take a chainsaw to him, he says.

But my mind is on other things. I am obsessed by the idea of
a woman and the miracles of the flesh.

How about that girl? I say.

Which one? he says.

That one you were fucking that day when I came... You still
fucking her?

You can't be that desperate, he says.

I am, I tell him. You have no idea how desperate I am. Bring
her in, I say. Persuade her to hold my dick. I am going nuts in
this fucking place. I'll pay her... I'll pay her well.

But this only troubles him. I'll get you a Walkman, he
promises. He knows this brilliant boy shoplifter you can give lists
to like Santa Claus.

Fuck the Walkman, I say. Bring the girl.

She is rough as fuck, he tells me.

Rougher the better, I gasp out.

He brings me a paper I do not want to read. Shows me the
headlines.

Who gives a fuck? I say. Please, I beg him, just bring me the
girl.

But my request makes him nervous. He takes a can from his
duffel bag and starts into another session. He will not bring her.
He considers me to be above such fodder.

Once he is gone there is the suspense of the rest of what is
left. The sag that goes deeper and deeper. Out in the ward, far
away in the other world, you can hear the strange sounds. I close
my eyes. Wait and try not to measure. Just lie there and wait.

My father never comes.

He used to tell us things, mostly when he was drunk. We must
establish a deeper anatomy, he used to say. We, who are the
melancholy midgets of the latterday.

My sister and I, we sat there and listened. We knew the score.
We could measure one glance from his downcast eyes and read

the whole history in a split second. We sat and were drawn in. We were all in the game, whether we liked it or not.

He had tried a lot of different ways that led into dead-ends. We are not, he used to tell us, necessarily hoping for a victorious outcome. Losing has its place. Never forget that. The great losers are the ones that count for the most. Not me, he added. I only rub shoulders with the lesser losers.

We were as quiet as mice. It was a kind of peace.

I am trying, he told us, to retrieve irons from the fire.

I don't think we ever spoke. I can never remember us saying a word to him. We simply understood it was our place to watch and wait and listen. My sister felt sympathy for him. I always thought him a fool. When he was drunk he talked shit. This is what drunks do. He tried one thing and lost. Then he tried another. Lost again. My mother kept going.

You have to give her credit for something. She was a woman of real beauty and that is not always an easy thing to support. Strange things happen. For a beautiful woman, a lot of the time things are out of control. The forces of life crowd around and make her open to threats. My mother could never walk into a room where men were, without a change taking place. Even as kids we could feel it. The butcher used to gaze at her as if his back was broke. The electrician gaped. Only the plumber, who was old and bitter, smiled his sour smile and nodded to my father as if he had seen the signs and remained unconvinced.

I think that was when it was still on the rails. The old man was out early and home late. That was the stone fireplace period. He was much in demand and the money was coming in. He bought a car to go with the green van. New furniture appeared about the house. Every Friday he brought her something, some little thing to show that he remembered how lucky he was. He had split up with his father and he was trying to prove something. They seemed to be happy. She used to clean the house and move lamps about and cook big meals for him when he came in out of the winter dark. He bought her a white fur hat when it snowed and sheepskin gloves. I think he was a foolish man. I think he knew he was a fool. I think he got nervous from waiting for the bubble to burst.

My father was trying to be a one man band. He went to

collect the stone from the quarry; he would select the various pieces and load them onto the van; unload them at the other end; then build the fireplace. He would come home late and sit up till all hours working out different designs. Preparing estimates. Paperwork, he said. The back garden filled up with small piles of stones that were left over. All kinds of different stones: Cotswold; Pennant; green Westmorland slate; Welsh slate; cobbles. When my mother complained, he promised to get a yard. Business was booming, he said, and in the spring he would take on a labourer. Some kid who could drive the van and give him that extra hand. But it never happened.

That was the spring I started school. After the Easter it was early mornings and the long walk. My sister in the pushchair and me hanging on. We were late a lot. My mother was not, she told us repeatedly, a morning person. Changes occurred. On one of the jobs one of the customers, a man named Rowles, would not pay for his fireplace and my father smashed the headlamps of his car with a hammer. The police were called and things went badly. He lost heart and sold his van. Then he took a job as a surveyor on some site near London. This meant that he left home at four am Monday and got back about eight pm the following Friday. My mother was alone in that big house. My sister and me were with her, but she was there like a light burning in a dark window. Gentlemen callers began to knock on the door. Many of them were men my father knew. Snell was another who showed up during that time.

At the wedding it came out that my mother and Bobby Snell had known each other before their marriages. Fate had kept them apart, according to Snell in his little speech. He had met his first wife, the former Joanie Dawes, banged her the first night and got her with child. There was no evading marriage. My mother and him, despite their love, had called it a day. About two years later she met my father. She was still only twenty. Snell came back into the picture when she was twenty seven. Their love had endured.

You look at Snell and wonder what it can be. Is it the haircut? Or the glibness? And my mother, is she just some poor thing who made her bed and feels she must go along?

This is Sunday and it is raining. I can see all the wet streets of the town when I close my eyes. All I want, for the rest of my life, is for things to be painless and quiet. I would settle for that: an evening that lasts forever. Some quiet bar and a pocket that never empties. Blues music, very slow, and no mirrors. No clock. The shank of the evening with the grey and the blue piled against the window.

But where I am is going no place and I know it. This is the place where you climb into the cockpit and the night locks round you. From then on you have to balance blindfold on the slackening rope.

My father used to say: I been half a my life trying to work it – how it feels after three beers and a single malt. Hold your breath... Get on the rope and pray. You pray and pray and close your eyes. If you fall, you go straight through the hoop.

He'd be drunk... gone past the point of return.

It is all deep snow and the dark night now, he once told me.

A small thing can alter the entire balance. Should I, for instance, spy a bird in the sky. Or a detached white cloud go sailing across the blue. Some element, however fragmentary, that is outside this shithole... Especially the birds... Mostly gulls... The odd pigeon... Then the spirit flies out of me and tries to pursue them to the ends of the earth.

Chris comes. It is a duty and he is dutiful. The time here sits heavy on his head. He belches and fidgets but stays faithful. Face like a bladder. The boredom of the sober mind threatens to bury him. He gazes at the window as if he longs to leap out. Then he sneezes. Smiles. Clasps his hands. Unclasps them. His elbows rest on his knees and he stares down at the floor. He can think of nothing he wants to say to me.

There is an old man in the adjacent ward who gets out of his bed and wanders. He wears one of these weird hospital gowns and you can see his balls. Skinny legs and red face. A blank angriness and a stiffbacked stagger. He comes to the door and peers in. Blinks to adjust his vision. Nobody comes to visit him. They have nowhere to put him and must keep him where he is. An old man who is like a lost monkey at the wrong zoo, he bothers me and it would cheer me up no end if I could get out of bed and cut his throat. Bundle him up in a sheet and push him out through the window.

Down at the far end of his ward there is an old man who is turning to bone. His skin has the fine smoothness of mother of pearl. A mask. His eyelids are like clamshells. He mumbles through dreams and barely breathes. Every other day his son comes and sits by his bed. They have the same shaped skulls. Same noses. The son watches the father, checks his watch, settles into his vigil. When the time is up he stands up and leaves. No words pass between them.

The rest are no more than intermittent ghosts.

I still think about Sandra. I can see her in my mind's eye and she is striding the corridors in a white dress. A sky-blue belt and a swirling skirt. I long for an endless series of things that will not happen. I cannot even cough without the bones of my body shuddering beneath the pain. In my heart of hearts I try to deny her, as if this might somehow spite the world. Sleep keeps passing me on the outside. Then there are the long windy lulls of the gaps between the visits. The long white nights. When my eyes close it is all hoarse whispers and creaks and saddle sores. Dull cramps in the abdomen. A total absence of solicitude.

The head nurse comes in one morning when Chris is there. She no longer wears her uniform. She is trying to talk me back onto the tracks. Health club skinny with cropped hair, you would think you were buggering a beautiful boy if you got lucky.

Discharge is getting closer. They need the bed. I am to go with mamma and her new husband. They have a house with many rooms and one of them awaits me.

Till you're strong again, mamma says. Me and Bobby will take care of you. Snell nods. Stands in the shadows and looks thoughtfully out through the window and nods.

The day comes. Men come for me and they wheel me along the corridors. Down in the lift. Out through the flower stall of faces where the new waiting room is like a railway station in an old film of the Crimean War. These are the fairy tales of our times, the coming and going of the sick and the cured. Out in the carpark the fresh air feels like a mantle of ice on my skin. Trapped amongst the cars, under a bright blue sky.

Mr and Mrs Snell are not happy. She turns once to hiss at him and he snarls something back. I never asked aught of them, I tell myself by way of consolation. Perhaps the old pussy and the worn-out tool have hit the buffers. I sit and wait. One of the porters comes and helps them get me into the back of the car.

The days are there to be cut out of the white cardboard. The house is all about the ability to understand what money can do; it is in the same district where we once lived, but in a grander street. It is detached and the garden is bigger. It has a name: Four Winds. There is marble in black and white squares to the hallway; a mahogany newell post and dark blue Wilton carpet on the stairs.

O I love my home, mamma says, and you feel that she wants to touch the walls, hang on the curtains. Embrace things.

I go up the stairs arse backwards and limp along the passage to my room at the back of the house. The carpet muffles everything.

The room smells of paint. There is a bed, a green chair set by the window, bright curtains; the walls are painted oatmeal and the woodwork bright green; a yellow and white duvet covers the bed.

Everything is brand new, mamma assures me. She stands in the passage and looks in. Snell is behind her. He rests his chin on her shoulder and moves his face to a smile.

What you think, Champ? he says.

We got a television coming, mamma promises me. I look around. Nod. Look around again and nod. Stagger to the window and look out. Turn, nod, slump into the chair.

Pretty nifty, huh? Snell says.

You bet! I tell him. You bet!

Mamma points to the wardrobe let into the wall. All new stuff in there, she tells me. Shirts, underwear... A dressing gown...

I close my eyes and wait until I hear the door close.

Most of the night I lay and stare. This is the time that I have, I tell myself. Study the ceiling and try to work out the way things may work out with time. I piss into a bottle and shit in a pot. In the morning my mother brings her sad face to my doorway and looks in. Going down the stairs, on his way to work, Snell is whistling a tune he may once have sung with the band at the old Pavilion on the Pier. In his tuxedo, up there on the bandstand, staring out over the bobbing heads of the dancers as they went round and round. The slowly turning mirrored ball catching and fraying downward the mauve and green and orange lights. Making shadows of gauze on the ballroom floor.

Later on I hear my mother's voice, raised for my benefit, bid him farewell at the door. He grunts something back at her. I hear the car drive away. She comes up to see me. Her smile is thin. We are like two ghosts who are left from a used-up world. She asks if everything is okay. I shrug. She frowns and sits down on the bed.

I brought the wedding snaps, she says. From the honeymoon, really. She points. Look at that blue sky... Look at the sea...

And I stare at the images they made for the camera. The hands raised to shade seaward gazing eyes. The smiles of a summer morning on a white balcony; the pensive reflection of the evening, with the sun just dropped from the pink and orange sky and the white become pale lavender on the balcony in shadow and the distant hill chinchilla grey. One palm tree, dark against the twilit sky.

You must think it's funny, Bobby and me, she says. I study the photos without speaking. She watches me. I can feel her eyes on me. Out of the corner of my eye I see her rubbing nervously at her wedding ring with the forefinger of her right hand. Then she moves it to the diamond of the ring above. With an abrupt movement, she thrusts this diamond under my nose.

This ring set Bobby back five grand, she hisses at me. I can see the wrinkles on the back of her hand. I smile.

It shows how much he must love you, I tell her.

Your father never bought me a thing, she says. Her mouth has grown bitter. A thin line. She frowns and stands and moves her hands to smooth at her thighs.

I stare at her and suddenly understand why my father hated dancehalls.

The TV comes in the afternoon. We'll get you a wheelchair, she says, and I can take you for walks. I switch on the set and stare and say nothing until she leaves. Something that feels like a form of terror starts up with a dull rumbling somewhere inside what is left of me.

Must have fallen into one those half vacancy, half dreaming in the mosquito net kind of a sleeps. Sitting in the chair, mumbling to the spirit and sort of splitting hair, you suddenly slip away and it ends up nowhere you have ever been before. Then the pause. The held breath. When I snap out of it, Snell is standing in the doorway. His eyes are on me. His expression is serious.

Just me and you, kid, he says. Chance for a little chat while your old lady is out of the way. He pauses. I think he wants me to speak. I stare at him. His eyes are gloomy and mean. Then I smile and nod my head as if I wish to encourage him. He gestures with a sweep of the right hand.

This room and board business, he says, I hope you understand it is *not* going to be permanent. Now he is looking at the window. Your mother and me, he says, we got, you know, lives to lead...

I hold up my hand. Nod and smile at him. Fine by me, Bobby Boy, I tell him. Soon as I am on my feet... I make the flight sign for departure.

He frowns. He suspects I am insincere. Only, your mother... The words run out and he flaps a hand. Half smiles. You know how it is, she wants to, you know, nurse you... Sees you all busted up and...

Again the flapping hand.

She's got a soft heart, I tell him. She always did. Soft heart was always her trouble... All those years you were fucking her behind my old man's back. Now she wants to make it up. Wants the old Redeemer to nod kindly and forget all the bad stuff. Wants a clean slate when they have that big Rollcall...

The eyes come back to meet mine. What you on about? he asks. He shifts his feet and tries to look tough. Points a single finger at me. Smart Aleck, he says. You don't know anything. We could have left you to rot, he tells me. I smile at him. A poor attempt at insolence. He ignores it.

Just so you get the picture, he says.

I smile again and nod.

Okay, I tell him. I think I got it.

I doze off again when he is gone. With these tablets for pain you never know the time of the day you are in. My mother comes into the room. I can smell her before the drowse lifts. She calls my name and I open my eyes. The room is dark.

Where's Snell? I ask her.

She stares. Was Bobby here?

I nod. My mouth is dry as a bone, I tell her. This fucking head ache is splitting my skull. Like a fucking axe. These fucking tablets don't even touch it.

She comes over to me and touches my shoulder. I can smell the gin on her breath. There are tears in her eyes.

This pain, I tell her, is driving me nuts. You got to do something to stop this pain. It feels like all my bones are burning. Like my skull is on fire...

The tears trickle down her powdery cheeks.

Snell wants me out, I tell her.

Don't worry, she tells me, you are not going anywhere. She sniffs and steps away from me. Smiles to reassure me.

It's his house, I point out.

Don't worry, she says, I can take care of him. She turns to leave.

Don't forget the water, I tell her. She brings me water and I wave her away.

I tell Chris when he comes: Snell gave me notice.

You can stay with me, he says.

I stare at him. You! I say. The sixteen hour a day man! How the fuck will you look after me?

If you are disabled you can get a nurse, he tells me. They come every day and check on you. He stares into my eyes. He is sincere. I am to be his purpose in life.

I'll look after you, Poll, he says. His voice grows hoarse from too much emotion. We'll get a wheelchair, he says. It'll be better in my place. I don't think your mother likes me coming here every day.

Fuck her, I say. Take no notice of her.

I study his hands with their dirty nails. Fingers like bread rolls. My mood gets dark.

Get lost, I tell him.

But the word, disabled, gives me much food for thought. Chris is like every Herculean dope since the world began: he means well.

Jesus, I say, very soft and heartbroke. He gets up and puts his hand on my shoulder.

Don't worry, Poll, he tells me again. Old Chris will look after you. He is sincere as fuck.

Fuck you! I tell him. Just leave me alone.

Then I go into my phantom of the opera mode.

This is another day. Chris tells me this story: It is Saturday. The sky is grey, but not menacing in any way, or threatening rain, merely the sombre, still, used but still-warm bathwater sort of a day that you often get in September around the second or third week of a new football season. Same sort of thing as a dogday, but without that vein of lead.

Chris opens his eyes. Dark eyes, the browny black of fresh bit licorice; a pale face with freckles; dark ginger hair cropped short. He stares and steadies his thoughts, tries to come to terms. Then he lifts his head from the pillow, throws off the blanket and sets both feet on the bare floor. This is the day off. He is naked; his skin is white as chalk. Dirt-rimmed fingernails of prussian blue. He scratches his head, yawns, rises and goes over to the window. Looks out and sees it is not raining. Sniffs and turns away. He goes back to the bed and stands. He looks down at the rumpled sheet.

He stares intently and it enters into him like an infusion, a righteous determination. Some definite thing to be set alongside the sullen rage that is more or less constant. Very like finding the Wrath of God.

It is a bad time. Most of the time (especially the sober) is bad for him. Even sleep, the dreams coming and going, brings an unseemly procession of bad omens. The world of shit; all things that come under your touch become shit.

His dark eyes stare steadily at the window. There is steady grey light, the autumn sun is veiled by a thin high layer of mottled cloud. Cheeks like white dough. Freckles. Hair the same colour as a Rita Hayworth wig. Big arms, the muscle softened and smoothed out beneath the layer of flab. Big hairless legs. Under the blubber and beer belly, a torso of tremendous strength. He stands up and tries to draw the slump out of the bulging gut. Raises both arms. Sniffs deep at the stagnant air. Lowers them to his sides and closes his eyes. Struggles to steady things in his head. Then dives suddenly and tries to touch his toes. Fails and tries again. Gasps and wobbles. Sits on the bed. His lips move, as if he is trying to memorise the lines of some ancient curse.

Later on, he opens a tin of beans, tips them into his greasy frying pan and sets it on the gas ring; finds a match to light it. When he judges them hot enough, he takes the pan from the ring and eats them with a spoon; crams home two slices of white bread. Half a litre of coke completes the breakfast. Then he gets dressed.

Just before noon he attempts twenty press-ups and fails at number eighteen. The girl comes at one pm and Chris goes at her like a maniac. He is cold sober and the girl is frightened by him. She leaves without clearing up.

At four o'clock he walks across the town to the Locomotive Hotel.

The Pieman is there. He sits on a tall stool at the corner of the bar. He is at the stage we call merry and breathing with small gasps through his mouth. The pint he is drinking is Strongbow. The room is subdued, about a dozen men scattered about at tables. The TV is going. The Pieman drinks alone. He is in repose, staring at nothing through half-closed eyes, hardly a shudder of breath. He is dressed in a vast t-shirt and big arse jeans with seams slit to the knees. His feet and hands are small. When the new pint comes he takes the head off it and closes his eyes. Chris watches. He orders a half pint of Guinness and takes it to the table nearest the door. The grey smoky air, the drab slowness enclosed by walls and windows, all of it seems to have flowed in out of the September afternoon. He sips the drink. Watches and waits.

The TV goes on and on. The football scores come up on the screen. The Pieman keeps on sipping and guzzling. Just stares at nothing and sinks his cider in silence. When the news comes on he goes out for a piss. Some of the drinkers leave. The atmosphere sags.

Chris, in his extra large denim shirt, worn loose like a coat, and his grey t-shirt and brown uniform pants, studies the palms of his hands, the grain of the wood, the dirt under his fingernails. Strapped to his hairless left leg, between knee and ankle (three separate strips of Elastoplast), is the brand new carving knife he bought in Hypervalue two weeks earlier. The handle of the knife has been closely bound with darning yarn and he has been careful to handle the implement only when wearing surgical gloves. He leaves his Guinness untouched and waits. The grey twilight. The wall lights are switched on. By this time, he says, he is getting nervous as fuck.

Some of the drunks, who had gone away at the end of the

afternoon, come back. Others with fresh faces and clean collars enter. Chris pushes the Guinness to one side and buys a pint of Stella. Drinks it straight down and orders another. Goes back to his seat. The Pieman is still in his place. Still guzzling. The light from the lamp at his end of the bar falls on him and outlines his bulk like golden pollen. Out in the street, the last of the setting sun casts a dull apricot glow. The Fat Boy is into his seventeenth pint and beginning into a light sweat. He stares languidly about the room. Everybody gives him a wide berth.

When the street is almost dark the men with the clean collars start to leave for town. They go outside to wave down taxis along Broadway.

Then the Pieman gets down from his seat and goes out. When he returns there is a woman with him. She is a blonde of forty or so dressed like a widow who wants to remarry with a younger man. She walks as if her shoes may be hurting her. The Fat Boy picks her up and sets her down on his stool; buys her a double Bacardi and a bottle of Pepsi. Whenever she speaks he smiles and nods. The two of them leave at ten thirty. The Pieman winks at the barman as he goes past. The woman laughs at something he says. Chris sees off his second Stella and slips out after them.

They, the Pieman and the woman, are walking along Nora Street. The Pieman stops by a car parked alongside the blank wall of the old brewery. Chris watches from the corner. The woman and the Pieman get into the back of the car. The street is quiet. A dead end. Chris walks towards the car, staying close to the blank wall of brown brick. When he reaches the car he sees that the nearside rear door is open. The Pieman is sprawled on his back on the back seat. The woman is fellating him. His legs press her close and his hands clutch at her bobbing head. The car door is open and the woman's feet hang out over the gutter. Chris can read the price on the yellow labels pasted under both arches between the high heels and the almost new soles. On her left ankle a fine gold chain catches the spent lamplight. Stooping quickly, he grabs hold of both ankles and drags her onto the pavement. When she sits up he kicks her hard in the face. The Pieman roars and struggles to get his body off the seat of the car. Chris pulls up his trouser leg and removes the carving knife from its Elastoplast strips. He leans into the car and then it all stops.

It is as if, he says, his arms are made of cotton wool. The Pieman roars at him again. Chris turns and nearly trips over the woman who is sat on the pavement, feeling her bloody gums for teeth. Then he drops the knife and runs away.

We sit in silence. He is ashamed. He holds his face in his hands. I couldn't do it, Poll, he tells me. I didn't have it in me.

Mamma gives me one of her nasty smiles. This is another day. I have seen her pull this one with my father many times. He was always a sucker. Inborn guilt, I suppose. She always knew it was there.

Pimp! she says. Don't ever call Bobby that. I'm not going to stand for you calling him that.

We are both drunk. She nods as if she can see into my secret heart and I decide that love is not something I feel for her. She takes a good sip of gin. Bobby is no pimp, she says and tries to look tragic. You got a lot to learn, she says. You think it is all plain sailing. All black and white...

I look at her and lose interest. All those years, the two of them, attempting to make their time seem precious.

You, she says, of all people... You and that Appleby's wife. I know. Know all about that business.

You know fuck all, I tell her. She smiles. Nods. She thinks she has found my Achilles' heel. And that other one, she says, that Italian woman.

I try to study her with dispassionate eyes. My father always called them 'vessels of grief'. A huge, unsympathetic boredom comes over me at the thought of all the trouble it is to be involved with them. And how much easier it must be to be queer or celibate. My sister hated her from an early age.

Don't do what I did, mamma told her. Don't marry some dope. Not even if he *has* got a nice smile. If he's poor, dump him. This kid is poor, I'm telling you. I can smell it on him.

She was talking about Martin Foster. He was poor. He was dull and poor. He advertised poverty, which was why my sister chose him.

You get too close to them, my mother said, and let them get their claws in you, you can catch it off them... Believe me, I been there. My own mother never said a word to me. Never warned me.

She thought getting married was enough. She thought your father had lovely blue eyes. And he did. Back then he had the brightest blue eyes you ever saw. A glib tongue, too. So we went the usual route: the one room and the pram in the corner. Some shitty little house in a shitty street. Two rooms. Guaranteed to kill all the lovelight off, believe me. I chose your father because I was a fool. And there were rich men panting after me... Plenty of them...

Go away, I tell her. I want to be left alone.

Chris comes. A fine, bright morning in late September. There is a dew sparkling on the lawn; the leaves on the trees in the other gardens are starting to change to browns and yellows.

I got you a wheelchair, he says. I found it in one of the storerooms, he explains. I'll take you for a spin.

He lifts me as if I weighed no more than a child. I can smell the beer on his breath. Can feel his immense strength and his love for me... can feel it flow into me. I press my face into his chest and he carries me along the passage to the head of the stairs at the first landing. My mother is at the foot, looking up.

You be careful with him, she says.

Don't worry, Mrs O, Chris says. I got him safe.

She frowns. Don't call me that, she says. You ought to know better than to call me that.

Sorry, Chris says. He winks at me. I forgot.

I hang on and he carries me down the stairs.

The wheelchair looks brand new. It stands on the carpet in the front room: black and silver tubing, silver spokes and pale grey tyres, dark green leather seat and backrest. He points out the features to me; shows how the brake works and the means of steering.

Come on, he says, I'll take you round the block.

My mother holds the front door open for us and we go out into the morning. The air is fresh and the sky is like new paint.

I should have a shawl, I tell him. One of those fucking plaid shawls like the old invalids... This is no good, I tell him.

I am frightened. There are tears in my eyes.

I am going to kill myself, I tell him.

Come on, Poll, he says, stop fucking about... You got to accept it. I'll take care of you, you got my word.

I got it worked out exactly, I tell him. Not tablets. Tablets are too chancy. I don't want to be swallowing a bottle of sleeping tablets and waking up. A gun would be good, but where could I get hold of a gun? That would be my favoured way, a gun. Muzzle right up in the roof of the mouth and *Boom!* But my plan is to take his car. He loves that car. It's a special year or something. He got its history all the way back to 1967. Keeps that fucking thing immaculate. If I can get his keys... He comes home every Wednesday afternoon for lunch. Him and my mother go into the front bedroom. They watch these pornographic films and have a jump. It's a ritual. Then he goes to play golf. He leaves his keys and his change on the sideboard in the dining room. If I can get into that car...

Chris is looking at me hard. He finds it hard to credit what I am saying. He is trying to see into my soul. He smiles at me. What he wants is me to smile back... Show I am only kidding.

Come on, Poll, he says. You'll outlive the lot of us. Being crippled is not the end of the world...

He smiles to encourage me, but I don't smile back.

Part Four

Chapter Thirteen

I see him before he sees me. Recognise the car. The Jaguar man. His face, when he gets out, bears a mask to make clear an extreme perplexity. His eyes are so busily avoiding mine that for a moment I think he means to sack me.

Tommy, he says. His hands come to rest on my shoulders. The eyes look away, then swivel back and lock with mine.

Tom, he says. The lips compress and bunch through a moment of arrest.

Then he blurts out: I got bad news. Your boy killed hisself.

We stare into each other's eyes. I shift my gaze and note the square grimness of his jaw, how it is set. Our eyes meet again. Lose track. I look at the evening that is all around where we stand. See the traffic crossing the Penarth Road bridge. Nothing comes readily to mind that I might say to move the moment onward. Then, at the last gasp, the slump inside my head that is like a violent discharge of cold shit.

This afternoon, he says. Drove a car over the cliff at Southerndown.

Maybe I groan or cry out at this point, it is hard to remember. He gets back into his car.

Take a couple of days off, he tells me. And drives away into the twilight.

My friend Mr Mack comes to mind. He has a bar filled with strong drink that will help hold me up. I turn about on the pavement to get bearings. Set my face towards the last strip of pale light above the blue hill. The feathery dusk is settling everywhere. The face of Mr Mack is steady in my mind's eye. The room where he presides, with its infinity of sorrow and tender silence. The gentle grey of the last light at the windows; the softened glow of the lamps where they press against the yellow walls. The drinker turns to his next drink. The entry to the harbour. The journey to the map room. I stare down at the pavement as my feet move to carry me hence.

Mr Mack is waiting. He knows. He looks up from behind his counter as I come into the outer gloom of the bar. This is such a magnificent face for sorrow to abide. Silence is all he needs and that steady grey drizzle of perpetual Irish sorrow burns into you like a brand. Like a thousand years of rain and lamentation. He takes the bottle he has kept at the ready and pours me a tumbler of Jameson's whiskey.

Your missus rang me, he says.

I accept the drink and gulp it down. Rap the glass down for a refill.

Harry just told me, I say.

Sit down, he says. He refills the glass.

I'm okay, I tell him. I'll be okay in a minute. And drink it off.

You're white as a ghost, he says.

I stare at him. Where is he? I say. Where have they got the body?

He takes the glass from me and puts it under the counter.

Enough of the hard stuff, he says and pulls me a pint.

Why don't you phone her, he says. I got the number.

He hands me a slip of paper. I take it and stare at the number written down. Give me another Jameson's, I tell him, and I will.

He complies.

She cries on the telephone. She is my ex-wife now. Sobs, gasps and a long litter of words strewn into the immensity of our separating gulf. We have no idea of the true hugeness until that hugeness comes. Then we know we are lost. She is lost. The moment of the death hits me and I have to hold the wall to stay on my feet. Her voice is like a torrent of loss. Then nothing. I close my eyes and count to ten. Then her voice, coming at me again.

Say something, she says. Why don't you speak?

But there is nothing in me. Not a single word, only blubbering that bubbles up from somewhere and wrenches itself free from my throat. Then tears. Then a vision of the universe as stars trapped on the head of the pin. You are looking in and it is looking back at you. It is grief. She is sobbing, the words lost to the writhing of her tongue in its agony. Fuck it, I mutter and hang up.

Later on there is a moon and I am wandering alone on the lonely riverbank. The light leaks into the greater night and stains the few clouds that have gathered. The moonlight ages the land and I am caught up in the ancientness of all things. The river holds the moon like the body of a child. On either side of where I stand the bridges fall over the water with the solemn purpose of iron bars. My feet yearn to stamp the world to dust. My hands clutch the empty air. I am on the path that runs through the dogshit grass. The bare branches of trees. The streetlamps and the mystery of streets. I can feel the death, the stalking presence somewhere in the night that is stilled to my pace to hold me. Or whatever it is that will keep me alive and busted open until the fisheyed dawn. With the cold iron rail of the bridge beneath my elbows. All the substance of existence as frail as woodash. Veins, braincells, the marrow of bones and the ends of the nerves, all snared to the slack plight of this single breath. Then the next. The balance of flesh and blood in air. You can feel it all around. Like bees buzzing. Death.

It is still October and the sun comes up. A cold breeze makes its way over the water to where I stand.

Death.

I turn away. The air on my skin. The river muttering its way to the sea.

Here I am in another day, I tell myself. It is Wednesday.

There is a suit to buy. Black shoes. Black socks. Black socks are a necessity. Even more than a black tie and the white shirt. No man should ever go to the funeral of a son in anything other than black socks. And the white shirt must be of Sea Island cotton.

First, though, there is the visit to the barber for haircut and shave. The barber is this kid with spiky black hair. A shop with three chairs and all of them empty. He looks up at me as I walk through the door. Long face and very dark eyes. Stands up and seems to peer into me, like a matador. His towel is his cape. He points to the middle chair. Our eyes meet in the mirror. He gestures dismissively.

Who the fuck been cutting this? he demands.

We stare. Just cut it short, I tell him.

It's a mess, man, he tells me.

I know it is, I tell him. I'm a mess. Just cut the hair. Then I want a nice shave.

He moves very light on his feet. He dances around the chair, very intense and serious as he snips at the raggedness. His lips move to mutter. The eyes hardly ever blink.

No work? he asks.

Day off, I tell him and that ends all conversation. He reminds me of the actor who plays the killer of the big industrialist who is going to build the new factory to give work to the sharecroppers and fieldhands in the film *In the Heat of the Night*. Mississippi, or somewhere. The one who runs the all-night diner and is fucking the redneck's underage sister. The longfaced boy who will avail Sam Woods none of the icecold lemon pie when he calls at midnight on his rounds. That place, the diner, sticks in the memory; a dim-lit lantern hung to draw restless moths from the great darkness of the empty land.

The barber, when he is finished, looks displeased with the haircut. He is jumpy with irritation. This is a dead neck of the woods. The rent is cheap. What he wants is a shop full of gimmicks, where young kids come to talk about Saturday, and all he gets is an old man like me who has been cutting his own hair with scissors from the junkshop. Before him it was a laundrette. The corner of Clive Street, next to the carpet vendor.

It's the best I can do, he says.

I nod and hand him a fiver. Nobody expected a miracle, I tell him. Keep the change.

The skin in my cheeks still prickles from the closeness of the shave. A paroxysm of wellbeing as I button up my coat and he brushes at the shoulders. I pause at the door to call back something, words, but he is already sweeping up the scant cuttings, watching himself in the mirror, screwing himself deeper and deeper.

I buy the black socks first and take them into the toilets on the

Hayes to put them on so that I can buy new shoes. Buy a black suit off the peg. The coat fits and I tell him to pack the pants untried.

All I need, I tell myself, is to bundle the bones appropriately for the single performance. A sack of shit, tied in the middle, as my old man used to say. The man in black.

I treat myself to some toothpaste and a new toothbrush and get a taxi to take me and my bags to the Bird in Hand.

Mrs Mack is behind the bar. Three customers, solitaries, who glance up at my entrance and go back to resume their careful journeys into the day. She pulls a face. Oh Tommy... she says. Shakes her head and bites at her lower lip. Extends the grimace as if she would like to suffer for me. I nod and shrug.

Terry won't be long, she tells me. He had to go to the bank.

She pulls me a pint and I slap a crisp tenner on the bar. With a silver dollar I could ape Randolph Scott. Have one with me, I tell her. She glances at the clock. Screws up her eyes.

I'd consider it an honour if you would drink with me, I tell her. It is like someone else speaking. We hate the sight of each other. I'll have a large gin, she says.

Of course, I say. I'll have one too. Not gin, whisky.

And toss it off at a single gulp. Then a swig of the beer. These are the time-honoured movements. Like dancesteps. We submit like sheep. The time pours in and swirls all around us. When I close my eyes I can feel it. White smoke. Then the world as we know it. She stands with her back to the till. She holds her drink as if it might be poison. We are mute. Marooned.

Mr Mack comes in at five past one. He comes up to stand alongside me and signals for his wife to serve him. He carries a black briefcase and wears a grey pinstripe suit.

What's all this? I say.

It's bullshit, he says. I had to go to see them at the brewery.

Bullshit baffles brains, I say.

He shrugs. They want blood, he says. I don't think I baffled anybody. Fuck 'em. He looks at me. There is an intensity to his gaze that makes me uncomfortable.

How *you* feeling?

I shrug. Half smile. Look away. Then the deep breath, life goes on routine.

Take it easy on the hard stuff, Tom, he warns me.

I will, I promise.

Then he pulls the *Echo* out of his briefcase and offers it to me.

It's in here, he tells me. There's a picture of the car. The funeral is Monday.

I need a bath, Terry, I tell him. I got all these new clothes and I haven't washed my arse for three months.

He nods. Okay, he says. Proffers the *Echo* for me to read.

I shake my head and push it away.

Any chance of that bath right now?

Follow me, he says and we go upstairs.

In the evening I go to see Bernie. We stare and the way he looks away tells me that he, too, has heard the news. He takes off his glasses and his eyes are as solemn as armpits. He nods at the *Echo* on the floor by his chair. I just been reading about it, he says. You seen it?

He picks up the paper and offers it to me. I shake my head.

I don't know what to say, he tells me.

I hold up my hand to stop him. It is a relief to say nothing. It is always peaceful sitting with him, he is a genuine solitary who expects nothing. He was able to name every capital city of every state in what he called the Union, and so was I. It was what we had in common. Nebraska, he would suddenly say, and I'd come back with an immediate Lincoln. He also knew William Holden's real (non-acting) name. Stuff about the Bowery Boys...

You want a drink? he asks me. I shake my head. What about your old man? he asks. This is something that has been troubling me. I stare at my hands.

The funeral, he says. Someone will have to tell him.

I bring my hands up to cover my face.

Maybe your missus will tell him, he suggests.

He is not on the fucking phone, I tell him. Besides, she hates him worse than I do.

And don't forget your daughter, he says.

I hold up both hands, close my eyes, and shudder hard.

Have a drink, he says. I got some Bushmills. You look fucking terrible.

It is the twilight hour and I had meant to stay sober, but I accept the glass of whisky he pours; succumb, you might say, from sheer terror. A night of sobriety, just me and the anguish, is not something I have ever been anxious to suffer. Now Julia, my daughter, comes back to haunt me. The guilt that dogs, from the ancient of days, condenses and drips into the cavern of my skull.

Just roll me up in a fucking carpet and dump me out on the tip, I tell him. It's the only place a man will get some peace.

I glug at the whisky. He nods wisely and tops up the glass.

Later on, when the bottle is empty, I retreat from there and wander in a legless fashion along Corporation Road. My limbs feel numb but my head is racing in frantic spurts. My father. We have not spoken in many years. Even with a telephone, communication would be no easier. Would probably be harder. The blind silence would strike me dumber than stone. Delirious hilarity would dismember my tongue. I can see him in my mind's eye, the finger of righteousness raised towards heaven.

All I want to do is hide. Down by the river, in the willows along the bank. Scampering and frantic, like Judas after the betrayal.

Wilson is waiting in the hallway as I enter the house. He smiles as if he would encourage me.

How you feeling? he enquires. We heard about your loss, me and the boys... Gestures vaguely to encompass house and tenants. We had a whip-round. We...

Then he lunges like a fencer and presses a manilla envelope into my grasp. From me and the boys, he says. His eyes are wide open and blank. He is like a man being tortured in front of his mother. It is the first time we have spoken in months. I nod and stare at the thing in my hand. Tears start up in my eyes and a howl escapes me. I lumber across the marble floor and embrace him like a long-lost brother. He shoves me away and runs for his life.

Coming awake, my eyes dully taking stock, I mutter: Jesus Jesus... I retch and cough twice and think about my next strong drink. Get out of where I am and keep on running. Down endless back lanes and tortuous side streets. Some vast city where I could be strange for as long as I lived. Till the pump packed in and I fell down and nobody knew me.

There is hard rain. I can hear it on the skylight.

There is a knock at the door. Just as I am about to piss into the bottle. I pause. Then another knock followed by Wilson's voice.

It's me, he says. The bossman is downstairs. He wants to see you.

Harry is waiting in the hall. He is wearing a grey suit and a black tie. He looks bored. How's things? he asks me. He straightens his tie. You look terrible, he says. Eyes like...

Spare me, I say.

I expect you need money, he says. He looks at me. I shrug and look away. He takes a white envelope from his inside pocket and holds it out to me. I take it from him.

One fifty, he informs me. It'll keep you going. Who's paying for the funeral?

There's my father, I tell him. I don't think he knows. He's not on the phone... The words come out as if my jaw is fractured.

He looks at me as if I am the kitten he wished he had drowned in the bucket.

I'll run you out there, he says.

Give me a minute to shave, I plead. I don't want him seeing me looking like this.

He looks at his watch, gives me a three-quarter sidelong glance, then the curtest of nods. Get a move on, he says. And bring your coat, it's pissing down.

I cut myself. The blade is new and my hands shake. A lot of blood from so small a nick. The mirror I gaze into is flecked with blight.

The face hangs in it like a pallid bloom. Unwholesome as a toadstool. I staunch the bloodflow with toilet paper and wear the new suit and the new shoes, but keep the old shirt. I put on my cap, which is grey Donegal tweed.

Harry is waiting in his car. What about your coat? he asks me.

He starts the car. How far is it? he asks.

Ten miles, I tell him and add the directions.

A rotten fucking day, he observes. How will you get back? Is there a bus?

I think there's a bus, I tell him.

I'll just drop you, he tells me. Give him my regards.

I will, I tell him, but I know I won't.

Outside it is a foul, bleak morning, with the rain flinging itself down in scattering handfuls from scraps of dark cloud scudding.

We go on, out through Ely and onto the old Cowbridge Road.
Dread chokes me. A clock in my head marking off every yard of
the way. I bring up my hands to shut out the light.

You okay? Harry asks.

Jesus, I say. It feels like my head is full of shit. Like I got shit
in my veins.

He turns his head to look at me.

He sniffs and nods thoughtfully. We drive to the edge of town
in silence. Up the Tumble and out through St Nicholas before he
speaks. How is he, your old man? he asks me.

Still breathing, far as I know.

I haven't seen him since Sammy Rees' funeral, he tells me.

He looks at me. He's a character, your old man, he says.

I make no reply to this. We turn off the main road and head
north. It feels like being reeled into some bad shit. The hedges
flying backwards; the wipers on the windscreen; the sense of the
sodden autumn all around.

Fuck me! I say, it must be years since I saw a field!

We go down the hill, veering east. Past the row of cottages. He
stops the car outside the gate. We both get out into the pouring
rain. Harry runs around to the back of the car and opens the boot.
He takes out a red and white golf umbrella and thrusts it at me.

Here, he says, for fuck sake, take this.

Then he is on his way before I can say a word.

There is the wooden gate; five bar, tied with pale grey sashcord
where the bottom hinge was; a strand of barbed wire undulates
along the length of the top rail. Then there is the path, a bramble
wilderness on the right hand side where the blackcurrant bushes
were (still are when you peer into the depths). Gooseberries, too,
are in evidence when you look hard. One stunted apple tree
being dragged under. The subversion of returning wildness that
comes with the ceasing of husbandry. A strip of rank grass runs
along the other side. Conical heaps of grey clinkers and ash from
his stove. Like molehills. A green plastic watering can.

I walk as slow as I can without coming to a halt. My head is
going Jesus Jesus Jesus. The apples are rotting on the branches.
The greenhouse, all but glassless, contains a virile upthrust of
nettles. The prize tomato man, I think. His trusty spade of forty

years leans askew, the handle rotting, rust on the worn down blade that once gleamed like a headsman's axe. Junk spills out of the old railway sheds. Doors hang on by hinges that have all but pulled from the frame. Rain drips in where the felt is peeling off the roof. All the signs of being near the end. I put my head into the shed and take it in, the lost visions of the thrifty man. A lifetime of bits and pieces and fragmentary things left over from this or that enterprise and set aside to wait their turn to come in handy one day. One day! One sunshiny day that never comes...

The rain drips in and the wind clamours behind my back. The house itself looks as if it is trying to hide; to screw itself into the earth and pull the grass back over to cover up where it went. His pale blue car rusts and bears silent testimony to the foolhardiness of all wise men. From whose number I exclude myself. I gaze out over the field, its barrenness. The single leafless oak. And it seems that all of my life was dragging me to where I stand. Some bewildering destiny, some story about the the unerring inevitability of the eventual betrayal. I can feel every day of my life bearing down.

The rain is falling hard on my bald patch, with the red and white umbrella still rolled up. Useless. The rain... All my life, this fucking rain...

Smoke issues from the single pot on the chimney. Discouraged smoke. A thin hair of smoke dragged east and lost. I go round to the back of the house and look in through the kitchen window. His back is to me. Sitting in his rocking chair, the rockers chocked with blocks of kindling. There is smoke in the room. A fire is struggling in the stove and the cold air in the flue is forcing back the smoke. Thick smoke the colour of sheepwool spews from the open flap; now the glimpse of a single languid orange flame that squirms and falls away again. My father sits and patiently feeds the mouth of the stove with sticks chopped thin. He leans forward and blows gently to keep it alive. There is, I tell myself, still time to turn away. But then he turns and sees me. Rises swiftly and comes to the door. When he kicks open the door of the porch he is clutching a shotgun.

Who is it? he demands. I am standing not ten feet from him.

It's me, I tell him.

Who's me? he snarls. He cranes his neck. Old head, like a

tortoise. I watch the way his mouth works. The bitter element. Move closer to him. That's a good question, I say. It's Tommy, I tell him, but by now he knows. I can see that his eyes are yellowed over with a snot of cataracts. He was always deaf.

You look like Ike Clanton, I tell him. Put the fucking thing away before it goes off.

He sniffs and looks down at the shotgun. Turns away to rest it in the corner of the porch. Come in, he says. I'll put the kettle on.

We go in and he points to the stove. First fire since last spring, he says. The flue is cold... but I'll get it going.

He fills the kettle and plugs it in. Goes to the sideboard and selects two cups. I got no milk, he tells me.

We face each other. The chasm is there. I am still clutching the red and white umbrella with both hands. At port arms.

Elliott's dead, I tell him. He blinks, twice, the way a heron blinks. What? he says, and thrusts his better ear towards me.

Elliott, I say again. He's dead.

He stares at me through the smoky air; then his gaze goes past me and he is lost somewhere. He lowers his head and when he looks up at me again his face is the perfect mask for sorrow. Made of bone. Then he turns and walks towards the window that overlooks the field. He rests his hands on the sill and his shoulders shake. The kettle comes to the boil and the switch clicks off. He turns to face me.

Aw, he says. Nothing else. The eyes close and he wipes at them with the back of his hand. Jesus, he says. Shakes his head, very slow, and sits on the bed. He is crying like a baby.

Then I start to cry too.

In all my life we were never easy in each other's minds. Our expression of grief, such as it is, is shortlived. He blows his nose and stands up. Watch the fire, will you? he says. I'll make the tea.

We are both glad of the distraction. I look into the bowels of the stove and drop sticks to feed it; gently blow to fan the fragile flame and ember. The flame takes hold. The new wood gives it faith.

It is necessary to build a flame fierce enough to force ignition into the wet, hard cobbles of anthracite in the grey iron bucket on the quarry stone hearth. It gets easier to do once the body of heat is there. The thin sticks crackle. Sparks fly. The smoke goes up.

When it is going good I close the flap of the stove and turn to survey the room. It is like a dismembered memory. Something rearranged as a puzzle. He has turned it into a cave, a hole in some hillside where he can attempt to resolve the complexity of the solitary life. We are still at the edges. I spot the giltframed photo of my mother's face when it was young and lovely. There is in it an infinity of innocence I had never realised. Much regret, too, and softness. The moment. Her calm smile; the light falling onto her left side, brow and cheek, her dark hair bobbed, her white blouse buttoned to the throat. We, my father and I, are separately lost into our own quiet. He pours tea into the cups and hands one to me.

Points to a stiffbacked chair.

How did it happen? he asks.

Car crash, I tell him.

I didn't know he had a car.

He borrowed it, I tell him.

Fucking deathtraps! he says with vehement bitterness.

We sit drinking tea.

After a while he asks how I got there.

Harry Rivers dropped me off, I tell him.

Who?

I repeat the name and his face clouds with disapproval. He never liked Harry.

How will you get back? he asks.

Bus, I suppose, I tell him. Or walk.

The hard part is over for me. The duty part. The rain slashing at the window seems like nothing now.

There's a bus at five past twelve, he tells me. You'll get fucking drowned if you walk.

The wind drives hard at the window and we both turn our heads.

What a day! he mutters. Then he gets to his feet and takes down a blackfaced alarm clock. Gives it a couple of winds and puts it back.

Keeps perfect time, that clock, he says. Bought it from that shop used to be at the bottom of Bridge Street. It's gone now. A man named F. Kiss had it. He was a Hungarian.

How long have you had that shotgun, Dad? I ask him.

He looks at me, the old hard blank I know so well.

Not long, he says. You want to get down there in plenty of time.

He points to the clock. It's quarter to. You want to be down there before twelve.

You frightened of rustlers? I ask him.

We fall into silence. I find myself watching the clock on the shelf. He puts some coal into the stove, popping the cobbles in one by one, about half a dozen.

Fire, he says, nodding. The one thing man craves. If I didn't have this stove and plenty of coal... Christ only knows. I got a telly but I never watch it. I hate it.

He points to the TV. You got one? he asks.

I shake my head. Never use them, I tell him.

I like the wireless, he says. I like to hear the world news. Stuck out here, no bastard to talk to...

The funeral is Monday, I remember to tell him.

He nods and stands. I'll get my mac and walk down with you, he says. What time?

Eleven, I tell him. That funeral home by the brook.

I'll be there.

Neither of us speaks as we walk to the gate. We go through and stand by the side of the road in the rain.

I'll have to buy black shoes, he says. I just hope it's not raining. I hate funerals in the rain.

His face lightens when the bus comes around the bend. He points.

Here she comes, he says. He offers me his hand before I get on.

A hard calloused hand, like cold leather. He turns away as I mount the step. He walks back along the path as the bus pulls away. He turns but there is no wave.

A journey on one of these small country buses heading back into town closely resembles a prolonged glimpse into dreams. There are things you remember and things you don't. The wet fields look strange yet familiar. The way the road gleams in the rain. The handful of passengers clutching things. Then you reach the edge of the town and you can see what is taking place. The development. Supermarkets and showrooms. A new world in the ancient fields. The new glass and the steel that will not stain under ancient rain. The face for the world to gaze on. Some people get off. The driver watches them. Cropped head. Red face. An ardent gumchewer. When they are off he closes the door and turns back to the way ahead. Passengers on, or passengers off, he never speaks. A nod or the shake of his head; a belligerence close to hostility. He might have a poker up his arse from the way he sits and peers out past the wipers. After hurtling between the wet hedgerows, now we hit the traffic. The roofs in the rain are old as the hills. Rain is what makes this dump what it is. It is why we hate it. I sit tight and stare out and wish in a way that the journey on that bus might go on forever.

The rain has eased by the time I get out in Westgate Street. This is loose time. Lunchtime for the working donkey. There is money in my pocket. This, I tell myself, is the life. The wind gusts along the alleyway. The boy, his face, comes back to haunt me. He was always bleak of eye, even as a child. Winter mornings, off to school like a skinned kitten. And my old man, his isolation, his rage. Grinding his false teeth in his personal wilderness. Alone with his alarm clock. Trying to work out how far back, calculating like a miser.

The street is cold to me. I stand on the pavement and stare. As always, the possibility of loose ends is endless. A man can sink and sink. How wonderful the simple thing, to be drunk and then drunker. Go home and sober up, then back out and in and drunk again. They should write anthems to it. Take bottles of strong liquor home. Hide them in cupboards. Under the pillow. Booze till you bust, then the bullet in the brain.

All those future twilights coming and going and you as dry and quiet as a bag of salt. These thoughts ever come to tempt us. It is the common affliction; it is not money that will lead us into the devil's lair, nor arse that is easy, either, but rather the old step off through the door on the dark landing. I see my father and I see myself a way I never want to be. Stand and consider the awful and alien intimacies that befall the lives of families.

The bus is gone. Sucked on and in. The passengers will by now be about their expeditions to buy butter or pay gas bills. Or sit in the arcades and stare at the life. Every day, like cutting a way from the trappings with a blunt axe.

The red and white umbrella is still clutched tight. I study it. A golf umbrella that belongs to Mr Rivers. I draw a deep breath and cut across St Mary Street. Through the market and into the side entrance of the Old Arcade. Two pints in here and a single whisky.

Some of the substance falls back into place. I can almost bear to look in the mirror when I go for a piss. Repeat this dose in The Cottage and then get a taxi to the Bird in Hand.

I smile as I step into the bar and Mrs Mack smiles back at me. No matter how she smiles, no matter what's behind it or what the occasion might be, she always smiles the smile of the whore. To this I have no response but to lower my gaze. Mr Mack is more serious.

Did you see your father? he asks me.

I nod. Duty done, I say and point to the Jameson's.

How is he? he asks. I haven't seen him for donkey's years.

Now I smile at him. Nod, too, as if happy.

He is fine, I tell him. The old fellow is in fine fettle. Made me a cup of tea and everything... Shook my hand.

How did he take it? Mrs Mack asks me. Was he upset?

I look from face to face.

I believe he was, I tell them. And then nod emphatically. Yes, I say, he may well have been upset. He always quite liked Elliott. When he was a little boy...

Mr Mack is watching me closely. A special sort of watch, not like the hawk way of watching. Sorrow is there, a big measure of his look is sorrow. It comes to me, the knowledge that this man is the only man in the world I can trust completely. The only one who has always and unfailingly given me the benefit of the doubt.

There was a line in a song my father used to sing when I was a child: '... and light a penny candle from a star...' His voice was weak. Not unmelodious, but commonplace and without strength. Sentimental stuff about America, or Ireland. He tried his best to sound like Bing Crosby. I used to love him singing those songs. *Little Redwing*; *Home on the range*; *My old Kentucky Home*, stuff that brought a certain comfort to me as a child. It was all part of something that was trying to be the happy home.

And this is on my mind as I come out of the Bird and make my way to Corporation Road. I buy a candle. A white wax candle with a white cotton wick. The Asian woman who serves me watches my face with quiet intensity. She knows me, my face, and she is waiting for me to get the usual cans of German lager, or the monstrosity whisky they sell, but I fox her. Just the candle and a box of Swan Vestas. I find a jam jar in a cupboard in the cellar of the house and take it to my room. Loving was always the sure way to misery. I am not sure how much love there was for the dead son (all things through all our lives were tempered by a certain lack of communication and some traces of what may have been hostility), but now the misery is in me like a lead weight. In my gut. I feel sick with it.

I set the chair directly under the skylight. I strike a match and light the white wick and watch as the wax moistens and glistens and the shadows recoil to the edges of the room. Drip hot wax into the jar and press the butt of the candle into it. Set the jar on the chair. The flame is the same gold as the bar on the wing of a cock goldfinch. The candle core makes the rest of the room gloom. I sit on my bed and stare at the flame. The votive candle. To what?

To be someone's child is never easy. The inevitable. All things for the first time, and the softness of you when you are more or less all underbelly. The wind and the proximity of possible harm. The candle burns and it feels, when I close my eyes, that I can feel its heat, hear the flame hiss in the air. The rain is gone away and the wind only moans softly over the roof slopes. Valleys and ridges. I sit on my arse and feel myself drop away down and down the deepest well there is. The candle is my parachute. Soon the sloth of removal is swept clear of me. I am alone. Skinless. I start to cry. But there is a certain calm to it. It might be an act, I tell myself. The tears bear no relevance to what I am or might yet turn into. Inside the skull there is a swirl of what might be emotion that feels like the surge of smoke in the lampglass when the lamp is first lit. The tears count for nothing. What I am means nothing more than this dim awareness... hardly a thing. A life that is more or less fuck all. The candle is there in the jar. The room is there, all around me. The dark is crowding about the skylight and looking in where I sit. It is a question of what I am and what it left for me. Breath. Blood. But who shall receive blessing?

When I come to, the candle is out and the enormous night is astride my chest. It shifts to my shoulder when I sit up. Crawls over the crown of my head. Gnaws at my face. This is not the white horse nightmare my mother used to tell me about. This is the cold wet black sack she told me they would wrap me in. That comes after the dream where you fall and fall (*come la quaglia*) on the first thorns at the desert edge. All in front of you, the blinding heat shimmer of the parched land. You blink heavy and exhausted lids, raise a palsied hand to a broken heart and feel it sink. You know.

I go out of the house and see if there is a moon to be found. Drunks are singing old songs several streets to the west. To the east, the river. Cars cross the bridge both ways. Sparse signs. If there is a moon, what cloud there is obscures it.

Chapter Fourteen

Streaky sky at the skylight. An old ceiling, scraped back to the bare plaster. All the ancient and flaky bits scoured away and dumped. Very high, this sky, and forbidding. The colour of the early light is the colour of white wine left overnight in the glass and lifted to the east at sunless dawn. Squinting through. Fucking Monday. This, I tell myself, is all the life we have.

The wind is strong. Insistent, yet lacking true direction (an inconsistent and variable wind), it buffets the roof over my head and roars and hisses through the gaps in the slates. Winter will soon be with us. The cold air in the room already speaks of its imminent entry. This is the morning they bury the corpse. It seems (somewhere in my dull recollection) I may have dreamed last night of the corpse. Pale as milk with blue shadow; the penis pink as a ripe boil, and bloated. The eyes with copper pennies on them. Polished with Brasso.

There is the shave to be accomplished. I should go to the barber. Sit in the chair and suffer the attentions of a stranger at my face. But I have a new blade and I must wash my neck. Rub the soapsuds hard into the hollows and gullies of my ears. Move on to the next move. Each task a column to be built grain by grain from the damp salt.

The kitchen is empty and I can boil a kettle in peace. The bare bulb in the thin grey atmosphere. Wait with bated breath lest some intruder comes. Listen the while for pins dropping. Suck deep that stinking and stale air. Thinking, fuck you all and thanks for nothing. You feel old and soiled. You want to take an axe and go for people in the street. The boiled water must be carried to the bathroom on the first floor. Shave. Look hard at the face that the mirror rejects out of hand. There is so much in these old faces that is gone that empty will no longer suffice to describe the loss. The was and the never was. Bloat and bladder and red-vein eyeball. Blood. I cut myself. A sullen spot that beads and runs (worms) down the wet cheek. A pink line on the pallid map, from cheek to point of chin. And drips. They say (I think they say) that blood brings good luck to an enterprise. The task at hand. Razors and fish hooks and Old Bloater at the looking glass. Look in, look out. Don't flinch. The eyes dull as snot. My lips go through the motions of mumbling as I staunch the flow of the blood with paper and leave for the room above.

Lay the black suit on the bed. There is no rain at the skylight and I thank the Lord for this. Gentle rain might suit the purpose of the day; might even declare an atmospheric drama to the shuffle of feet on the wet road and lend a mysterious sheen to the tilted umbrellas. A degree of solemn grace. Some soft grey drizzle, like fine ash falling through the grey, might be okay. Just enough to bead the wax on the black hearse. The new shirt is cold on my back. Get into the suit. Polish at the shoes with the bright yellow duster. Maroon stitching along the edges. The smooth black polish in the new tin. I sit under the skylight and dab and polish. Spit and dab and polish etc. The old trick from the army days. Another gust of wind. A soft gust. Exhausted. Enough (a last gasp) to send a shiver through a clump of conifers and nothing else.

I know the place. The conifers. It comes up in my mind's eye. A desolate place, this hillside, on the best of days. Memories of long ago, when the boy in the box was just a child. The earth will be wet where they pile it. They dig the graves by machine these days. Yellow JCB or orange (Jap) Kubota. Take out the main bulk in ten minutes where it would have took a good man half a day. If the ground is soft, of course, and not too many stones. They still send down a man to trim the sides. Planks and struts and waling boards. And sweat. Jesus, you think. Finality. The supper at Emmaus comes to mind. Close my eyes and all about me in that room the air seethes.

The first thing I see moving (the only thing) is the blackbird. Perched there, rocking, tail to beak, on the topmost tip of the stunted yew. Then the rain comes, as if it had bided quietly all morning to greet our arrival. Spot the little silver tap in its sentry box housing of unpainted wood. Redundant except in the hot dry summers that never materialise. There is a quiet to the place and a sterility of limits. The neat little toilet block is the only building; rustic brick (multi-coloured Coed Ely) with a white mortar joint cut off flush; bathstone quoins and reveals to doorway and windows. Sprocketed hips to the steep pitched roof and Welsh slates. Impervious. Harry pulls up behind the line of cars. He stares straight ahead. We sit in silence and wait for the coming of the hearse. The noise of the rain on the roof of the car reminds me.

Tin roof, I say. Takes me back. Harry looks at me. I point up. The rain on the tin roof, I say. Old memories. The old man and long wet days in the cement shed. Trying to fathom a way out...

I laugh, a short bark of sound without conviction.

His eyes are fixed steadily on the hill. He says nothing. His hair is freshly cut and his white shirt immaculate. I turn to look at the hill; scrubby fields with neither sheep nor cattle grazing, rusty scabs of bracken, a dull blue scalp of ragged trees to scrape the sky. My voice speaks my thoughts: Sometimes I think that all our lives have been fucked up by the rain.

I turn to look at him. You think back, I say, over a lifetime... all the things it fucked up...

Harry stretches his arms, grits his teeth, but says nothing. He brings up his hand to cover a yawn.

This kid, I say. (What is there to say?) It is like being in a balloon. He is willing me to shut up.

So young, I say. The obvious. It is what we are. Words are fuck all. Nothing.

I can only manage a loose gesture, a movement of the hands. No more than a spasm to cover the hugeness of what is left out. The vast desert that separates father and son.

Fuck all, I say quietly, and a small wind moves the body of the yew.

The blackbird flies away. The dark portion of the sky is moving east. Like a lid sliding off. The west lightens. A brief white sun turns the wet twigs to streaks in the hedge. People are starting to get out of the cars. Harry raises his eyes to the rearview mirror.

Here they come, he says.

A strip of wet road that runs due west and ends abruptly at the grey iron fence. Beyond the fence lies the motorway. Cars hurtling north and south, glimpsed through the bare trees. The sky in the west is clearing. The Garth mountain is bare. Stony grey. The sky over it is palest blue. Cloudless and bare as bone. The two gravediggers are dragging a green canvas tarpaulin to cover the mound of wet earth beside the open grave as we approach. This accomplished, they pick up their spades and move away. The coats on their backs are wet through. The rectangular hole. Two planks to each of the long sides, resting on bearers at either end.

I get a glimpse of Lillian's face as the car goes by. She sits alone. Her head is lowered. She wears a black pill box hat, but no veil. Snell is in his own car, the woman beside him must be his daughter. The hearse is parked alongside the grave. When they bring out the coffin, Harry steps away from me and I am all alone. I move forward. Lillian gets out of her limousine and I stand beside her. She turns her head but does not look at me. I spot my father. He is like an old crow in his new black suit, his face pinched and bony. Bleakeyed, he stares in my direction. I might be a sheet of glass. My mother is in this ground. We are all together, once more reunited on this unwholesome hillside, under an October sky.

Splintered from the block, this is how we meet again, these hillsides.

There is no priest. The funeral parlour men, with their tight grey suits and red beerfaces carry the coffin from the hearse to the graveside like a battering ram. Strap it with the webbing belts and set it to rest on the bearers. Four of them. A pause for last considerations, then the bearing pieces are withdrawn; the webbing slips through their hands and down it goes. Draw up the straps and step away. One of their number offers a trowel of the wet earth to my wife. The mother first. She walks like blind woman and takes it from him. Stares down. Her face is the colour of unbaked dough. She trembles, then steadies herself. Twists her wrist and the brown earth lumps fall off the trowel and clump soft as toads on the coffin lid. Then it is my turn. The mind is barren. A bare board. For all of my days up and down on the face of the world, I know nothing. I stare where the hill cuts off the sky and try for some thing. Anything, some brief emotion, grief, however small, to register the moment. I am empty. A scraped clamshell. A lost shoe. Numb. I make the task with the trowel and earth and stare in where it falls. Turn away and look into my wife's eyes. She moves as if to come to me and for a moment I almost come to the belief she is about to touch my hand. But she looks down and turns away instead. The man who handed me the trowel takes it back. It is over.

I stay where my feet are. Snell comes to comfort her. My father goes to where she is. Says something. She is weeping. He looks at me but there is nothing. They move away like a shoal of fish. The shuffle of feet on the road back to the hub where the cars are.

Harry turns, catches my eye. Lillian is back in her limousine, her face in her hands. I spot Snell; my father, with his back to me. Harry points to his car. I shake my head. You go on, I tell him. I catch up and drift with them as they shuffle east.

I think I'll stay for a bit, I tell him. I'm not going back with them. I spread my hands to indicate some measure of the bewilderment and loss. He nods and touches my arm and goes. The cars go down the hill and I am left alone but for the two men backfilling the grave.

There is a wooden bench to the northwest side of the hub; darkstained hardwood, a bright brass plate bears the donor's name; it is protected by a stand of thick conifer from the prevailing wind. A place to take the weight off. I sit down and stare to the east, where the older section lies, the grander monuments, angels and crosses etc. The sun is out. The pale light catches the wet grass as it shudders under a sudden gust of wind. I study my hands and bring them together for warmth. I am consciously straining after something. I close my eyes to see if it lies in the darkness in my head. Some small, elusive thing. No more than a grey moth, perhaps, in the blackest night. For a moment I think it may be there, a brief flicker – then gone. But I can't be sure. But it seemed to be there. Whatever it might have been seemed, for a moment, to be almost there...

Once, long ago, when I was young and foolish and newly married with a lovely wife and two lovely children, one of each,

I was as happy as the day was long and it was summer or winter according to the measure of her smile and I truly believed our only way was to be the true happiness, our measure of joy and earthly delight a certain thing.

I open my eyes. My hands are cold. My knees are stiff and I am busting for a piss.

Chapter Fifteen

I am in the mystery now and there can be no respite. Most nights I walk the narrow streets that skirt the main roads. Itinerant and woebegone, I expect nothing and find nothing. An old man in another late autumn, still bent on the last lost cause.

One night in City Road, a wet night, one of those nights when drizzle swarms in the lamplight and clogs the air, I happen to pass the shebeen they have where you look straight in and I see this girl in a white t-shirt at one of the tables. She is blonde and neat and her lips are full and red and she is smiling at a boy. The boy is blowing the smoke from a drag on his cigarette into the air above the table and sighting her along the bridge of his nose as his head tilts back. He looks a nice, even-tempered kid. About twenty four; the girl looks under twenty. She is not quite beautiful but her tits are, and the white t-shirt is the perfect means to afford them a proper and respectful emphasis. Tits like this are by no means commonplace and I stop to stare through the misted window at the little scene within. The rain is falling on my head but I am fascinated by her. The boy interests me too. I am trying to work out how it might go. Something reminds me of some thing out of my own past life. The easiness between them makes me envious. She is nice but not great, but by no means simply a piece of arse. He is a nice-looking kid. But she is not vital to him, nor he to her. He could reach across and touch her anywhere and she would not jump and squawk and make a fuss. She might welcome the familiarity. Might even touch the hand that touched her. Clasp it in a casual fondness.

And I am still stood there, sort of daydreaming, when the boy sees me. There am I, this old man with the face of a drunkard, wet through with October rain, staring at a girl in a white t-shirt who shares his company. This is a boy who still thinks the world is an oyster. Our eyes meet and he frowns. Then he looks back at the girl. She smiles at him. It might be close to adoration, that smile. The boy takes his glass of beer and drinks and smiles back. The girl in the white t-shirt touches his hand. She never sees me.

I move on and walk as far as the crossroads. Traffic at the lights, vapours and lights and rain. Along Newport Road, the buildings that swarm up into the night with lit windows and dark windows. To the south is the dark church with its spire and farther east the dark uneven sprawl of masonry that is the closed up Infirmary. The girl in the white t-shirt is still in my thoughts. But there is no lust in it. Women are beginning to frighten me with their absolute strangeness and secrecy. I think of the boy and wonder what the next few beers will do to his mood. Drunk or sober, it is a hard path through the dark wood. Then comes the intimate time and the minefield of compromise. I remember my ex-wife as she was when I first knew her. It is not easy for me. The recollection of her kisses, the shock of their luxurious intimacy. That amazing journey into the strange land.

I walk into town as the rain comes down harder still. I reach the railway bridge and pause to wipe my face. Queen Street lies in front of me. The rain falls through the wet leafless branches of the trees they planted. Not a soul in sight.

There is nothing now, I know, that can save me from the bottomless hole of celibacy. Whatever I was, I am all but done. The vast obscurity that is set to swallow us all: the bricklayer who nailed his trowel to the wall and waits to starve.

I go into the Park Lane Bar and I don't know why. The place is dead, even by middle of the week's standards. A place of misery. The barman comes out from behind a screen, serves me and goes back. There are four others in the room. I take my bottle of beer to a table and sit down. Pour some beer in the glass but leave it untouched. Stare down at my hands. My hands are the key to the mystery. I think now of my son who is dead. Of his mother, who now belongs to another man. Then my own father comes to mind. I remember his shotgun. This is the vital factor. It would be easier to see myself as a lost straggler. Written off. But it will not leave me, this stubborn burr, this unyielding sense of obligation. The scales of justice. The inescapable duty. I have been nursing it for days, been through it and over it time and time again. Step by step. The whole thing down pat.

When I come out of the bar I walk west. I am wet through but the rain is not cold. I am going to my father's house. I walk to the bus station and catch a bus to the edge of the town. Out through the districts through the wet streets until the bus sets me down alongside a hedge that borders a dark field. Another crossroads. I keep going west, face into the driving rain. But now I am like a pilgrim. The narrow country road and its winding. It is a considerable distance to walk. I sweat within my sodden clothes. My legs keep going. I am emptied out, by and large, and death would be a lot easier, or so it seems, but my purpose does not waver. I keep plodding. Cars go by. Headlights like gunbarrels. Fields and wayside trees and the rain in my face. A long, long way.

It must be close to midnight when I finally arrive at his gate. Yet more mysteries: the field beyond the gate, the house, the orchard trees. The rain ceases as I stand there and the clouds part to reveal stars. The sweat makes me feel greasy and warm and my legs are trembling. Now I pause to consider the next hurdle. My father's face. My father's voice. Chasms of cloud. Snowfields. The old hatreds carried over from the old lives. I climb over the gate and walk slowly down the path. Nothing now can impede my purpose.

My father sits at the table in the kitchen. His face is like a thing made out of pale thin bone; the pale fragility of a moth as it floats in the light of the table lamp. There is a book open in front of him. His eyes are closed. Both hands rest palm down on the oilcloth that covers the table. The room is dark all about him. I watch for a moment to see if he breathes. Then a finger, the ring finger, twitches, and his old bony frame of a chest heaves a breath from the air. His eyes open and he stares ahead. He might be calmly plotting the strategy for a final campaign, going over the need for coal and provisions for what may be his last winter in the world. The death that is in him has come to the fore. He might, you almost feel, disintegrate and float away as a puff of dust into the dark beyond the lamplight. It is as if he might be working out the theorems that make up the geometry of time remaining. With one eye forever on the clock running down. Then he coughs. The right hand comes up to cover his mouth. A shudder racks him. Then he turns his head and looks right at me. He gets up and crosses to the window. He moves very slow, as if the bones are unwilling. I watch as he presses his face to the glass. I tap lightly on the glass and he starts. His lips clench about the toothless mouth. When he opens the door he is holding the shotgun. He switches on the porch light. His teeth are in. Who's there? he says.

I step into the light. We stand facing each other. He nods and lowers the shotgun. You look wet, he says. I follow him into the kitchen. Been raining? he says.

A bit, I say, but it is stopped now.

Better dry yourself, he says. You'll catch pneumonia.

He rests the shotgun against the wall and hands me an old towel. I wipe at my face and hair. He is watching me.

What do you want? he asks me.

To borrow your gun, I tell him.

I only got two cartridges left, he tells me.

That's plenty, I say.

He points to the gun. Take it, he says.

A cup of tea? he asks me.

Water will do, I tell him.

Get out of those wet clothes, he says. I'll see what I can find'll fit you. You staying the night?

I nod. If that's okay.

I'll get some blankets. Did you walk?

I nod. Most of the way, I tell him.

Must be gone midnight, he says.

It is late, I tell him. Where's the dog?

He points where the dog lies in front of the stove. The black dog watches me with solemn eyes.

She didn't bark, I say.

She knows you, he says. Dogs know.

I go over to the dog and touch her warm fur. Pat her head. Fondle her. The logs in the stove, burned to the ghosts of ash, crumble and collapse. There are chopped sticks on the hearth. I feed two of them into the stove. There is a pause, then a crackle as the flames take hold of the dry wood, then the small flame.

I better get these things off, I say. Get me an old shirt or something, will you? I'm knackered. It is a long way to walk. I am out of condition.

You are lost, he says. You been lost for years.

There is nothing to say. I lay the towel over the back of the chair and start to undress.

He points to the book on the table. It is a photograph album.

I'll get the blankets, he says and goes out.

I stand naked and look at the photograph. I am in the picture. As are my two children and my wife. There is sunlight and shadow. Leaves on young fruit trees against a wall. Shadows from morning sun. A low table with cups and jugs and a teapot. My dead son aged about ten; his sister aged about eight. He is smiling at the camera, she is not: she frowns. My wife looks serious. She sits with her legs drawn up. I am staring down at my hands. My hair is black and glossy. I look thoughtful. We all know it is over. Elliot has his thumbnail rubbing against his lower teeth to modify his smile of awareness. My former wife is very beautiful. Her hands are loosely clasped on her knees. Her face gives nothing away. She is perfectly composed. I stare at the snapshot and hardly know what it is that comes over me. A scene that I no longer recall, waiting all these years to show me again what was lost. I go to the sink and drink some water from my cupped hands. Then I take the towel from the chair and start to wipe myself dry.

My father comes back with a dry shirt and an old woollen dressing gown as thick and heavy as an army greatcoat. He averts his eyes while I dress. You can sleep on the settee in the front room, he tells me.

We'll build up the fire and dry your things. He brings a wooden clothes horse and kicks the dog to make her move. I'll make a nice pot of tea. You can have a drop of whisky in it. Some sugar... Maybe I can find a lemon somewhere... Put your wet clothes on the horse.

Sleep sucks me in and I go under without dreams.

When I wake I hear the old man chopping sticks. The fire is blazing in the stove and the kettle is on. There is sunlight streaming in.

My clothes are still damp.

They'll dry soon, my father promises. I'll make a pot of tea, he says, the kettle won't be long.

The dog stands in the morning sunlight under the damson tree. She wags her tail. Her black coat gleams.

We can have beans on toast, my father says. Beans on toast be okay? You sleep okay?

I watch him; the sharp deft blows of the axe as he splits slender kindling sticks from the block of wood.

Like a log, I tell him.

When we have eaten he shows me the gun. Demonstrates for me how to break it down. Stock. Breech. Two barrels. The two shells. Then he puts it back together. You try, he says.

I take it apart. The separated parts on the table. I take them and make a gun again. Take it apart.

I'll give you a bag to carry it home, he says. He goes out and comes back with a canvas carpenter's tool bag. He wraps the parts of the gun into pieces of an old white shirt and then the wrapped parts into a blanket torn in half. He ties up the bundle in three places with old brick line. It could be a ritual like morning mass. Deft fingers. The second best bricklayer the town ever saw. He puts the bundled gun into the canvas bag. Hefts it. Hands me the two shells.

Keep them safe, he says. There's a bus at ten o'clock.

My father walks with me to the gate. The dog comes too. We stand in the gateway and watch the road. Neither of us speaks. That there is much to say is never in doubt, but the words, as ever, are not easy to come by. The black dog sniffs at the roadside weeds. She is content; she has found her place in the world. The morning is fine and the air sparkling after the rain.

When the bus comes into sight he touches my arm.

Here she comes, he says. We shake hands. I pat the dog's head.

He nods to the gun in the bag and smiles. Tough hombre, he says.

It is not a matter of complexity, strange to say, it is one of complete simplicity. I go to work and come back to my room. I eat in the Silver Fox Diner and stay sober. I fool around with the shotgun. The different parts. Make it whole and break it down again. Put it back. Hold the shells in my hand and stare and think hard. Try to perceive some kind of destiny, as if it is a game for gods and mortals and fate is caught up in it. A sort of drama. The way the gunbarrel gleams in the light of the naked bulb. The quiet of the attic room. Painstaking, I go through the solitary routine until it is as smooth and commonplace as the morning shit.

A full week goes by. The sobriety is making me tense. I had never known the length of the hours could stretch and stretch the way they do. I buy a second hand suitcase in a junkshop at the bottom of Clive Street. Sugar-bag blue glazed cardboard, there is a genuine Canadian Pacific sticker and the initial B on it. We are in November now. I work the Saturday morning and come back to the room. I place the shotgun in the suitcase. The shells are in the pocket of my funeral suit coat. I shave with great care. Study my face in the mirror. I dress in the suit and put on my new black funeral shoes. Sit on the side of the bed and wait for it to get dark.

When I am leaving, Wilson sees me coming down the stairs with the suitcase. Going away? he says. I say nothing. It is a mild dry night. Bonfire Night. Fireworks are already going off and the air smells of woodsmoke. I have eaten nothing all day and I can feel the tension like a current running through my bones. Nerves. I walk to the bus station and catch a bus to Constellation Street.

The plan is in my head like a play. I walk the length of Clifton Street carrying the suitcase that holds the gun. The shells are in my pocket wrapped in a white handkerchief. The whole business is very solemn and must be precise.

I go into the lighted bar of the Locomotive Hotel and he is there. Instantly recognisable, at the end of the bar. Big, as Hurfoot said, as the side of a fucking house. I am happy to see him He looks like somebody I would be happy to kill. To rub out, as my father might put it. The place is not crowded. I carry my suitcase up to the bar and buy a bottle of Worthington and a single whisky. Then carry bottle, both glasses and suitcases to a table by the door. I am calm. I sit and take sip of the pale ale and sniff the whisky. I watch the man at the bar. My victim. A gross-looking bastard, yet his hands are small and his movements possess a degree of deftness that might be construed as close to delicacy. When he tilts his glass to drink. Or passes the barmaid money from the pile in front of him on the bar. Or looks at his watch. When he gets off his stool and goes out for a piss his movements are not as ponderous as his bulk might lead you to expect. I look about the room. There is not one face that I know.

When he comes back from the piss he gives me a cursory glance. Funny eyes. Peculiar colour. His face is very pale, as if he hardly ever saw sunlight. I watch the silent television and can feel him watching me. I turn my head and our eyes meet. He looks at the suitcase but says nothing. He gets back onto his stool. Lifts his glass and drinks, pours it down his throat as you might empty a bucket of slops down a drain. Sets the glass down and points for the barmaid to fill it again.

I nurse my beer. A new barmaid comes in. A fresh face. Blonde hair, close to platinum, very red lipstick, cheap little eyes made up to look big. A black velvet choker sets her off.

Stragglers come in. Others leave.

By nine o'clock the fat man is drunk. He staggers as he gets off the stool and clutches at the counter. He laughs. Small mouth and white teeth. He shakes his head when the barmaid comes for his glass.

Had enough, he says. Time I was off.

I follow him out of the door. He turns into Nora Street and I follow. The street is empty. I open the suitcase and take out the gun. Take the shells from my pocket and press them home. No nerves. Icy calm. I leave the suitcase against the wall and follow him with the gun at the ready. He goes slowly along and his shadow is huge on the blank wall of the old brewery. There is a red car just caught in the edge of the lamplight. He stops at the car and feels for the lock with his key. Then he turns his head and sees me. He stops what he is doing and faces me.

Mr Harris? I say. I show him the gun. Time to settle up, I say.

Who the fuck are you? he says.

What difference does it make? I say. Point the gun at his chest. There is no fear in his eyes. He looks at the gun. Looks at me.

What's going on? he says. Then he smiles. Is that thing loaded? he asks me. You sure it's loaded?

It's loaded, I assure him. You got lovely teeth, I tell him. I was lost, I tell him. I was lost a long time.

He smiles and I smile. You going to shoot me? he asks me.

Too true, I tell him. Too fucking true. Now I have found you, my friend, I am almost home. Then I raise the barrel a notch and press the trigger. It goes off and his face disappears before my eyes. What remains of the skull resembles a squashed fig. His body goes back against the car and starts to sink. His hands raise themselves as if they wanted to straighten his tie, but don't make it and fall back. He slumps very slowly like a sack of shit.

Then I think I must faint. I think for a moment I must pass out. Not black but white. When I come to the gun is still in my hand but I am backed up against the long wall. It feels as if I have woken up from a different dream.

I look around me. There is nobody in the street. I am still calm. The plan is still clear in my head. I am slightly astonished by how simple it was. I prod him with my foot. The blood is oozing up from his neck, black and thick and slow, just like crude oil.

I still think of her. She was my one and only love. Thinking of her as she is now and as I am now is hard, but the memories of the old times are insistent. There is some part of me, some stubborn part, that cannot give it up. It is not hope anymore, just the nursing of an ancient dream. And not fucking or kissing or anything as ridiculous as that, just for her to look at me with love in her eyes once again before I die. And touch my face with a real tenderness.

It is winter now. The old man at the desert's edge sits down on a stone and he can hold up the past and present to the light and see it all as a counterfeit banknote. He has come to understand that in the end we are all alone with only the merciless stars to steer by.

Most nights I walk about the different districts of the town. Sobriety is something I have found. Rediscovered, you might say. The different streets carry their different messages as I take note of brick and stone and slate. Shadowy figure. Almost a beggarman. Or a scarecrow. Wrinkles about each eyesocket, grey winter stubble, a bald patch like a dinner plate.

There are moments when the dusk falls in some exhausted street and I stop to observe. It is the mousegrey air before the dark of a December afternoon, with night gathering pace as the lights brighten in the windows of the Agral Stores or the Divine Products or the bar of The Exchange. It might be a Saturday, with all the young whores getting ready to be real again in third floor attic rooms, embracing the magical deceptions of high heel shoes and stockings to lure cross-eyed men who try to squint up dogleg stairs. Men with strange dicks and faces like fog. You stand and gaze up at the underside of heaven. The last flight of strung out gulls, that serve as the curtains for the days that are lost, have passed over and gone. They have passed over the tiny roofs of the tiny houses, over church spires and banks, flagpoles and parked cars, hovel and mansion house, out past the edge of the shore and over the polluted Channel to vanish into the musselshell blue of the night. Only the clouds, and what starlight there is, remain.

You stand on the corner of some street and once the lamplight is established you are locked into the rigid framework of a play.

I still have the gun in my possession and still harbour the miraculous possibilities of the remaining shot. Some things fade away, remain obscure, but the vital things are no longer mysteries. I am sure of death now. Once you are sure of death, in absolute terms, all things are possible. Nothing much can happen and if it does, who will care? You walk, you wear holes in your shoes. Trapped in a desert of dogshit and dust, we soak up each other's lives like sponges.

There is a place about four miles north of where I live. If you follow the river bank, you come upon a small clearing in a wood on the west side, just south of the Black Bridge. There is a ring of river stones in the sand where many fires have been lit. It was there when I was a child and it will be there when I am dead. It is a place that has been tattooed on the maps of dream and nightmare all my life.

Winter is the best time for such journeys. In the morning there is mist over the water like a white veil. I stand in the clearing and wait for the dark.

Sometimes I light a small fire. Gather straws and small twigs to build into a combustible structure inside the ring of stones. Set it alight and feed it, build it into something that will last. Then I sit down on the log and look into the flames. There is fear on my mind. A trembling unease that won't let me alone. A terrible desire to be forever running from the encroachment of catastrophe the next second may bring. I know it is nothing from nothing leaves nothing from now on. What I have discovered is the true detachment of torment. Beseech though I may with all my heart, no angel will come.

Acknowledgements

Many thanks to Dai Smith for his encouragement and friendship; to Des Barry for wise words in the margins and to David Gould for helping me with those new-fangled machines.